BARUNDIN STONEHEART is now the king of the dwarf realm of Zhufbar. His ascension should herald hearty celebration, but it only brings the ancient dwarf bitterness and rage. For Barundin's father Throndin was slain on the field of battle. A death caused by the cowardice of a manling, no fate for an honourable dwarf. Honour now demands that Barundin must seek vengeance on his father's betrayer, no matter how long it takes.

But dwarf history is littered with countless grudges and oaths of vengeance. Every action, every battle gives birth to hundreds more. Can Barundin ever hope to plough through all these grudges and still lead his people to victory over their many enemies?

GRUDGE BEARER

Gav Thorpe

A BLACK LIBRARY PUBLICATION

First published in Great Britain in 2005 by
BL Publishing,
Games Workshop Ltd.,
Willow Road, Nottingham,
NG7 2WS, UK

Cover by Adrian Smith.

Map by Nuala Kennedy.

10 9 8 7 6 5 4 3 2 1

A CIP record for this book is available from the British Library

ISBN 13: 978 1 84416 197 3
ISBN 10: 1 84416 197 8

Distributed in the US by Simon & Schuster
1230 Avenue of the Americas, New York, NY 10020.

Printed and bound in Great Britain by
Bookmarque, Surrey, UK.

See the Black Library on the Internet at
www.blacklibrary.com

Find out more about Games Workshop
and the world of Warhammer at
www.games-workshop.com

THIS IS A DARK age, a bloody age, an age of daemons
and of sorcery. It is an age of battle and death, and of the
world's ending. Amidst all of the fire, flame and fury
it is a time, too, of mighty heroes, of bold deeds
and great courage.

AT THE HEART of the Old World sprawls the Empire, the
largest and most powerful of the human realms. Known
for its engineers, sorcerers, traders and soldiers, it is
a land of great mountains, mighty rivers, dark forests
and vast cities. And from his throne in Altdorf reigns
the Emperor Karl-Franz, sacred descendent of the
founder of these lands, Sigmar, and wielder
of his magical warhammer.

BUT THESE ARE far from civilised times. Across the
length and breadth of the Old World, from the knightly
palaces of Bretonnia to ice-bound Kislev in the far north,
come rumblings of war. In the towering World's Edge
Mountains, the orc tribes are gathering for another assault.
Bandits and renegades harry the wild southern lands of
the Border Princes. There are rumours of rat-things, the
skaven, emerging from the sewers and swamps across the
land. And from the northern wildernesses there is the
ever-present threat of Chaos, of daemons and beastmen
corrupted by the foul powers of the Dark Gods.
As the time of battle draws ever near,
the Empire needs heroes
like never before.

Grey
Mountains

Zorus
Forest

Karak-Norn

The
Vaults

Tilea

Karak-
Izor

Karak-
Hirn

Border

Princes

The Black Gulf

Badlands

Dragon Back
Mountains

Ekrund

Blind River

The Marshes
of Madness

Karak-
Azgal

The Desolation
of Nagash

Blight Water

Misty
Mountain

The
Sour
Sea

Karag
Orrud

To The Legendary

GRUDGE ONE
Hard as Stone

THE TWISTED, BAYING *creatures came on in a great mass, howling and screaming at the darkening sky. Some shambled forwards on all fours like dogs and bears, others ran upright with long, loping strides. Each was an unholy hybrid of man and beast, some with canine faces and human bodies, others with the hindquarters of a goat or cat. Bird-faced creatures with bat-like wings sprouting from their backs swept forward in swooping leaps alongside gigantic monstrosities made of flailing limbs and screeching faces.*

As the sun glittered off the peaks of the mountains around them, the host of elves and dwarfs stood grimly watching the fresh wave of warped horrors sweep down the valley. For five long days they had stood against the horde pouring from the north. The sky seethed with magical energy above them, pulsing with unnatural vigour. Storm clouds tinged with blue and purple roiled in the air above the dark host.

At the head of the dwarf army stood the high king, Snorri Whitebeard. His beard was stained with dirt and blood and he held his glimmering rune axe heavily in his hand. Around him his guards picked up their shields, axes and hammers and closed around the king, preparing to face the fresh onslaught. It was the dwarf standing to Snorri's left, Godri Stonehewer, who broke the grim silence.

'Do you think there'll be many more of them?' he asked, hefting his hammer in his right hand. 'Only, I haven't had a beer in three days.'

Snorri chuckled and looked across towards Godri. 'Where did you find beer three days ago?' the high king said. 'I haven't had a drop since the first day.'

'Well,' replied Godri, avoiding the king's gaze, 'there may have been a barrel or two that were missed when we were doling out the rations.'

'Godri!' snapped Snorri, genuinely angry. 'There's good fighters back there with blood in their mouths that have had to put up with that elf-spit for three days, and you had your own beer? If I survive this we'll be having words!'

Godri didn't reply, but shuffled his feet and kept his gaze firmly on the ground.

'Heads up.' someone called from further down the line, and Snorri turned to see four dark shapes in the sky above, barely visible amongst the clouds. One detached itself from the group and spiralled downwards.

As it came closer, the shape was revealed to be a dragon, its large white scales glinting in the magical storm. Perched at the base of its long, serpentine neck was a figure swathed in a light blue cloak, his silvered armour shining through the flapping folds. His face was hidden behind a tall helm decorated with two golden wings that arched into the air.

The dragon landed in front of Snorri and folded its wings. A tall, lean figure leapt gracefully to the ground from its saddle and strode towards Snorri, his long cloak flowing just above the muddy ground. As he approached, he removed his

*helm, revealing a slender face and wide, bright eyes. His skin
was fair and dark hair fell loosely around his shoulders.*

'Made it back then?' said Snorri as the elf stopped in front
of him.

'Of course,' the elf replied with a distasteful look. 'Were you
expecting me to perish?'

'Hey now, Malekith, don't take on so,' said Snorri with a
growl. 'It was a simple greeting.'

The elf prince did not reply. He surveyed the oncoming
horde. When he spoke, his gaze was still fixed to the north.

'This is the last of them for many, many leagues,' said
Malekith. "When they are all destroyed, we shall turn
westwards to the hordes that threaten the cities of my
people.'

'That was the deal, yes,' said Snorri, pulling off his helmet
and dragging a hand through his knotted, sweat-soaked hair.
'We swore oaths, remember?'

Malekith turned and looked at Snorri. 'Yes, oaths,' the elf
prince said. 'Your word is your bond, that is how it is with
you dwarfs, is it not?'

'As it should be with all civilised folk,' said Snorri, ramming his helmet back on. 'You've kept your word, we'll keep
ours.'

The elf nodded and walked away. With a graceful leap he
was in the dragon's saddle, and a moment later, with a thunderous flapping of wings, the beast soared into the air and
was soon lost against the clouds.

'They're a funny folk, those elves,' remarked Godri. 'Speak
odd, too.'

'They're a strange breed, right enough,' agreed the dwarf
king. 'Living with dragons, can't take their ale, and I'm sure
they spend too much time in the sun. Still, anyone who can
swing a sword and will stand beside me is friend enough in
these dark times.'

'Right enough,' said Godri with a nod.

The dwarf throng was silent as the beasts of Chaos approached, and above the baying and howling of the twisted monsters, the clear trumpet calls of the elves could be heard, marshalling their line.

The unnatural tide of mutated flesh was now only some five hundred yards away and Snorri could smell their disgusting stench. In the dim light, a storm of white-shafted arrows lifted into the air from the elves and fell down amongst the horde, punching through furred hide and leathery skin. Another volley followed swiftly after, then another and another. The ground of the valley was littered with the dead and the dying, dozens of arrow-pierced corpses strewn across the slope in front of Snorri and his army. Still the beasts rushed on, heedless of their casualties. Now they were now only two hundred yards away.

Three arrows burning with blue fire arced high into the air.

'Right, that's us,' said Snorri. He gave a nod to Thundir to his right. The dwarf lifted his curling horn to his lips and blew a long blast that resounded off the valley walls.

The noise gradually increased as the dwarfs marched forwards, the echoes of the horn call and the roaring of the Chaos beasts now drowned out by the tramp of iron-shod feet, the clinking of chainmail and the thump of hammers and axes on shields.

Like a wall of iron, the dwarf line advanced down the slope as another salvo of arrows whistled over their heads. The scattered groups of fanged, clawed monsters crashed into the shieldwall. Growling, howling and screeching, their wordless challenges met with gruff battle cries and shouted oaths.

'Grungni guide my hand!' bellowed Snorri as a creature with the head of a wolf, the body of a man and the legs of a lizard jumped at him, slashing with long talons. Snorri swept his axe from right to left in a low arc, the gleaming blade shearing off the beast's legs just below the waist.

As the dismembered corpse tumbled down the hill, Snorri stepped forward and brought his axe back in a return blow, ripping the head from a bear-like creature with a lashing snake for a tail. Thick blood that stank of rotten fish fountained over the king, sticking to the plates of his iron armour. Gobbets caught in his matted beard, making him gag.

It was going to be a long day.

The throne room of Zhufbar echoed gently with the hubbub of the milling dwarfs. A hundred lanterns shone a golden light down onto the throng as King Throndin looked out over his court. Representatives of most of the clans were here, and amongst the crowd he spied the familiar face of his son Barundin. The young dwarf was in conversation with the runelord, Arbrek Silverfingers. Throndin chuckled quietly to himself as he imagined the topic of conversation: undoubtedly his son would be saying something rash and ill-considered, and Arbrek would be cursing him softly with an amused twinkle in his eye.

Movement at the great doors caught the king's attention. The background noise dropped down as a human emissary entered, escorted by Hengrid Dragonfoe, the hold's gatewarden. The manling was tall, even for one of his kind, and behind him came two other men carrying a large ironbound wooden chest. The messenger was clearly taking slow, deliberate strides so as not to outpace his shorter-legged escort, while the two carrying the chest were visibly tiring. A gap opened up in the assembled throng, a pathway to the foot of Throndin's throne appearing out of the crowd.

He sat with his arms crossed as he watched the small deputation make its way up the thirty steps to the dais on which his throne stood. The messenger bowed low, his left hand extended to the side with a flourish, and then looked up at the king.

'My lord, King Throndin of Zhufbar, I bring tidings from Baron Silas Vessal of Averland,' the emissary said. He was speaking slowly, for which Throndin was grateful, as it had been many long years since he had needed to understand the Reikspiel of the Empire.

The king said nothing for a moment, and then noticed the manling's unease at the ensuing silence. He dredged up the right words from his memory. 'And you are?' asked Throndin.

'I am Marechal Heinlin Kulft, cousin and herald to Baron Vessal,' the man replied.

'Cousin, eh?' said Throndin with an approving nod. At least this manling lord had sent one of his own family to parley with the king. In his three hundred years, Throndin had come to think of humans as rash, flighty and inconsiderate. Almost as bad as elves, he thought to himself.

'Yes, my lord,' replied Kulft. 'On his father's side,' he added, feeling perhaps that the explanation would fill the silence that had descended on the wide, long chamber. He was acutely aware of hundreds of dwarfs' eyes boring into his back and hundreds of dwarfs' ears listening to his every word.

'So, you have a message?' said Throndin, tilting his head slightly to one side.

'I have two, my lord,' said Kulft. 'I bring both grievous news and a request from Baron Vessal.'

'You want help, then?' said Throndin. 'What do you want?'

The herald was momentarily taken aback by the king's forthright manner, but gathered himself quickly. 'Orcs, my lord,' said Kulft, and at the mention of the hated greenskins an angry buzzing filled the chamber.

The noise quieted as Throndin waved the assembled court to silence. He gestured for Kulft to continue.

'From north of the baron's lands, the orcs have come,' he said. 'Three farms have been destroyed already, and we believe they are growing in number. The baron's armies are well equipped but small, and he fears that should we not respond quickly the orcs will only grow bolder.'

'Then ask your count or your emperor for more men,' said Throndin. 'What concern is it of mine?'

'The orcs have crossed your lands as well,' replied Kulft quickly, obviously prepared for such a question. 'Not only this year, but last year at about the same time.'

'Have you a description of these creatures?' demanded Throndin, his eyes narrowing to slits.

'They are said to carry shields emblazoned with the crude image of a face with two long fangs, and they paint their bodies with strange designs in black paint,' said Kulft. This time the reaction from the throng was even louder.

Throndin sat in silence, but the knuckles of his clenched fists were white and his beard quivered. Kulft gestured to the two men that had gratefully placed the chest on the throne tier, and they opened it up. The light of a hundred lanterns glittered off the contents – a few gems, many, many silver coins and several bars of gold. The anger in Throndin's eyes was rapidly replaced with an acquisitive gleam.

'The baron would not wish you to endure any expense on his account,' explained Kulft, gesturing to the treasure chest. 'He would ask that you accept this gesture of his good will in offsetting any cost that your expedition might incur.'

'Hmm, gift?' said Throndin, tearing his eyes away from the gold bars. They were of a particular quality, originally dwarf-gold if his experienced eye was not mistaken. 'For me?'

Kulft nodded. The dwarf king looked back at the chest and then glowered at the few dwarfs that had taken hesitant steps up the stairway towards the chest. Kulft gestured for his companions to close the lid before any trouble started. He had heard of the dwarf lust for gold, but had mistaken it merely for greed. The reaction had been something else entirely, a desire for the precious metal that bordered on physical need, like a man finding water in the desert.

'While I accept this generous gift, it is not for gold that the King of Zhufbar shall march forth,' said Throndin, standing up. 'We know of these orcs. Indeed, last year they were met in battle by dwarfs of my own clan, and the vile creatures took the life of my eldest son.'

Throndin paced forward, his balled fists by his side, and stood at the top of the steps. When he next spoke, his voice echoed from the far walls of the chamber. He turned to Kulft. 'These orcs owe us dear,' snarled the king. 'The life of a Zhufbar prince stains their lives and they have been entered onto the list of wrongs done against my hold and my people. I declare grudge against these orcs! Their lives are forfeit, and with axe and hammer we shall make them pay the price they owe. Ride to your lord, tell him to prepare for war, and tell him that King Throndin Stoneheart of Zhufbar will fight beside him!'

THE TRAMPING OF dwarf boots rang from the mountainsides as the gates of Zhufbar were swung open and the host of King Throndin marched out. Rank after rank of bearded warriors advanced between the two great statues of Grungni and Grimnir that flanked the gateway, carved from the rock of the mountain. Above the dwarf army swayed a forest of standards of gold and silver wrought into the faces of revered ancestors, clan runes and guild symbols.

The thud of boots was joined by the rumbling of wheels and the wheezing and coughing of a steam engine. At the rear of the dwarf column, a steamdozer puffed into view, its spoked, iron-rimmed wheels grinding along the cracked and pitted roadway. Billows of grey smoke rose into the air from the fluted funnel as the traction engine growled forwards, pulling behind it a chain of four wagons laden with baggage covered with heavy, cable-bound, waterproof sacking.

The autumn sky above the World's Edge Mountains was low and grey, threatening rain, yet Throndin was in high spirits. He walked at the head of his army, with Barundin to his left carrying the king's own standard, and marching to his right the Runelord Arbrek.

'War was never a happy occasion in your father's day,' said Arbrek, noticing the smile on the king's lips.

The smile faded as Throndin turned his head to look at the runelord. 'My father never had cause to avenge a fallen son,' the king said darkly, his eyes bright in the shadow of his gold-inlaid helmet. 'I thank him and the fathers before him that I have been granted the opportunity to right this wrong.'

'Besides, it is too long since you last took up your axe other than to polish it!' said Barundin with a short laugh. 'Are you sure you still remember what to do?'

'Listen to the beardling!' laughed Throndin. 'Barely fifty winters old and already an expert on war. Listen, laddie, I was swinging this axe at orcs long before you were born. Let's just see which of us accounts for more, eh?'

'This'll be the first time your father has had a chance to see your mettle,' added Arbrek with a wink. 'Stories when the ale is flowing are right enough, but there's nothing like seeing it firsthand to make a father proud.'

'Aye,' agreed Throndin, patting Barundin on the arm. 'You're my only son now. The honour of the clan will be yours when I go to meet the ancestors. You'll make me proud, I know you will.'

'You'll see that Barundin Throndinsson is worthy of becoming king,' the youth said with a fierce nod that set his beard waggling. 'You'll be proud, right enough.'

They marched westwards towards the Empire until noon, the towering ramparts and bastions of Zhufbar disappearing behind them, the mountain peak that held the king's throne room obscured by low cloud.

At midday Throndin called a halt and the air was filled with the noise of five thousand dwarfs eating sandwiches, drinking ale and arguing loudly, as was their wont when on campaign. After the eating was done the air was thick with pipe smoke, which hung like a cloud over the host.

Throndin sat on a rock, legs splayed in front of him, admiring the scenery. High up on the mountains, he could see for many miles, league after league of hard rock and sparse trees and bushes. Beyond, he could just about make out the greener lands of the Empire. As he puffed his pipe, a tap on his shoulder caused him to turn. It was Hengrid, and with him was an old-looking dwarf with a long white beard tucked into a simple rope belt. The stranger wore a hooded cloak of rough-spun wool that had been dyed blue and he held a whetstone in his cracked, gnarled hands.

'Grungni's honour be with you, King Throndin,' said the dwarf with a short bow. 'I am but a simple traveller, who earns a coin or two with my whetstone and my wits. Allow me the honour of sharpening your axe and perhaps passing on a wise word or two.'

'My axe is rune-sharp,' said Throndin, turning away.

'Hold now, king,' said the old dwarf. 'There was a time when any dwarf, be he lowly or kingly, would spare an ear for one of age and learning.'

'Let him speak, Throndin,' called Arbrek from across the other side of the roadway. 'He's old enough to even be my father – show a little respect.'

Throndin turned back to the stranger and gave a grudging nod. The peddler nodded thankfully, pulling off his pack and setting it down by the roadside. It looked very heavy and Throndin noticed an axe-shaped bundle swathed in rags stuffed between the folds of the dwarf's cloak. With a huff of expelled breath, the dwarf sat down on the pack.

'Orcs, is it?' the peddler said, pulling an ornate pipe from the folds of his robe.

'Yes,' said Throndin, taken aback. 'Have you seen them?'

The dwarf did not answer immediately. Instead he took a pouch from his belt and began filling his pipe with weed. Taking a long match from the pouch, he struck it on the hard surface of the roadway and lit the pipe, puffing contentedly several times before turning his attention back to the king.

'Aye, I seen them,' said the dwarf. 'Not for a while now, but I seen them. A vicious bunch and no mistake.'

'They'll be a dead bunch when I catch them,' snorted Throndin. 'When did you see them?'

'Oh, a while back, a year or thereabouts,' said the stranger.

'Last year?' said Barundin, moving to stand beside his father. 'That was when they slew Dorthin!'

The king scowled at his son, who felt silent.

'Aye, that is right,' said the peddler. 'It was no more than a day's march from here, where Prince Dorthin fell.'

'You saw the battle?' asked Throndin.

'I wish that I had,' said the stranger. 'My axe would have tasted orc flesh that day. But alas, I came upon the field of battle too late and the orcs were gone.'

'Well, this time the warriors of Zhufbar shall settle the matter,' said Barundin, putting his hand to the axe at his belt. 'Not only that, but a baron of the Empire fights with us."

'Pah, a manling?' spat the peddler. 'What worth has a manling in battle? Not since young Sigmar has their race bred a warrior worthy of the title.'

'Baron Vessal is a person of means, and that is no mean feat for a manling,' said Hengrid. 'He has dwarf gold, even.'

'Gold is but one way to judge the worth of a person,' said the stranger. 'When axes are raised and blood flows, it is not wealth but temper that is most valued.'

'What would you know?' said Throndin with a dismissive wave. 'I'd wager you have barely two coins to rub together. I'll not have a nameless, penniless wattock show disrespect for my ally. Thank you for your company, but I have enjoyed it enough. Hengrid!'

The burly dwarf veteran stepped forward and with an apologetic look gestured for the old peddler to stand. With a final puff on his pipe, the wanderer pushed himself to his feet and hauled on his pack.

'It is a day to be rued when the words of the old fall on deaf ears,' said the stranger as he turned away.

'I am no beardling!' Throndin called after him.

They watched the dwarf walk slowly down the road until he disappeared from view between two tall rocks. Throndin noticed Arbrek watching the path intently, as if he could still see the stranger.

'Empty warnings to go with his empty purse,' said Throndin, waving a dismissive hand in the peddler's direction.

Arbrek turned with a frown on his face. 'Since when did the kings of Zhufbar count wisdom in coins?' asked the runelord. Throndin made to answer, but Arbrek had turned away and was stomping off through the army.

THE SOLEMN BEATING *of drums could be heard echoing along the halls and corridors of Karaz-a-Karak. The small chamber was empty save for two figures. His face as pale as his beard, King Snorri lay on the low, wide bed, his eyes closed. Kneeling next to the bed, a hand on the dwarf's chest, was Prince Malekith of Ulthuan, once general of the Phoenix King's armies and now ambassador to the dwarf empire.*

The rest of the room was hung with heavy tapestries depicting the battles the two had fought together, suitably aggrandising Snorri's role. Malekith did not begrudge the king his glories, for was not his own name sung loudly in Ulthuan while the name of Snorri Whitebeard was barely a whisper? Each people to their own kind, the elf prince thought.

Snorri's eyelids fluttered open to reveal cloudy, pale blue eyes. His lips twisted into a smile and a fumbling hand found Malekith's arm.

'Would that dwarf lives were measured as those of the elves,' said Snorri. 'Then my reign would last another thousand years.'

'But even so, we still die,' said Malekith. 'Our measure is made by what we do when we live and the legacy that we leave to our kin, as any other. A lifetime of millennia is worthless if its works come to nought after it has ended.'

'True, true,' said Snorri with a nod, his smile fading. 'What we have built is worthy of legend, isn't it? Our two great realms have driven back the beasts and the daemons and the lands are safe for our people. Trade has never been better, and the holds grow with every year.'

'Your reign has indeed been glorious, Snorri,' said Malekith. 'Your line is strong; your son will uphold the great things that you have done.'

'And perhaps even build on them,' said Snorri.

'Perhaps, if the gods will it,' said Malekith.

'And why should they not?' asked Snorri. He coughed as he pushed himself to a sitting position, his shoulders sinking into thick, gold-embroidered white pillows. 'Though my breath comes short and my body is infirm, my will is as hard as the stone that these walls are carved from. I am a dwarf, and like all my people, I have within me the strength of the mountains. Though this body is now weak, my spirit shall go to the Halls of the Ancestors.'

'It will be welcomed there, by Grungni and Valaya and Grimnir,' said Malekith. 'You shall take your place with pride.'

'I'm not done,' said Snorri with a frown. His expression grim, the king continued. 'Hear this oath, Malekith of the Elves, comrade on the battlefield, friend at the hearth. I, Snorri Whitebeard, high king of the dwarfs, bequeath my title and rights to my eldest son. Though I pass through the gateway to the Halls of the Ancestors, my eyes shall remain upon my empire. Let it be known to our allies and our enemies that death is not the end of my guardianship.'

The dwarf broke into a wracking cough, blood flecking his lips. His lined faced was stern as he looked at Malekith. The elf steadily returned his gaze.

'Vengeance shall be mine,' swore Snorri. 'When our foes are great, I shall return to my people. When the foul creatures of this world bay at the doors to Karaz-a-Karak, I shall take up my axe once more and my ire shall rock the mountains. Heed my words, Malekith of Ulthuan, and heed them well. Great have been our deeds, and great is the legacy that I leave to you, my closest confidant, my finest comrade in arms. Swear to me now, as my dying breaths fill my lungs, *that my oath has been heard. Swear to it on my own grave, on my spirit, that you shall remain true to the ideals we have both striven for these many years. And know this, that there is nothing so foul in the world as an oath-breaker.'*

Malekith took the king's hand from his arm and squeezed it tight. 'I swear it,' the elf prince said. 'Upon the grave of high king Snorri Whitebeard, leader of the dwarfs and friend of the elves, I give my oath.'

Snorri's eyes were glazed and his chest no longer rose and fell. The keen hearing of the elf could detect no sign of life, and he did not know whether his words had been heard. Releasing Snorri's hand, he folded the king's arms across his chest and with a delicate touch from his long fingers, Malekith closed Snorri's eyes.

Standing, Malekith spared one last glance at the dead king and then walked from the chamber. Outside, Snorri's son Throndik stood along with several dozen other dwarfs.

'The high king has passed on,' Malekith said, his gaze passing over the heads of the assembled dwarfs and across the throne room. He looked down at Throndik. 'You are now high king.'

Without further word, the elf prince walked gracefully through the crowd and out across the nearly empty throne chamber. Word was passed by some secret means throughout the hold and soon the drums stopped. With Throndik at their head, the dwarfs entered the chamber and lifted the king from his deathbed. Bearing Snorri's body aloft on their broad shoulders, the dwarfs marched slowly across the throne chamber to a stone bier that had been set before the throne itself. They lay the king upon the stone and turned away.

The doors to the throne room were barred for three days while the remaining preparations for the funeral were made. Throndik was still prince and would not become king until his father had been buried, so he busied himself with *sending messengers to the other holds to bear the news of the king's death.*

At the appointed hour, the throne room was opened once more by an honour guard led by Throndik Snorrisson and Godri Stonehewer. As once more the solemn drums echoed through the hold, the funeral procession bore the high king to his final resting place deep within Karaz-a-Karak. There were no eulogies, there was no weeping, for Snorri's exploits were there for all to see in the carvings upon the stone casket within his tomb. His life had been well spent and there was no cause to mourn his passing.

On Snorri's instructions, the casket had been carved with dire runes of vengeance and grudgebearing by the most powerful runelords in the hold. Inlaid with gold, the symbols glowed with magical light as Snorri was lowered into the sarcophagus. The lid was then placed on the stone coffin and bound with golden bands. The runelords, chanting in unison, struck their final sigils onto the bands, warding away foul magic and consigning Snorri's spirit to the Halls of the Ancestors. There was a final crescendo of drums rolling in long echoes along the halls and corridors over the heads of the silent dwarfs that had lined the procession route.

Throndik performed the last rite. Taking up a small keg of beer, he filled a tankard with the foaming ale and took a sip. With a nod of approval, he reverently placed the tankard on top of the carved stone casket.

'Drink deep in the Halls of the Ancestors,' intoned Throndik. 'Raise this tankard to those who have passed before you, so that they might remember those that still walk upon the world.'

BY MID-MORNING the following day, the dwarf army had left the World's Edge Mountains and was in the foothills that surrounded the Zhuf-durak, known by men as the River Aver Reach. The thudding of the cargo-loco's steam pistons echoed from the hillsides over the babbling of the river, while the deep murmuring of dwarfs in conversation droned constantly.

At the head of the column, Throndin marched with Barundin and Arbrek. The king had been in a silent mood since the encounter with the peddler the day before. Whether he was deep in thought or sulking because of Arbrek's soft admonishment, Barundin didn't know, but he was not going to intrude on his father's thoughts at this time.

A distant buzzing from the sky caused the dwarfs to lift their heads and gaze into the low cloud. A speck of darkness from the west grew closer, bobbing up and down ever so slightly in an erratic course. The puttering of a gyrocopter's engine grew louder as the aircraft approached and there were pointed fingers and a louder commotion as the pilot pushed his craft into a dive and swooped over the column. Almost carving a furrow in a hilltop with the whirling rotors of the gyrocopter as he dipped toward the ground, the pilot swung his machine around and then passed above the convoy more sedately. About a half a mile ahead, a great trailing of dust that rose as a cloud into the air marked the pilot's landing.

As they neared, Barundin could see the pilot more clearly. His beard and face were soot-stained, two pale rings around his eyes from where his goggles had been. Those goggles dangled from a strap attached to the side of the dwarf's winged helms, hanging down over his shoulder. Over a long chainmail shirt the pilot wore a set of heavy leather overalls, much darned and patched.

The pilot regarded the king and his retinue with a pronounced squint as he watched them approach.

'Is that you, Rimbal Wanazaki?' said Barundin.

The pilot gave a nod and a grin, displaying broken, yellowing, uneven teeth. 'Right you are, lad,' said Wanazaki.

'We thought you were dead!' said Throndin. 'Some nonsense about a troll lair.'

'Aye, there's a lot of it about,' replied Wanazaki. 'But I'm not dead, as you can see for yourself.'

'More's the bloody pity,' said Throndin. 'I meant what I said. You're no longer welcome in my halls.'

'You're still mad about that little explosion?' said Wanazaki with a disconsolate shake of the head. 'You're a hard king, Throndin, a hard king.'

'Get gone,' said Throndin, thrusting a thumb over his shoulder. 'I shouldn't even be talking to you.'

'Well, you're not in your halls now, your kingship, so you can listen and you don't have to say a word,' said Wanazaki.

'Well, what have you got to say for yourself?' said the king. 'I haven't got the time to waste with you.'

The pilot held up one hand to quiet the king. Reaching into his belt, he pulled out a delicate-looking tankard, no bigger than twice the size of a thimble, so small that only one finger would fit into its narrow handle. Turning to the gyrocopter engine, which was still making the odd coughing and spluttering noise, he turned a small tap on the side of one tank. Clear liquid dripped out into the small mug, which the pilot filled almost to the rim. Barundin's eyes began to moisten as the vapours from the fuel-alcohol stung them.

With a wink at the king, the disgraced engineer knocked back the liquid. For a moment he stood there, doing nothing. Wanazaki then gave a small cough and Barundin could see his hands trembling. Thumping a fist against his chest, the pilot coughed again, much louder, then stamped his foot. Eyes slightly glazed, he leaned forwards and squinted at the king.

'It's orcs you're after, am I right?' said Wanazaki. The king did not reply immediately, still taken aback by the engineer's curious drinking habit.

'Yes,' Throndin said eventually.

'I've seen them,' said Wanazaki. 'About thirty, maybe thirty-five miles south of here. Day's march, no more, if it's a step.'

'Within a day's march?' exclaimed Barundin. 'Are you sure? Which way are they heading?'

'Course he's not sure,' said Throndin. 'This grog-swiller probably doesn't know a mile from a step.'

'A day's march, I'm telling you,' insisted Wanazaki. 'You'd be there by midday tomorrow if you turn south now. They were camped, all drunk and fat by the looks of it. I seen smoke to the west, reckon they've been having some fun.'

'If we go now, we could catch them before they sober up, take them in their camp,' said Barundin. 'It'd be an easy runk and no mistake.'

'We don't need some gangly manlings – we can take them,' said Ferginal, one of Throndin's stonebearers and a cousin of Barundin on his dead mother's side. The comment was met with a general shout of encouragement from the younger members of the entourage.

'Pah!' snorted Arbrek, turning with a scowl to the boisterous dwarfs. 'Listen to the beardlings! All eager for war, are you? Ready to march for a day and a night and fight a battle? Made of mountain stone, are you? Barely a full beard between you and all ready to rush off to battle against the greenskins. Foolhardy, that's what they'd call you if you ever lived long enough to have sons of your own.'

'We're not scared!' came a shouted reply. The dwarf that had spoken up quickly ducked behind his comrades as Arbrek's withering stare was brought to bear.

'Fie to scared – you'll be dead!' snarled the runelord. 'Get another thousand miles under them legs of yours and you might be ready to force march straight into battle. How are you going to swing an axe or hammer without no puff, eh?'

'What do you say, father?' said Barundin, turning to the king.

'I'm as eager to settle this grudge as any of you,' Throndin, and there was a roaring cheer. It quieted as he raised his hands. 'But it'd be rash to chase off after these orcs on the words of a drunken outcast.'

Wanazaki gave a grin and a thumbs up at being mentioned.

Throndin shook his head in disgust. 'Besides, even if the old wazzock is right, there's no guarantee the orcs would be still around when we got there,' the king continued. There was a rumble of disappointment from the throng. 'Most importantly,' Throndin added, raising his voice above the disgruntled grumbling, 'I made a promise to Baron Vessal to meet him, and who here would have their king break his promise?'

As THEY MARCHED westwards to their rendezvous with the men of Baron Vessal, the dwarf army crossed the advance of the orcs. The signs were unmistakable: the ground trampled and littered with discarded scraps and even the air itself still filled with their taint, emanating from indiscriminate piles of orc dung. The most veteran orc-fighters inspected the spoor and tracks and estimated there to be over a thousand greenskins. Even with just eight hundred warriors, all that duty would spare from the guarding of Zhufbar, Throndin felt confident.

Even if Vessal had only a handful of men, the army would be more than a match for the greenskins.

As the evening twilight began to spill across the hills, several campfires could be seen in the distance along a line of hills.

About a mile from the camp, the leading elements of the dwarf army encountered two men on the trail. Two horses were tethered to a tree and a small fire with a steaming pot was set to one side of the road. They were dressed in long studded coats and bore bulky harquebuses. Throndin could smell ale. They looked nervously at each other and then one stepped forward.

'Ware!' he shouted. 'Who would pass into the lands of Baron Vessal of Averland?'

'I bloody would,' shouted Throndin, stomping forward.

'And you are?' asked the sentry, his voice wavering.

'This is King Throndin of Zhufbar, ally to your master,' said Barundin, carrying his father's standard to the king's side. 'Who addresses the king?'

'Well,' said the man with a glance behind him at his companion, who was busily studying his feet, 'Gustav Feldenhoffen, that's me. Road warden. We's road wardens for the baron. He said to challenge anyone on the road, like.'

'A credit to your profession,' said Throndin, giving the man a comforting pat on the arm. 'Dedicated to your duty, I see. Where's the baron?'

Feldenhoffen relaxed with a sigh and waved towards a large tent near one of the fires. 'The baron's in the centre of the camp, your, er, kingliness,' said the road warden. 'I can take you, if you'd like.'

'Don't worry, I'll find him right enough,' said Throndin. 'Wouldn't want you leaving your post.'

'Yes, you're right,' said Feldenhoffen. 'Well, take care. Erm, see you at the battle.'

The king grunted as the road warden stepped aside. Throndin waved the army forwards again and passed the word to his thanes to organise the camp while he sought out the baron. Tomorrow they would march to battle, and he was looking for a good night's sleep before all the exertion.

THE SUN WAS barely over the horizon and Baron Vessal looked none too pleased about a visit from his dwarf ally. For his part, Throndin was dressed in full battle armour, his massive double-bladed axe propped up against his leg as he sat on the oversized stool, and he seemed eager to get going. Vessal, on the other hand, was still in his purple bed robes, scratching at his stubbled chin as he listened to the dwarf king.

'So I suggest you use your horsey men to go ahead and look for the orcs,' Throndin was saying. 'When you've found them, we can get after them.'

'Get after them?' said the baron, eyes widening. He smoothed back the straggling black hair that was hanging down around his shoulders, revealing a thin, almost haggard face. 'Not to be indelicate, but how do you propose you'll catch them? Your army is not built for speed, is it?'

'They're orcs, they'll come to us,' Throndin assured him. 'We'll pick somewhere good, send a bit of bait forward – you for example – and then draw them in and finish them.'

'And where do you propose to make this stand?' asked Vessal with a sigh. He had drunk more wine than he was used to the night before and the early hour was not helping his headache.

'Where have the orcs been lately?' Throndin asked.

'Up and down the Aver Reach, heading westwards,' replied Vessal. 'Why?'

'Well, we'll set up somewhere west of where they last attacked and wait for them,' said Throndin. The king scowled as the sound of the first pattering of rain trembled across the canvas of the tent.

'Surely such hardened warriors are not troubled by marching in a little rain?' said Vessal, raising his eyebrows.

'Don't rain much under a mountain,' said Throndin with a grimace. 'Makes your pipe weed soggy, and your beard all wet. Rain's no good for a well-crafted cannon, nor the black powder needed to fire it. Some of them engineers are clever, but I still haven't met the one who'd invented black powder that'll burn when it's wet.'

'So we stay in camp today?' suggested Vessal, his enthusiasm for the idea plain to see.

'It's your folk getting killed and robbed,' Throndin pointed out. 'We can kill orcs whenever we like. We're in no hurry.'

'Yes, I suppose you're right,' agreed the baron. 'My tenants tend to get argumentative about taxes when there's orcs or bandits on the loose. The sooner it is settled the quicker things can return to normal.'

'So, get your army ready to march and we'll head west as soon as you like,' said Throndin, slapping himself on the thighs as he stood up. He grabbed his axe and swung it over his shoulder as he turned.

'West?' said Vessal as the dwarf king was heading for the flaps of the door. 'That'll take us into the Moot.'

'Where?' said Throndin, turning around.

'Mootland, the halfling realm,' Vessal told him.

'Oh, the grombolgi-kazan,' said Throndin with a grin. 'What's the matter with that?'

'Well, they're not my lands, for a start,' said Vessal, standing up. 'And there'll be halflings there.'

'So?' asked Throndin, scratching his beard and shaking his head.

'Well…' began Vessal before shaking his head as well. 'I'm sure it will be fine. My men will be ready to march within the hour.'

Throndin gave a nod of approval and walked out of the tent. Vessal slumped back into his padded chair with a heavy sigh. He glanced towards the table where he had been dining with his advisors and saw the piles of half-eaten chicken and the nearly empty goblets of wine. The thought of the excess the night before made his stomach heave and he shouted for his servants to attend him.

By the time the baron was ready, dressed in his full plate armour and mounted atop his grey stallion, the dwarfs were already lined up along the trail. The rain rattled from their armour and metal standards like hundreds of tiny dancers on a metal stage, jarring every hangover-heightened nerve in Vessal's body. He gritted his teeth as Throndin gave him a cheery wave from the front of the column and raised his hand in return.

'The sooner this is over with, the better,' the baron said between gritted teeth.

'Would you rather we did this alone?' asked Captain Kurgereich, the baron's most experienced soldier and head of his personal guard.

'Not after sending them all of my bloody money,' snarled Vessal. 'I thought they'd be only too happy for some help killing the orcs that slew the king's heir. They were meant to send back my gift.'

'Never show a dwarf gold, my old grandmother used to say,' replied Kurgereich.

'Well the old hag was a very wise woman indeed,' growled Vessal. 'Send out the scouts and then leave me in peace. All this, and bloody halflings as well.'

Kurgereich turned his horse away to hide his smirk and cantered off to find the outriders. Within minutes the light cavalry had ridden off and soon some fifty knights and the baron's two hundred infantry were trudging along the road, which had started to resemble a shallow stream in the continuing downpour.

Over the tramping of feet, a bass tone rose in volume as Throndin led his host in a marching song. Soon eight hundred dwarfs in full voice made the banks of the Aver tremble as they advanced to the rhythm of the tune. At the end of each couplet the dwarfs crashed their weapons on their shields, the sound reverberating along the line. As they fell in behind the baron's men, the dwarfs' war horn joined the chorus, its long blasts punctuating every verse.

It was mid-afternoon when they sighted smoke on the horizon, and within two miles they came across a halfling village. Across the rolling hills, low, sprawling houses were spread between dirt tracks next to a wide lake. As they came closer, they could see uneven windows and doors carved into the turf of the hills themselves, surrounded by hedged gardens over which tall plants could be seen waving in the rain-flecked breeze.

Baron Vessal called a halt and dismounted, waiting for Throndin to join him. Heinlein Kulft stood beside him, holding the sodden banner of his lord. Barundin accompanied his father, proudly hefting the standard of Zhufbar and exchanging a glance with Kulft. A reedy voice drifted out of the bushes that lined the road.

'Dwarf and tall folk in Midgwater, by my old uncle, I wouldn't believe it hadn't I seen it with me own eyes,' the voice said.

Turning, Barundin saw a small figure, shorter even than he, with a thick mop of hair and side burns that reached almost to his mouth. The halfling was dressed in a thick green shirt that was dripping with rain. His leather breeches were around his ankles and he glanced down and then tugged them back up, tying them at his waist with a thin rope belt.

'You caught me unawares,' the halfling said, jutting out his chin and puffing out his chest.

'Who is your elder?' asked Kulft. 'We must speak with him.'

'He's a she, not a he,' said the halfling. 'Melderberry Weatherbrook, lives in the burrow on the other side of the lake. She'll be having tea 'bout now, I would say.'

'Then we'll be on our way, and leave you to your...' Kulft's voice trailed off at the stare from the halfling. 'Whatever it is you're doing.'

'You after them orcs?' the halfling asked.

Throndin and Vessal both looked sharply at the halfling but it was Barundin who spoke first.

'What do you know, little one?' the king's son asked.

'Little one?' snapped the halfling. 'I'm quite tall. My whole family is, 'cept for my third cousin Tobarias, who's a little on the short side. Anyways, the orcs. My uncle Fredebore, the one on my grandfather's side, was out fishing on the river with some friends and they saw them. Rowed back sharpish they did, 'bout lunchtime. Them orcs is heading this way they reckons.'

Vessal absorbed this news in silence, while Throndin turned to Arbrek, who had joined them. 'What do you think?' the king asked his runelord.

'If they're coming here, no point in marching when we don't have to,' Arbrek replied. 'Good hills for the cannons, plenty of food and ale, if the tales of the grombolgi are true. Could be worse.'

Throndin nodded and turned to the halfling. 'Is there somewhere we can camp, close by to the lake?' he asked.

'Stick yourselves in old farmer Wormfurrow's field,' the halfling told them. 'He died last week and his missus won't be complaining, not with her being up at farmer Wurtwither's place these days. No one's seen her since the funeral, four days ago.'

'Right then,' said Throndin. 'I'll go see Elder Weatherbrook, everyone else make camp in the fields.'

'I'll come with you,' said Vessal. 'My lands border the Moot, I know these folk a little better than you.'

'I'll be glad of the company,' said Throndin with a glance at Barundin. 'Help with the camp, lad. I don't think waving standards around is going to impress anyone around these parts.'

Barundin nodded and started walking back towards the other dwarfs. Kulft looked to the baron, who waved him away with barely a glance.

'Shall we go?' the king asked. Vessal nodded. As they began to walk up the road, Throndin stopped and patted his belt. With a frown, he turned back down the road but the halfling was nowhere to be seen.

'The little kruti's had it away with my pipe,' the king exclaimed.

'I did try to warn you,' said Vessal. 'I'm sure you'll get it back soon enough, just don't accuse anyone of thieving – they don't take to it in the Moot.'

'But he stole my pipe!' growled Throndin. 'Theft's theft! I'm going to be bringing this up with the elder when we see her.'

'It won't help,' said Vessal, motioning with his head for them to continue up the road. 'They just don't understand. You'll see.'

* * *

THE WHITE STONE of the city's walls was marked with soot as
flames and smoke poured across the sky from the burning
buildings inside the elven settlement of Tor Alessi. Tall spires,
their peaks glittering with silver and gold, disappeared in the
thick clouds, towering many hundreds of feet into the smoke-
choked heavens.

A double gateway protected by three slender towers was
battered and scorched, and stone blocks fell to the ground as
boulders hurled through the sky crashed into them. By the
gates themselves, short armoured figures hauled an iron-
shafted battering ram forward.

Flocks of white arrows dove down onto the dwarf army
from the cracked battlements above, punching through raised
shields and oiled chainmail. Withering fire from repeating
bolt throwers hurled branch-like missiles into the ranks of the
assembled throng, cutting down a dozen dwarfs at a time,
ripping holes through the packed mass pressing towards the
beleaguered gate towers.

Above the dwarfs the barrage of rocks from the siege
catapults continued, as armoured warriors surged forwards to take the places of the fallen. With a resounding
crash, the battering ram slammed into the thick white
timbers of the right-hand gate, sending splinters and
shards of metal into the air. With a bellowed order, the
dwarfs hauled the ram back, some of them dragging aside
the dead to make way for the iron-rimmed wheels of the
war machine.

With a collective grunt that could be heard above the
crackle of flames and the shouts of the wounded and dying,
the dwarfs pushed forwards once more, the serrated spike of
the ram again biting into the wood, ripping between the
planks of the gate and shearing through the bars beyond.
With a triumphant roar the dwarfs stormed forwards,
throwing their weight against the ram and forcing the
breach in the gate even wider. Drawing their axes, the

dwarfs continued to hack at the planks until there was enough room to force their way through.

A storm of arrows swept through the gateway, embedding themselves into helmeted heads and piercing iron rings of mail shirts. At the centre of the dwarfs' charge was a figure decked in ornate plate armour and shining mail, a purple cloak flowing from his shoulders. His face was hidden behind the metal ancestor mask of his helm, his long white beard flowing from beneath it, clasped with golden bands.

The warrior's armour glowed with runes, and the sigils upon his great two-handed axe pulsed with magical energies as he thundered into the elf line, the arcane blade slicing through armour, flesh and bone with ease.

None of the other dwarfs knew who the mysterious warrior was or where he came from, and over the long years of fighting none could recall when he had first appeared. Like an avenging spirit he had turned up at the first battle against the elves, when the ancient alliance had been shattered with discord. As tales of the fighter's prowess spread, he was given a simple name, but one that now conjured up images of bloodshed and vengeance – the White Dwarf.

BARUNDIN SCOWLED AND rounded on the halfling barmaid stood behind him.

'If you pinch my backside one more time...' he growled. But Shella Heartyflanks was unconcerned. With a leer and a wink, she turned away and swept between the tables of the small inn, enthusiastically waving her jugs at the dwarfs that had taken up residence for the evening.

All day Barundin had been pestered by complaints from the other dwarfs. His father, in his wisdom, had immediately deferred all halfling-related matters to the prince and closeted himself away with Arbrek and his other advisors. Since then, Barundin had not had a moment's peace.

He'd been forced to set up a standing guard around the baggage train after reports that the light-fingered Mootfolk had been helping themselves to ale, tobacco, bed sheets, black powder and all manner of sundry items. His father had told him not to hurt any of the halflings, but to gently but insistently keep them at arm's length.

Then there had been the episode with the two young halflings that had been found in an act of intimacy under Norbred Sterneye's wagon, and Barundin had been forced to resort to a bucket of water to resolve the situation before some of the older dwarfs exploded with indignation.

Just as he had been losing the will to live, the invitation had been passed around that the Red Dragon Inn was willing to provide free ale and food to the bold protectors of Midgwater. Barundin, while thankful for the show of generosity, had then been engaged in a long and complicated process of planning how to get eight hundred thirsty dwarfs into an inn no bigger than a forge fire, whilst making sure there were enough bodies left behind to protect the camp from the acquisitive attentions of the halflings.

When he had finally managed to enjoy the tavern's hospitality himself, late into the night after many others had retired to bed, he had been less than thrilled to find that the old halfling, Shella, had taken a fancy to him. He was sure his buttocks would be black and blue all over from her playful yet painful signs of affection.

It was with some relief then that a table near to the nook was vacated and Barundin hurriedly occupied the space with a sigh. The relief was short-lived though, as the doors opened and his father strode in, bellowing for a mug of the finest ale. Baron Vessal stooped through the low doorway behind him, followed by his marechal, Kulft.

The trio saw Barundin and headed across the inn towards him, the manlings bent at the waist to avoid the beams across the ceiling. Barundin pushed himself to his feet to make space for the new arrivals, as Shella brought over three foaming tankards and slammed them onto the table. She reached across to ostensibly wipe at a spillage, and Barundin tried to squeeze himself into the bricks of the wall as the halfling pressed herself against him in an attempt to push past.

When she was gone, they settled down, and Barundin managed to clear his mind and concentrate on his beer, blocking out the occasional conversation that passed between the others. He vaguely heard the rusted hinges of the doors squeaking again and felt his father tense next to him.

'By Grungni's flowing beard…' muttered Throndin, and Barundin looked up to see what was happening.

In front of the door stood the peddler, still swathed in his ragged travelling cloak, his heavy pack across his shoulders. He glanced around the inn for a moment, until his eyes lingered on Throndin. As he crossed the room, the pedlar pulled his pipe from his belt and began stuffing it with tobacco. By the time he had reached their table, he was busily puffing away on the pipe.

'Hail, King Throndin of Zhufbar,' the dwarf said with a short bow.

'Is this a friend of yours?' said Vessal, eyeing the newcomer suspiciously.

'Not at all,' growled Throndin. 'I believe he was just leaving.'

'It is by the hospitality of the grombolgi that I stay, not by the invite of the King of Zhufbar,' the pedlar replied as he worked his way onto the end of a bench, shoving Kulft into the baron.

The king said nothing and an uneasy quiet descended, broken only by the crackling fire nearby and the murmuring from the other tables.

'So, you'll be fighting tomorrow then?' said the stranger.

'Aye,' replied Throndin, staring into his mug of ale.

'It's a fine body of warriors you've got here,' the stranger said. 'Are you sure it'll be enough though?'

'I think we can handle a few orcs,' said Barundin. 'We also have the baron's men. Why, do you know something?'

'I know many things, beardling,' said the pedlar before pausing to blow a trio of smoke rings that floated around Kulft's head. The baron's companion coughed loudly and swept them away with his hand.

The stranger looked at Throndin. 'I know that he who is as hard as stone, shall break as stone,' the pedlar said, looking at the baron. 'And he who is as hard as wood, shall break as wood.'

'Look here, vagabond, I don't like your tone at all!' replied Vessal. He looked at Throndin. 'Can't you control your people, casting aspersions all over the place like that?'

'He's not one of mine,' said Throndin with a grunt.

'Well, it seems that nothing can change in a day,' the stranger said, packing away his pipe and standing up. 'Even an old fool like me can tell when he's welcome, and when his wisdom falls on deaf ears. But you'll remember this, in a time to come, and then you'll know.'

They watched as he turned away and walked back towards the door.

'Know what?' Barundin called after him, but the stranger did not reply, and left the inn without a backward glance.

A PARTY OF halfling hunters returned in the early hours the next morning, warning that their predictions had been correct. The orcs were moving in force down the Aver, straight towards Midgwater.

Throndin was unconcerned, as this was exactly what he had hoped would happen. He walked out of the halfling village, ignoring the stray dogs running beside him, and looked across the fields to the east of the town where his army and the baron's men were readying themselves for battle.

The dwarfs held the northernmost fields, their flank secured by the rushing waters of the River Aver. Behind the dwarf army, atop a line of hills that had recently been home to several halfling families, now evicted for their own safety and Throndin's sanity, sat the four cannons that had been brought with them. The steam loco sat like a silent shadow behind them, its small cannon not yet fired up. The morning sun gleamed with a golden light from polished iron barrels and gilded ancestor faces, and Throndin paused for a moment to enjoy the sight.

In a staggered line, his warriors were spread across the field, groups of thunderers armed with handguns taking up positions behind fences and hedges, his crossbow-armed quarrellers on the slopes of the hills in front of the cannons. At the centre stood Barundin with the standard of Zhufbar, protected by the hold's Hammerers – Throndin's own bodyguard.

At the very end of the line was a mess of halflings, carrying bows, hunting spears and other weaponry. They had arrived at dawn, declaring their intent to fight for themselves, and Throndin had not had the heart to send them on their way. They had looked so eager, and many of them had a dangerous glint in their eyes that had caused the dwarf king to pause for moment. He had concluded that they were far better on the battlefield where he could see them than causing trouble somewhere else.

In consultation with Captain Kurgereich, Throndin had arranged for the halflings to be positioned between Throndin's axe-wielding hearth guard and the bodyguard of the baron, in an effort to keep them out of harm's way as much as possible,

To the south were arranged the baron's spearmen and halberdiers, with his knights held in reserve behind them, ready to counter-attack. The basic plan was to shelter under the cannonade for as long as possible, before the dwarfs marched forwards to finish the battle toe-to-toe. The baron was to ensure no swift-moving wolf riders or chariots swept around the end of the dwarf line and attacked them from behind. It was simple, and both Throndin and Krugereich had agreed that was for the best.

The waiting went on for several hours, through lunchtime (both elevenses and lunchtime in the case of the halflings), and into the afternoon. Throndin began to fear that the orcs would not reach Midgwater in the daylight hours, but the doubts had only begun to form when he noticed a dust cloud on the horizon. Soon after, the easterly breeze brought the stench of the orc horde wafting over the army, causing the horses to stamp and whinny and the halflings to choke.

At the merest hint of the orc smell, a strange mood came over the dwarfs, a race memory of holds being destroyed and ancestors being slain. They began a mournful dirge, which rippled along the line and gathered in strength, as Throndin walked out from his hammerers to stare at the approaching horde. The low blast of war horns accompanied the sombre hymn, echoing from the hills around the battlefield.

There were gasps of dismay from the manlings as the orcs came into view. There were many more than anyone had expected – several thousand brutal green-skinned savages. The horde stretched out from the riverbanks for a mile, their tattered banners and skull totems bobbing up and down above the green mass as they advanced.

Throndin could see their war boss, a broad warrior that stood over a head taller than the orcs around him, his face daubed in black war paint with only his evil red eyes showing through. He wore a great horned helm and carried a cleaver as long as a halfling was tall in each hand, their serrated blades glinting in the afternoon sun.

Upon seeing their foes, the orcs gave up a great clamour of shouting, and beat their weapons upon the fanged faces daubed onto their shields. Their harsh voices cut the air, the cacophony of bellowing drowning out the deep song of the dwarf army. Brassy horns and erratic drumbeats signalled the advance to begin anew and the orcs came pouring forward, waving weapons and shields in the air.

Throndin gestured for his stonebearers and they came forward, carrying between them a lump of granite, hewn into a long flat step carved with runes. Lowering it to the ground by the iron rings driven into its ends, they placed the grudgestone in front of the king. He gave them a nod and then turned to face his army, who fell silent.

'Here I place the grudgestone of Zhufbar, and here we shall stand,' he called out, his voice clear above the tumult of the orcs. 'I shall be victorious standing upon this grudgestone, or I shall be buried beneath it. No dwarf takes a step back from this line. Death or victory!'

With great ceremony Throndin took a step up onto the stone and unslung his broad-bladed axe. He hefted it above his head and a great cheer went up from the dwarfs. At his signal, the battle began.

With a loud roar, the first cannon opened fire and its ball went sailing over the heads of the dwarfs. Pitching off the turf in a great explosion of mud and grass, the ball skidded forwards and slammed through the orc line, ripping limbs from bodies and smashing bones. A great cheer went up from the men of the baron, while the dwarfs resumed their mournful hymn to Grimnir.

A succession of three loud reports signalled the start of the bombardment as the other cannons opened fire. Unconcerned by the mounting casualties, the orcs continued forward, screaming and cavorting in their excitement. The swish of crossbow quarrels and the rattle of handgun fire added to the noise of battle as the other dwarf troops loosed their weapons upon the charging greenskins.

Fully a third of the orc host had been wounded or killed by the time it crashed into the dwarf line. Fanged faces bellowing battle cries met stubborn bearded visages set with grim intensity.

The cleavers and mauls of the orcs clanged off mail and plate armour, while the axes and hammers of the dwarfs cleaved through flesh and pulverised bone. Despite their losses, the orcs pushed onwards, their numbers beginning to tell against the thin dwarf line. Thunderers wielded their guns like clubs while Throndin's axe sang through the air as he cleaved apart his foes.

The ground shook with a great pounding, and Throndin felt the thundering of many hooves. He turned to his right and glanced over the heads of his comrades, expecting to see Vessal's knights charging forwards to counter some move by the orcs to surround the dwarfs. To his dismay, he saw a wall of boar-mounted greenskins charging through the halflings, crushing them beneath their trotters and spitting them on crude spears.

'The baron, he has abandoned us!' cried Barundin, standing next to the king. The prince pointed over his shoulder and Throndin turned to see the humans retreating from the field. The orcs were advancing quickly across the now open field.

'The oathbreaker!' shouted Throndin, almost falling off his grudgestone.

The squealing of gigantic boars mingled with the crude shouts of the charging orcs drowned out Throndin's curses. Spears lowered, the boar riders smashed into Throndin's hammerers like a thunderbolt.

Crude iron speartips crashed against dwarf-forged steel armour while the boars trampled and gored anything in front of them. The hammerers swung their heavy mattocks in wide arcs, smashing riders from their porcine steeds and breaking bones. In the midst of the fighting, Throndin stood upon his grudgestone lopping off heads and limbs with his rune axe, bellowing the names of his ancestors as he did so.

A particularly large and brutal orc came charging through the mass, his heavy spear held above his head. Throndin turned and raised his axe to parry the blow but was too slow. The serrated point of the spear slid between the overlapping plates protecting his left shoulder and bit deep into royal flesh. With a roar of pain, Throndin brought his axe down, carving the orc's arm from its body. The spear was still embedded in the king's chest, with arm attached, as he took a step backwards, the world spinning around him. His foot slipped from the back of the grudge-stone and he toppled to the muddy ground with a crash.

Hengrid Dragonfoe gave a shout to his fellow hammerers and they surged forward around the king as more orcs poured into the fray, joining the boar riders. Barundin was caught up in the swirling melee, his axe cutting left and right as he fought to stand beside his father. The king's face was pale and deep red was spilled across his armour from the grievous wound. Throndin's eyes were still open though, and they turned to Barundin.

Feeling his father's gaze upon him, Barundin planted the standard into the dirt, driving it down through the turf of the field. He hefted his axe and lunged forward to meet the oncoming greenskins.

'For Zhufbar!' he shouted. 'For King Throndin!'

THE GOBLINS SCATTERED *as the lone figure approached, abandoning their looting of the corpses strewn across the narrow mountain valley. Dead orcs and goblins were piled five deep in places, around the bodies of the dwarfs they had ambushed, who had fought to the very end. The goblins backed away to the far end of the valley, fearful of the powerful aura that surrounded the newly arrived dwarf.*

He was dressed in rune-encrusted armour, a purple cloak hanging from his shoulders. His long white beard was banded with golden clasps as it spilled from his helm to his knees. The White Dwarf picked his way through the piles of the slain, his gaze sweeping left and right. Seeing the object of his search, he cut right, pushing his way past a mound of dismembered orc bodies. Within the circle of dead greenskins lay four dwarfs, amongst them a battered metal standard driven into the earth of the valley floor.

One of the dwarfs was sitting upright, his back to the standard, blood drying in his greying beard, his face a crimson mask. The dwarf's eyes fluttered opened at the approach of the White Dwarf and then widened in awe.

'Grombindal!' he wheezed, his voice cracked with pain.

'Aye, Prince Dorthin, it's me,' the White Dwarf replied, kneeling beside the fallen warrior and placing his axe on the ground. He gently laid a hand on the prince's shoulders. 'I wish I had arrived earlier.'

'There were too many of them,' the prince said, trying to pull himself up. Blood bubbled from a massive cut to his temple and he collapsed back again.

Dorthin looked up at the White Dwarf, his face twisted with pain. 'I'm dying, aren't I?'

'Yes,' the White Dwarf replied. 'You fought bravely, but this is your last battle.'

'They say you have come from the Halls of the Ancestors,' said Dorthin, one eye now clotted with fresh blood. 'Will they welcome me there?'

'Grungni and Valaya and Grimnir and your ancestors will more than welcome you,' said the White Dwarf. 'They will honour you!'

'My father...' said Dorthin.

'Will be very proud and aggrieved,' the White Dwarf interrupted him with a raised hand.

'He will declare a grudge against the orcs,' said Dorthin.

'He will,' said the White Dwarf with a nod.

'Will you help him avenge me?' asked the prince, his eyes now closed. His breath rattled in his throat, and with one final effort he forced himself to look at the White Dwarf. 'Will you avenge me?'

'I will be there for your father, because I could not be here for his son,' the White Dwarf promised. 'You have the oath of Grombrindal.'

'And we know that your oath is as hard as stone,' said the prince with a smile. His eyes closed once more and his body slumped as death took him.

The White Dwarf stood and looked across the battlefield before turning his gaze back to the fallen prince. He reached into his pack, unfolded a broad-headed shovel, and drove it into the ground.

'Aye, laddie,' he said as he started digging the first of many graves. 'Hard as stone, that's me.'

BARUNDIN'S ARM WAS beginning to ache as he chopped his axe into another orc head. His armour was dented and scratched from numerous blows, and he could feel broken ribs grinding inside him. Every time he breathed in, new pain flared through his chest.

It seemed hopeless. The orcs were all around them now, and the hammerers were virtually fighting back to back. Barundin glanced at his father, and saw blood frothing on his lips. At least the king was still alive, if only just.

A crude cleaver slammed into Barundin's helmet, dazing him for a second. He swung his axe in instinct, feeling it bite home. As he recovered his senses he saw an orc on the ground in front of him, cradling the stump of its left leg. He drove his axe into its chest, and the blade stuck.

As he tried to wrench the weapon free, another orc, almost twice as tall as Barundin, loomed out of the press, each hand grasping a wicked-looking scimitar. The orc grinned cruelly and swung the blade in its right hand at Barundin's chest, forcing the dwarf prince to duck. With a yell, Barundin yanked his axe free and brought it up, ready to deflect the next blow.

It never came.

A dwarf in shining rune armour crashed out of the orc ranks, his glittering axe hewing down foes in twos and threes with every swing. Orc blood stained his purple cloak and his flowing white beard was muddy and bloodied. With another mighty blow he cleaved the scimitar-armed orc from neck to waist.

Barundin stepped back in shock as the White Dwarf continued the assault, his axe a whirling, glowing arc of death for the orcs. Their clumsy blows rebounded harmlessly from his armour or missed entirely as the legendary warrior ducked and weaved through the melee, his every stroke disembowelling, severing and crushing.

Out of the corner of his eye, Barundin saw something moving, a golden light, and he turned to see the runelord, Arbrek Silverfingers. He had a golden horn in his hand, glowing with inner light. The runelord raised the instrument to his lips and blew a long, clear blast.

The deep blow reverberated across the battlefield, causing the ground itself to tremble. The note seemed to echo down from the clouds and rise up from the earth, filling the air with thunderous noise. The runelord took a deep breath and blew again, and this time Barundin felt the earth shaking beneath his boots. The shuddering grew in intensity and gaping cracks began to emerge in the tortured ground. Orcs and goblins toppled into the newly formed crevasses.

'Come on lad, don't just stand and gawp!' cried Hengrid raising his hammer above his head. Looking around, Barundin saw that the orcs were stunned, many of them on the ground clasping their ears, others pulling themselves out of holes and cracks.

Barundin snatched up the standard of Zhufbar in his left hand and charged forward with the hammerers, like the tail of a destructive comet behind the White Dwarf.

Hammers rose and fell onto orc skulls, while Barundin's axe bit into flesh and shattered bone. Within minutes, the orcs were broken, the tattered remnants of the horde fleeing faster than the dwarfs could follow.

The enemy vanquished, Barundin felt exhaustion sweep through his body and his legs weaken. He stumbled and then righted himself, aware that he was in front of his fellow dwarfs and needed to be strong.

He remembered his father and with a curse turned and ran back across the corpse-laden field to where the king still lay. Arbrek was beside Throndin, cradling his head and holding a tankard to the king's lips. Throndin spluttered, swallowed the beer, and heaved himself onto one arm.

'Father!' gasped Barundin as he came to a stop and leaned on the standard for support.

'Son,' croaked Throndin. 'I'm afraid I'm all done in.'

Barundin turned to Arbrek for some form of denial, but the runelord simply shook his head. The dwarf prince turned as he felt a presence behind him. It was the White Dwarf. With gauntleted hands, he removed his helm, his bushy beard gushing out like a waterfall. Barundin gave another gasp. The face that looked at him was that of the old pedlar.

The White Dwarf gave him a nod and then stepped past and knelt beside the king. 'We meet again, King Throndin of Zhufbar,' he said in a gruff tone.

'Grombrindal...' the king wheezed. He coughed and shook his head. 'I should have seen, but I refused to. It is not in our nature to forgive, so I can only offer my thanks.'

'It is not for gratitude that I am here,' replied the White Dwarf. 'My oath is as hard as stone, and cannot be broken. I only regret that the leader of the orcs escaped my axe, but I will find him again.'

'Everything would have been lost without you,' said Barundin. 'That oathbreaker Vessal must be held to account.'

'Manlings are weak by nature,' said the White Dwarf. 'Their time is so short, they fear to lose everything. Not for them the comfort of the Hall of Ancestors, and so each must make what he can of his short life and hold that life dearly.'

'He forsook his allies. He is nothing more than a coward,' growled Barundin.

The White Dwarf nodded, his gaze on Throndin. He stood and stepped up to Barundin, looking him in the eye. 'The King of Zhufbar is dead. You are now king,' the White Dwarf said. Barundin glanced over Grombrindal's shoulder and saw that it was true.

'King Barundin Throndinsson,' said Arbrek, also standing. 'What is your will?'

'We shall return to Zhufbar and bury our honoured dead,' said Barundin. 'I shall then take up the Book of Grudges and enter into it the name of Baron Silas Vessal of Uderstir. I shall right the wrong that has been done to us today.'

Barundin then looked at the White Dwarf. 'I swear an oath that it shall be so,' he said. 'Will you swear with me?'

'I cannot make that promise,' said the White Dwarf. 'The slayer of your brother still lives, and while he does, I must avenge Dorthin. In time, however, you may yet see me again. Look for me in the unseen places. Look for me when the world is at its darkest and when victory seems far away. I am Grombrindal, the White Dwarf, the grudgekeeper and the reckoner, and my watch is eternal.'

GRUDGE TWO
The Grudgesworn

THE DWARFS STOOD in a quiet group, King Barundin at their head, looking out over the battlefield. The pyres of orc bodies were now no more than dark patches in the mud and grass, and the grey sky was tinged with smoke from the halfling hearths around the battlefield.

Upon a bier decorated with golden knotwork and the stylised faces of hanging ancestor badges lay the body of King Throndin, held aloft by Ferginal and Durak. The king's stonebearers in life were now the carriers of his body in death. Beyond them, a large knot of halflings stood watching the ceremony, many of them weeping. Their scabrous little dogs even felt the mood, lying on the ground whining and yapping. For their part, the honour guard of dwarfs stood in stoic silence, their glimmering mail and long beards frosted by the cold air.

Arbrek stepped up to Barundin and gave a nod. The new King of Zhufbar cleared his throat and turned to the assembled mourners.

'In life, King Throndin was everything that a dwarf should be,' said Barundin. His gruff voice was deep and strong, the words well-rehearsed. 'Never one to forget a vow, his life was dedicated to Zhufbar and our clans. Now, as he looks upon us from the Hall of Ancestors, we give thanks for his sacrifice. I must now take up the burden that he carried upon his shoulders for those many long years.'

Barundin walked across to the shroud-covered body of the dead king. His face, pale and sunken in death, was framed by a shock of greying hair. Throndin's beard had been intricately braided into funerary knots, the better for him to look in the Halls of the Ancestors.

Throndin laid a hand upon his father's unmoving chest and looked eastwards, where the World's Edge Mountains reared up from beyond the horizon, disappearing into the low clouds.

'From stone we came and to stone we return,' said Barundin, his gaze focussed on the mountains in the distance. 'On this very field, a year ago, King Throndin gave his life. He died not in vain, for his life was taken avenging the death of his son and fulfilling his last oath.'

Barundin then looked at the dwarfs and pointed to the ground a short distance away. A hole had been dug, lined with carved stone tablets, and to one side on a small stand was Throndin's oathstone.

'Here my father took his last breath, to swear never to take a step back, never to surrender to our foes,' continued Barundin. 'He was true to his word and was struck down on this spot. As he swore then, so shall we obey his will. We have returned here from Zhufbar to see his wish carried out, after a due period of state and my true investiture as king. The clanhave paid their respects, we have received messages of courage from my fellow kings in the other holds, and my father has lay in state as appropriate to his station. Now it is time for us to wish him well on his journey to the Halls of the Ancestors.'

The bier-bearers marched forward with the body of the king, Barundin and Arbrek following them, and stood beside the open grave. Hengrid Dragonfoe joined them, a foaming mug of ale in his hand. It was halfling ale, nowhere near as good as dwarf ale, but the Elder of the village had been so adamant and sincere that Barundin had wilted under her impassioned request to provide the final pint. Arbrek had assured the king that his father would have been grateful for the gesture from the people he had died fighting to protect.

Hengrid handed him the mug and Barundin took a swig before placing the tankard on his father's chest. With great care Throndin's body was lowered into the grave until it rested on a stone plinth at its bottom. A covering stone, inlaid with silver runes of protection by Arbrek, was then lifted over the tomb, completing the blocky sarcophagus. Barundin took a proffered shovel and began to pile the earth from the grave onto the coffin of his father. When the funeral mound was complete, Ferginal and Durak took up the king's oath-stone and placed it at the top of the mound, marking the grave for all eternity.

'Stone to stone,' said Barundin.

'Stone to stone,' echoed the dwarfs around him.

'Rock to rock,' intoned the king.

'Rock to rock,' murmured the throng.

They stood in silence for a few moments, broken only by the yelps of dogs and the sniffling of the halflings themselves, each dwarf paying his last respects to the fallen king.

Finally, Barundin turned and faced the crowd of dwarfs. 'We return to Zhufbar,' the king said. 'There are fell deeds to be done, grudges to be written and oaths to be sworn. On this, the day of my father's end, I swear again that the name of Baron Silas Vessal of Uderstir is worth less than dirt, and his life is forfeit for his betrayal. I shall right the wrong that has been done to us by his treachery.'

BARUNDIN LED THE small host eastwards into the World's Edge Mountains and they took the southerly route towards Zhufbar, passing close to the ancient hold of Karak Varn. The dwarfs proceeded cautiously as they neared the fallen stronghold, keeping their axes and hammers loose in their belts. Small groups of rangers preceded them, wary of orcs and goblins and other foes who would look to attack them. On the afternoon of the second day, they reached the shores of Varn Drazh – Blackwater – a vast mountain lake that filled a crater smashed into the mountains millennia before.

The name was well earned, for the lake was still and dark, its surface rippled only by the strong mountain winds. As they marched along the shoreline, the dwarfs were quiet, wary of the creatures that were known to lurk in the depths of the water. Their unease grew as their course took them around Karaz Khrumbar, the tallest mountain surrounding the lake and site of the ancient beacon tower of Karak Varn. The blackened, tumbled stones of the outpost could still be seen littering the mountainside, gutted by fire nearly four thousand years earlier as orcs had attacked Karak Varn.

The fallen hold itself lay at the south-western edge of the lake, and the cliff face from which it had been delved could be seen rearing out of the mountain mists in the distance. Looking upon it, Barundin felt a tremor of emotion for his lost kinsmen, He could imagine the scene as vividly as if he'd been there four millennia ago, for the tale of the fall of Karak Varn had been a bedtime tale for him as a young dwarf, along with the stories of all the other dwarf holds.

The king could almost hear the sound of warning horns and drums echoing across the lake as the green skinned hordes had assaulted the small towers atop Karaz Khrumbar. They called in vain, for Karak Varn was already doomed. The mountains had shook with a ferocity never known and the great cliff had been rent in two, smashing aside the gates and allowing the cold waters of the Varn Drazh to pour into the hold, drowning thousands of dwarfs. Sensing the dwarfs' weakness, their enemies had gathered.

From below, in tunnels gnawed from the bedrock of the mountains, the rat-things had come, silently in the darkness, slitting throats and stealing away newborns. The dwarfs of Karak Varn had mustered what might they could against this skulking foe, but they'd been unprepared when the orcs and goblins had come from above.

The dwarfs of Karak Varn had fought valiantly, and their king refused to leave, but some clans realised their doom and managed to escape the trap before it fully closed. Some of those clans still wandered the hills, dispossessed until their lines died out or were absorbed by one of the hold clans. Others had sought shelter in Zhufbar or gone west to the Grey Mountains. None of the dwarfs that had remained in the hold had survived.

Now majestic Karak Varn was no more. Called Crag Mere, it was a desolate place, full of shadows and ancient memories. Barundin looked out across the water and knew that beneath the rock and water lay the treasures of Karak Varn alongside the skeletons of his forefathers' kin. Occasionally the engineers of Zhufbar would construct diving machines to explore the sunken depths of the hold, but few of these expeditions returned. Those who did spoke of troll infestations, goblin tribes and the vile ratmen clawing an existence out of the ruined hold. There was the odd treasure chest recovered, or an ancient rune hammer or some other valuable, enough to keep the stories fuelled and spark the imagination of others adventurous or foolhardy enough to dare the dangers of the Crag Mere.

Blackwater's name had taken on new meaning, and had become the site of many a battle between dwarfs and goblinkind. It had been here that the Runelord Kadrin Redmane had stood upon the shores, protecting his carts of gromril ore against an orc ambush. Seeing that his force was doomed, his final act had been to throw his rune hammer into the depths so that it would not fall into greenskins' hands. Many an expedition had sought to recover it, but it still lay in the murky waters.

It was on these bleak shores that the dwarfs finally slew Urgok Beard Burner, the orc warlord that had assailed the city of Karaz-a-Karak over two and half thousand years before in retaliation for the capture of their high king.

And so the history of Blackwater went on, skirmishes and battles punctuating short periods of peace. The latest had been the Battle of Black Falls, when the high king had led the army of Karaz-a-Karak against a goblin host. At the culmination of the battle High King Alrik was dragged over the falls into Karak Varn by the mortally wounded goblin chieftain Gorkil Eye Gouger.

Yes, mused Barundin, Blackwater has become an accursed place for the dwarfs.

* * *

As NIGHT CLOSED in, they set camp near the northern tip of Blackwater. Barundin was in two minds about whether to set fires or not, and consulted with Arbrek. The runelord and king stood at the water's edge, tossing stones into its unmoving darkness.

'If we light fires, it will keep wild animals and trolls at bay,' said Barundin. 'But they might attract the attention of a more dangerous foe.'

Arbrek looked at him, his eyes glittering in the dying light. He did not reply immediately, but laid a hand on Barundin's shoulder. Arbrek smiled, surprising Barundin.

'If this is the most difficult decision of your kinghood, then your reign will have been blessed by the ancestors,' said the runelord. His smile faded. 'Light the fires, for if a foe is to come upon us, better that we have more than just starlight to watch for their coming.'

'I'll set double guard, to be on the safe side,' replied Barundin.

'Yes, better to be on the safe side,' agreed Arbrek.

As night settled, the winds calmed and turned northerly. Over the crackling of the flames of the half dozen fires, Barundin could hear another noise, distant and more comforting. It was a dim, barely audible sound like a bass roaring and rattling from the north. He slept fitfully and when he awoke, his eyes were drawn to the still menace of the lake, his spine tingling with the sensation of being watched. He turned his eyes northward and saw the faintest of glows in the darkness beyond the nearest mountains, a dull, ruddy aura from the forges of Zhufbar. With happier thoughts, he fell asleep again.

The night passed without incident and as the sun crept over the eastern peaks, the dwarfs finished their breakfast and readied for the march. Gorhunk Silverbeard, one of Barundin's hammerer bodyguards, sought out the king as he brushed and plaited his beard. The veteran warrior wore the tanned hide of a bear across his shoulders, suitably tailored for his frame. If the stories were to be believed, he had killed the bear with only a small wooden hatchet when he was a beardling. Gorhunk had never confirmed or denied this, though he seemed happy with the reputation. That he was an accomplished and experienced fighter was obvious just from the two ragged scars that ran the length of his right cheek, turning his beard white in two stripes.

'The rangers have returned,' Gorhunk told his king. 'The path to the north is clear of foes, though they found spoor of wolf riders, a few days old.'

'Pfah! Wolf riders are nothing but scavengers and cowards,' spat Barundin. 'They'll give us no trouble.'

'That's true, but they can also fetch help,' warned Gorhunk. 'Where there are wolf riders, there'll be others. This place is crawling with grobi scum.'

'We'll set off as soon as is convenient,' said the king. 'Send the rangers out again. There's no harm in being forewarned.'

'Aye,' said Gorhunk with a nod. The hammerer turned and strode off into the camp, leaving Barundin to his thoughts.

With the fall of Karak Varn, Zhufbar had been left partially isolated from the rest of the old dwarf empire. Now they were surrounded by hostile orc and goblin tribes, while the ratmen were never too far away. It was a constant battle, and on a handful of occasions the hold had been seriously threatened with invasion. But they had survived these attempts, and the mettle of Zhufbar was as strong as ever. Barundin, as new king, was determined that his hold would not fail during his reign.

* * *

NOT LONG AFTER the sun had reached noon, the dwarfs passed into the chasm at the north end of Blackwater. Here the dark waters rushed over the edge of the cliff in a gushing waterfall, the mountainsides echoing with the roaring, foaming torrent. Behind the noise was another, more artificial sound: the pounding and clanking of machinery.

The walls of the waterfall were lined with scores of waterwheels, some of them massive. Gears, pulleys and chains creaked and groaned in constant motion, driving distant forge hammers and ore crushers. Stone viaducts and culverts redirected the waters into cooling tanks and smelters. Amongst the spume and spray, gantries of iron and bulwarks of stone dotted the landscape, the muzzles of cannons protruding menacingly from embrasures, watching over this vulnerable entrance into Zhufbar.

Steam and smoke from the furnaces was lifted high above the vale, gathering in a pall overhead. The air was thick with moisture and droplets formed on Barundin's beard and armour as they began their descent. The path wound back and forth along the chasm's southern face, in places curving down spiral steps hewn through the rock, in others crossing cracks and fissures over arcing bridges with low parapets. Beneath them, the glow of Zhufbar's forges tinged the watery air with a glinting red hue.

At the foot of the chasm, the road took a long spiral turn northwards to the main gate, overlooked by more fortifications. As the group neared, word was passed from watchtowers to the gate wardens. A deep rumbling made the ground reverberate underfoot, as water was redirected from the flow through the gate locks. Heavy iron bars and granite lockstones were separated from one another, and the gates swung open, driven by large gears and chains machined into the rock on either side of the gateway.

A lone dwarf stood in the gaping opening, which stretched five times his height. He planted his hammer at his feet and barred their passage. Barundin walked forward to initiate the ritual of entry.

'Who approaches Zhufbar?' the door warden demanded gruffly.

'Barundin, King of Zhufbar,' Barundin replied.

'Enter your hold, Barundin, King of Zhufbar,' the gate-keeper said, stepping aside.

As the dwarfs entered, they passed beneath a lintel stone as thick as a dwarf is tall, carved with runes and ancestor faces. It was the oldest stone in the hold, as near as could be reckoned from the ancient stories, and local tradition held that should a person pass beneath it without permission, it would crack and break, bringing the rocks down onto his head and sealing the entrance to the hold. Barundin was glad that the tale had never been tested.

Inside, the dwarfs passed into the entrance chamber. It was low and long, lit by lanterns set into alcoves every few feet. The walls were hewn into the shape of castellations, three tiers on each side, and dwarfs with handguns – the fabled thunderers – patrolled its length. Cannons and other war machines overlooked the entrance, ready to unleash lethal metal at any foe that managed to breach the gate. It could never be said that the dwarfs would be caught unprepared.

From the entrance chamber, Zhufbar spread out, north, east and south, up and down, in a maze of tunnels. Here, at the heart of the underground city, the walls were straight and true, decorated with runes and carved pictures telling the stories of the ancestor gods. In places it opened out into wide galleries overlooking eating halls and armouries, audience chambers and forge-halls. Armoured doors of stone and gromril protected treasuries containing wealth equivalent to that of entire human nations.

Dismissed by Barundin, the dwarf throng quickly dispersed, returning to their clan-halls and families. Barundin made his way to the chambers above the main hall, where the kings of Zhufbar had lived for seven generations. He swiftly undressed and washed in his chambers, hanging his mail coat on its stand next to his bed. Putting on a heavy robe of dark red cloth, he brushed his beard, using the troll-bone comb that had belonged to his mother. Taking golden clasps from a locked chest beneath the bed, he plaited his beard into two long braids and swept his hair back into a ponytail. Feeling more refreshed, he left and walked to the whispering chamber a short way from his bedroom.

Named for its amazing acoustics, the whispering chamber had a low, domed ceiling that echoed sound to every corner, allowing a large number of dwarfs to converse with each other without ever raising their voices. It was empty now except for a solitary figure. Seated at the near end of the long table was Harlgrim, thane of the Bryngromdal clan, second in size and wealth to Barundin's own clan, the Kronrikstok.

'Hail, Harlgrim Bryngromdal,' said Barundin, taking a seat a little way from the thane.

'Welcome back, King Barundin,' said Harlgrim. 'I take it that the funeral went without hindrance?'

'Aye,' said Barundin. He paused as a young dwarf maid entered, dressed in a heavy apron and carrying a platter of cold meat cuts and piles of cave mushrooms. She placed the food between the two dwarf nobles and withdrew with a smile. A moment later, a young beardling brought in a keg of ale and two mugs.

'We've received more messages from Nuln,' said Harlgrim as he stood and poured out two pints of beer.

Barundin pulled the platter towards him and began nibbling at a piece of ham. 'I take it that all is well?'

'It appears so, though it's hard to tell with manlings,' said Harlgrim. He took a swig of beer and grimaced. 'I miss real beer.'

'How is work on the brewery?' asked Barundin, tentatively sipping his ale. It wasn't that it was bad as such. It was still dwarf ale, after all. It just wasn't *good*.

'The engineers assure me that it is proceeding to schedule,' said Harlgrim. 'Can't work fast enough if you ask me.'

'So, is the Emperor still this Magnus fellow?' said the king, bringing the conversation back on topic.

'Seems so, though he must be getting on a bit for a manling,' said Harlgrim. He plucked a leg of meat from the platter and bit into it, the juices dribbling into his thick black beard. 'Apparently, the elves are helping him.'

'Elves?' said Barundin, his eyes narrowing instinctively. 'That's typical of elves, that is. They bugger off for four thousand years with nary a word, and then they're back, meddling again.'

'They did fight alongside the high king against the northern hordes,' said Harlgrim. 'Apparently, some prince, Teclis he's called, is helping the manlings with their wizards, or some such nonsense.'

'Elves and manling wizards?' growled Barundin. 'No good will come of it, mark my words. They shouldn't be teaching them that magic they're so proud of, it'll end in tears. Humans can't do runework, can barely brew a pint or lay a brick. I can't see any good coming from manlings having truck with elves. Perhaps I should send a message to Emperor Magnus. You know, warn him about them.'

'I don't think he'll listen,' said Harlgrim.

Barundin grunted and started on a piece of ham. 'What's in it for them?' the king asked between mouthfuls. 'They must be after something.'

'I've always considered it good sense not to think too long about the counsel of elves,' suggested the thane. 'You'll tie yourself in knots, worrying about that sort of thing. Anyway, it's not just elves he's looking to make friends with. This Magnus is setting up a foundry in Nuln, calling it the Imperial Gunnery School, according to his message. He's been told, rightly so, that the best engineers in the world live in Zhufbar, and he wants to hire their services.'

'What does the guild reckon?' asked Barundin, putting aside his food and concentrating for the first time. 'What's Magnus offering?'

'Well, the Engineers Guild hasn't met to formally discuss it, but they're going to bring it up at the next general council. They've already assured me that any extra commitment they undertake won't affect work here, especially on the brewery. Magnus's offer is very vague at the moment, but the language he uses sounds generous and encouraging. The poor souls have only just finished squabbling amongst themselves again. They're looking for a bit of stability.'

'Sounds like good sense to me,' said Barundin. 'These past few centuries have been troublesome indeed, with them fighting amongst themselves, allowing orcs to grow in numbers. Do you think it's worth sending someone to Nuln to have a proper talk with this fellow?'

'I believe the high king himself travelled to Nuln only five years ago,' said Harlgrim. 'I can't think of anything to add to whatever he might have said – he's a sensible dwarf.'

'Well, let's wait and see what they have to offer,' said Barundin. 'There's more pressing business.'

'The new grudge?' asked Harlgrim.

Barundin nodded. 'I need the thanes assembled so that we can enter it into the book and send word to Karaz-a-Karak,' said the king.

'The Feast of Grungni is almost upon us. It would seem right that we do it then,' suggested Harlgrim.

'That'd suit,' said Barundin, standing up and finishing his beer.

He wiped the froth from his moustache and beard and nodded farewell.

Harlgrim watched his king leave, seeing already the weight of rulership on his friend's shoulders. With a grunt, he also stood. He had things to do.

HAD THE LONG tables not been sturdily dwarf-built, they would have been sagging with the weight of food and ale barrels. The air rang with the shouts of the assembled thanes, the glugging of beer into tankards, raucous laughter and the trample of serving wenches hurrying to and from the king's kitchens.

They were seated in three rows at the centre of the shrine to Grungni, greatest of the ancestor gods and lord of mining. Behind Barundin, sitting on his throne at the head of the centre table, a great stylised stone mask glowered down at the assembled throng. It was the face of Grungni himself, his eyes and beard picked out in thick gold leaf, his helm crafted from glinting silver. Above the diners, great mine lanterns hung from the high ceiling, spilling a deep yellow light onto the sweating gathering below.

All across Zhufbar other dwarfs were holding their own celebrations, and beyond the great open doors of the shrine, the sounds of merriment and drunken dwarfs echoed along the corridors and chambers, down to the deepest mines.

Refilling his golden tankard, Barundin stood up on the seat of his throne and held the beer aloft. Silence rippled outwards as the thanes turned to look at their king. Dressed in heavy robes, his war crown on his head was studded with jewels, at the centre of which was a multi-faceted brynduraz, brightstone, a blue gem more rare than diamond. A golden chain of office hung around the king's neck, studded with gromril rivets and pieces of amethyst. His beard was plaited into three long braids, woven with golden thread and tipped with silver ancestor badges depicting Grungni.

As quiet descended, broken by the occasional belch, loud gulp or cracking of a bone, Barundin lowered his pint. He turned and faced the image of Grungni.

'Oldest and greatest of our kind,' he began. 'We thank you for the gifts that you have left us. We praise you for the secrets of delving and digging.'

'Delving and digging!' chorused the thanes.

'We praise you for bringing us gromril and diamonds, silver and sapphires, bronze and rubies,' said Barundin.

'Gromril and diamonds!' shouted the dwarfs. 'Silver and sapphires! Bronze and rubies!'

'We thank you for watching over us, for keeping our mines secure and for guiding us to the richest veins,' chanted Barundin.

'The richest veins!' roared the dwarfs, who were now standing on the benches, waving their mugs in the air.

'And we give greatest thanks for your best gift to us,' Barundin intoned, turning to the thanes, a grin splitting his face. 'Gold!'

'Gold!' bellowed the thanes, the outburst of noise causing the lanterns to sway and flicker. 'Gold, gold, gold, gold! Gold, gold, gold, gold!'

The chanting went on for several minutes, rising and falling in volume as varying numbers of dwarfs emptied their tankards and refilled them. The hall reverberated with the sound, shaking the throne beneath Barundin's feet, though he did not notice for he was too busy shouting himself. Several of the older thanes were running out of breath and eventually the hubbub died down.

Barundin signalled to Arbrek, who was seated to the king's left. The runelord took a keg of beer and carried it to the stone table in front of the face of Grungni. Barundin took up his axe, which had been propped up against the side of his throne, and followed the runelord.

'Drink deep, my ancestor, drink deep,' Barundin said, smashing in the top of the keg with his axe. With a push, he toppled the barrel so that the beer flowed out, spilling across the table and running into narrow channels carved into its surface. From here, the ale flowed down into the ground, through narrow culverts and channels, into the depths of the mountains themselves. Nobody now knew, if anyone ever had, where they ended, except that it was supposedly in the Hall of the Ancestors, where Grungni himself awaited those that died. From all across the dwarfs' empire, the tankard of Grungni was being filled this night.

With his duty done, Barundin turned and nodded to Harlgrim, who had been sitting at his right-hand side. The mood in the hall changed rapidly as the leader of the Bryngromdals unwrapped the thick leather covers of Zhufbar's book of grudges.

Barundin took the tome from Harlgrim, his face solemn. The book itself was almost half as tall as Barundin, and several inches thick. Its cover was made from thin sheets of stone bound with gromril and gold,

and a heavy clasp decorated with a single large diamond held it shut.

Placing the book on the table in front of him,
Barundin opened it. Ancient parchment pages crackled,
bound with goblin sinew. As each page turned, the
dwarfs in the hall murmured louder and louder, growling and grunting as seven thousand years of wrongs
against them turned before their eyes. Finding the first
blank page, Barundin took up his writing chisel and
dipped the tip of the steel and leather writing imple-
ment into an inkpot proffered by Harlgrim. The king
spoke as he wrote.

'Let it be known that I, King Barundin of Zhufbar,
record this grudge in front of my people,' Barundin said,
his hand rapidly dabbing the writing-chisel onto the
pages to form the angular runes of khazalid, the dwarf
tongue. 'I name myself grudgesworn against Baron Silas
Vessal of Uderstir, a traitor, a weakling and a coward. By
his treacherous act, Baron Vessal did endanger the army
of Zhufbar, and through his actions brought about the
death of King Throndin of Zhufbar, my father. Recompense must be in blood, for death can only be met with
death. No gold, no apology can atone for this betrayal.
Before the thanes of Zhufbar and with Grungni as my
witness, I swear this oath.'

Barundin looked out at the sea of bearded faces, seeing nods of approval. He passed the writing-chisel to
Harlgrim, blew gently on the book of grudges to dry the
ink, and then closed it with a heavy thud.

'Reparation will be made,' the king said slowly.

THE NEXT DAY, Barundin's loremaster, the king's librar-
ian and scribe, penned a message to Baron Silas Vessal,
urging him to travel to Zhufbar and present himself for
Barundin's judgement. The dwarfs knew full well that

no manling would ever be so honourable to do such a thing, but form and tradition had to be followed. After all, there was a centuries-long alliance between the dwarfs and the men of the Empire, and Barundin was not about to wage war upon one of the Empire's nobles without having his house in order.

None of the wisest heads in the hold could determine where Uderstir actually was, and so it was decided to send a contingent of rangers into the Empire to locate it. While preparations were being made for this expedition, another group of dwarfs was sent on the long, dangerous march south to Karaz-a-Karak. With them they carried a copy of Barundin's new grudge to present to High King Thorgrim Grudgebearer, so that it might be recorded in the Dammaz Kron, the mighty book of grudges that contained every slight and betrayal against the whole dwarf race. The Dammaz Kron's first grudge, now illegible with age and wear, had supposedly been written by the first high king, Snorri Whitebeard, against the foul creatures of the Dark Gods. Seven thousand years of history were recorded in the Dammaz Kron, a written embodiment of the dwarfs' defiance and honour.

For many days, as he awaited the return of the travelling bands, Barundin busied himself with the day-to-day affairs of the hold. A new seam of iron ore had been discovered south of the hold, and two clans staked rival claims to it. There were many laborious hours spent with the hold's records and Loremaster Thagri to reconcile the two claims and work out who held ownership of the new mine.

Barundin spent a day inspecting the work on the new brewery. The vats and mechanisms of the old brewery that had been salvaged had been carefully restored, while new pipes, bellows, fire grates and oast houses were being erected on the site of the old brewery. Engineers and their apprentices were gathered in groups, discussing the finer points of brewery construction, and arguing over valves and sluices with beermasters and keglords.

While work was still ongoing, and had been for several years, crude measures had been taken to supply the hold with sufficient beer. Part of the king's own chambers had been turned into a storehouse to allow the beer to mature, while many of the other clans had donated halls and rooms to the endeavour. However, the result was, by dwarf standards, thin and weak, and lacked the real body and froth of proper dwarf ale. Without exception, the new brewery was the single most observed engineering project the hold had seen since the first waterwheels were built thousands of years earlier.

Six days after they had set out, the messengers to Uderstir returned. As expected, their news was grim. It had taken them four days to find Uderstir, and upon arrival in the early evening of the fourth day, had found themselves unwelcome. They had called for Silas Vessal and he had come to the gatehouse to parley. They had politely explained the terms of Barundin's grudge and requested that the baron accompany them back to Zhufbar. They assured him that he was in their safe-guard and no harm would come to him until the king's judgement.

The baron had refused them admittance, cursed them for fools, and had even had his men pelt the dwarfs with stones and rotten fruit from the ramparts of his castle. As instructed, the dwarfs had left a copy of the grudge nailed to the castle gate, translated as well as possible into the Reikspiel spoken by most of the Empire, and had departed.

When he heard the news, Barundin was incensed. He had not expected Vessal to comply with his demand that he travel to Zhufbar, but to act with such brazen cowardice and insult made the king's blood boil. The next day, he brooded in his audience chamber with Arbrek, Harlgrim and several of the other most important thanes.

The king sat in his throne with his council on high-backed seats in a semi-circle in front of him.

'I do not wish a war,' growled Barundin, 'but war we must have for this despicable behaviour.'

'I do not wish for war, either,' said Thane Godri, head of the Ongurbazum clan.

Godri's interest was well known, for it had been the Ongurbazum that had been the first to send emissaries back into the Empire after the Great War against Chaos and the election of Magnus as Emperor. They were amongst the foremost traders in the hold and had recently negotiated several contracts with the Imperial court. It was they who had brought news of the new Gunnery School in Nuln, and the profit to be made.

'This Magnus seems a sensible enough fellow,' continued Godri, 'but we can't say for sure how he will react to us attacking one of his nobles.'

'Doesn't the insult done to us merit a response?' asked Harlgrim. 'Does not the late king demand that honour be restored?'

'My father died fighting with a coward,' said Barundin, thumping a fist onto the arm of his throne.

Arbrek cleared his throat and the others looked at him. He was by far the oldest dwarf in Zhufbar, over seven hundred years old and still going strong, and his counsel was rarely wrong. 'Your father died trying to avenge a fallen son,' said the runelord. 'It would honour him not to be hasty, lest his other son join him too swiftly in the Halls of the Ancestors.'

They pondered this in silence until Arbrek spoke again, with a glance at Godri. 'The thane of the Ongurbazum has a point. Your father would also not thank you for emptying the coffers of Zhufbar when we could be filling them.'

'What would you have me do?' growled Barundin. 'I have declared the grudge, it is written in the book. You would have me ignore this manling and pretend that he did not contribute to my father's death and slight my hold?'

'I would have no such thing,' said Arbrek, drawing a deep breath, his beard bristling, eyes glinting angrily under his bushy eyebrows. 'Do not put words in my mouth, King Barundin.'

Barundin sighed heavily and raked his fingers through his beard, looking at the others around the table. Straightening in his throne, he clasped his hands together and leaned forward. When he spoke, Barundin's voice was quiet but determined.

'I will not be known as an oathbreaker,' the king said. 'For less than a year I have ruled Zhufbar. I shall not have my reign begin with an unfulfilled grudge. Whatever the consequences, if war it must be, then war we shall have.'

Godri opened his mouth to retort, but said nothing as the doors to the chamber opened, letting in the hubbub of the corridor outside. Thagri the loremaster entered, carrying with him a small book in one hand, and the book of grudges under his arm. He had excused himself from the debate on the grounds that he had research to do that might have a bearing on the subject. The king, runelord and thanes watched expectantly as the loremaster closed the doors behind him and walked across the hall and up the steps. He sat down in the empty chair that had been left for him.

He looked around the group as if noticing their stares for the first time. 'My noble kinsmen,' he began, his white beard wagging as he spoke. 'I believe I have discovered something of import.'

They waited for him to continue.

'Well, what is it?' asked Thane Snorbi of the Drektrommi, a stout warrior even for a dwarf, known for his somewhat heated temper. 'Don't keep us waiting like a bunch of idiots.'

'Ah, sorry, yes,' said Thagri. 'Well, it appears that my predecessor, Loremaster Ongrik, was slightly amiss in his book-keeping. Your father, I have just found, recorded a last grudge several years ago. It was in his journal, but Ongrik witnessed it, which is why it wasn't with all the other documents.' He waved the smaller book he was carrying.

'Last grudge?' asked Godri, one of the youngest thanes present.

'It's an old tradition, not used much in recent centuries,' explained Thagri with a wistful smile. 'Your father was very much a traditionalist in that regard. Anyway, the last grudge was recorded by a dwarf as a vow to settle it before his death, or if he could not do so, then to bequeath the settlement of that particular grudge to his heir. It started during a bit of wrangling many, many centuries ago during the Time of the Goblin Wars, to avoid breaking an oath because of an untimely death during all the fighting with the grobi scum.'

'Are you suggesting that I record this grudge as a last grudge and avoid my responsibilities?' asked Barundin, eyes narrowing.

'Of course not!' spluttered Thagri, truly indignant. 'Besides, a king can't record a last grudge until he's been in power for a hundred and one years. If we let kings have last grudges all over the place, the system would become a complete joke.'

'So what does it have to do with this debate?' asked Harlgrim.

'The last grudge is the first grudge that the heir must try to right,' said Arbrek, speaking as if he had just remembered something. He looked at Thagri, who nodded in confirmation. 'Before you do anything else, you must avenge your father's last grudge or dishonour his wishes.'

'Why didn't he tell me he had done such a thing?' asked Barundin. 'Why did he only write it in his journal?'

Thagri avoided the king's gaze and fiddled with the clasp of the book of grudges.

'Well?' demanded Barundin with a fierce stare.

'He was drunk!' blurted Thagri with a desperate look in his eyes.

'Drunk?' said Barundin.

'Yes,' said the loremaster. 'Your father and Ongrik were close friends, and as I've read this very morning in my late master's own diary, the two of them drank with each other frequently. It appears that the pair of them, this particular day, had drunk rather more than was normal even for them and had begun reminiscing about the Time of the Goblin Wars and how they wished they had been there to give the grobi a solid runking. Well, one thing led to another. Ongrik mentioned the last grudge tradition and your father ended up writing it in his journal, swearing to avenge the depredations against Zhufbar.'

'What, precisely, did my father swear?' asked Barundin, his heart heavy with foreboding. 'He didn't vow to retake Karak Varn or something like that?'

'Oh no,' said Thagri with a shake of his head and a smile. 'Nothing quite that grand. No, not that grand at all.'

'Then what was his grudge?' asked Harlgrim.

'Well, a last grudge is not a new grudge at all,' explained Thagri, placing the journal on the floor at his feet and opening the book of grudges. 'It's an oath to fulfil an existing grudge. There was one in particular that your father was always annoyed by, particularly when he was in his cups.'

The loremaster fell silent and the others were quiet as they saw a pained expression twist Barundin's face.

The king wiped a hand over his lips. 'Grungankor Stokril,' he said, his voice barely a whisper.

'Grunga…' said Harlgrim. 'The old mines to the east? They've been overrun by goblins for nearly two thousand years.' He fell silent as he saw Barundin's look, as did the others except one.

'Dukankor Grobkaz-a-Gazan?' asked Snorbi. 'That's connected to Mount Gunbad now. Thousands, tens of thousands of grobi there. What did King Throndin want with that doomed place?'

The thane looked at the pale expressions on the other dwarfs and then stared at Thagri. 'There's a mistake,' insisted Snorbi.

The loremaster shook his head and handed Snorbi the book of grudges, pointing to the relevant passage. The thane read it and shook his head in disbelief.

'We have a war to prepare for,' said Barundin, standing. There was a fell light in his eyes, almost feverish. 'War against the grobi. Call the clans, sound the horns, sharpen the axes! Zhufbar marches once again!'

GRUDGE THREE
The Rat Grudge

THE HALLS AND corridors of Zhufbar rang constantly with the pounding of forge hammers, the hiss of steam, the roar of furnaces and the tramp of dwarf boots. To Barundin, it was a symphony of craftsmanship, suffused with the melody of common purpose and kept in beat by the rhythm of industry. It was the sound of a dwarf hold bent to a single goal: war.

The armouries had been opened and the great rune weapons of the ancestors brought forth once more. Axes with glimmering blades and fiery runes were polished; shields and mail of gromril carved with the images of the clans' ancestors were hefted once more. Hammers graven with gold and silver hung upon the walls. Battle helms decorated with wings and horns and anvils sat upon bedside tables, awaiting their owners.

The engineers were bent to their craft as the forges billowed with fire and smoke. Keg upon keg of black powder was made in the strong rooms, while artisans of all types turned their minds to great war machines, weapons and armour. Cannons were pulled from the foundries and lovingly awakened from their slumber with polish and cloth. Flame cannons, organ guns, bolt throwers and grudgethrowers were assembled and inscribed with oaths of vengeance and courage.

This was no mere expedition, no foray into the wilds for a skirmish. This was dwarf war, grudge-born and fierce. This was the righteous anger that burned within the heart of every dwarf, young and old alike. This was the power of the ancients and the wisdom of generations set on a single course of destruction.

Barundin could feel it flowing through his veins, even as the spirits of seventy generations looked upon him from the Halls of the Ancestors. Never had he felt so sure of his mind; never had his being been set on something so singular and yet so worthy. Although at first the thought of reclaiming Grungankor Stokril had filled the king with apprehension, it had taken but a few moments, thought to reconsider the idea.

Though it had begun as a necessity so that he might pursue his own goals, Barundin had become wedded to the idea of the purge of Dukankor Grobkaz-a-Gazan – the Warren of Goblin Ruin. It would be a fitting way to start his kingship, and would set the minds of his people for his whole reign. A conquest to reclaim the ancient mines would launch Zhufbar into a new period of endeavour and prosperity. It was more than a simple battle, a stepping-stone to his own needs. The destruction of the goblin kingdom in distant lands would herald his ascendancy to the throne of Zhufbar.

Though the war would be terrible, and the dwarfs implacable in the conflict, life in a dwarf hold did not turn quickly. The preparations for Barundin's march forth against the goblins had been going on for five years. Such an undertaking could not begin lightly, and no dwarf worth his gold would do so in a hasty, unprepared fashion.

While the engineers and axe-smiths, armourers and foundry workers had laboured, so too had Barundin, the thanes and the loremaster. From the depths of the libraries, the old plans of the mine workings of Grungakor Strokril had been brought into the light for the first time in a millennium and a half. With his advisors, Barundin pored for long weeks and months over the detailed maps. They postulated where the goblins would have dug their own tunnels, and where they might be trapped.

Rangers were sent into the tunnels eastwards, to gauge the numbers of the goblins and their whereabouts. Ironbreakers, veteran warriors of tunnel-fighting, spent time teaching their ways of war to young beardlings, tutoring them in axe-craft and shield-skill. The oldest of the Zhufbar throng taught the youngest the ways of grobkul, the ancient art of goblin-stalking. Miners were tasked with practising demolition as well as tunnel building, so that the goblin holes might be filled and reinforcements waylaid.

Amid all of this, the hold tried its best to continue life as normal. Barundin was assured that work was continuing apace on the brewery, and with no effect from the stronghold's new war footing. There were still trade agreements to be fulfilled, mines to be dug, ore to be smelted and gems to be cut and polished.

Despite the length of time it had taken so far, Barundin knew that soon his army would be ready. It would be a force the like of which Zhufbar had not seen in five generations. Of course, Abrek cautioned, such armies as those that had fought during the War of Vengeance against the elves, or had valiantly defended Zhufbar during the Time of the Goblin Wars, would never be seen again. Dwarfs no longer had such numbers, nor the ancient knowledge and weapons of those times. He warned against underestimating the threat of the goblins. However, the ancient runelord's pessimism did little to dent Barundin's growing hunger for the coming battles.

It was then, perhaps only weeks from the date the army was due to march forth, that troubling news was brought to Barundin's ears. It was from Tharonin Grungrik, thane of one of the largest mining clans, as Barundin held his monthly war council.

'I don't know what it is, but we've stirred something up,' Tharonin told them. 'Perhaps it's grobi, perhaps something else. There's always a young beardling or two goes missing now and then, lost their way most likely. These past few months, there's been more not coming back than in the ten years before. Seventeen went down and never returned.'

'You think it's the grobi?' asked Barundin, reaching for his alepot.

'Maybe, maybe not,' Tharonin told him. 'Perhaps some of them followed the rangers back from the east. Perhaps they found their own way through the tunnels. Who knows where they've been digging?'

'All the more reason why we have to press on with our preparations,' snorted Harlgrim. 'Once we're through with them, the grobi won't dare set foot within fifty leagues of Zhufbar.'

'There's been bodies found,' said Tharonin, his deep voice ominous. 'Not hacked up, not a shred of cloth nor a ring or trinket taken. That doesn't come across as grobi work to me.'

'Stabbed?' said Arbrek, stirring and opening his eyes. The other dwarfs had assumed he was asleep. Apparently he had been deep in thought.

'In the back,' said Tharonin. 'Just the once, right through the spine.'

'I'll wager a fist of bryn that it wasn't no grobi did that,' said Harlgrim.

'Thaggoraki?' suggested Barundin. 'The ratmen are back, do you think?'

The others nodded. Along with orcs and goblins, trolls and dragons, the thaggoraki, mutant ratmen also known as skaven, had contributed to the downfall of several of the ancient dwarf holds during the Time of the Goblin Wars. Twisted, cursed scavengers, the skaven were a constant menace, digging their own tunnels in the dark of the world, unseen by man or dwarf. It had been many centuries since Zhufbar had been troubled by them, the last of the skaven having been driven south by the goblins.

'We've laboured too long to be put off by guessing and hearsay,' said Barundin, breaking the gloomy silence. 'If it is the walking rats, we need to be sure. Perhaps it's just some grobi that've followed the expeditions back, like Tharonin says. Send parties into the mines, open up the closed, barren seams and see what's down there.'

'It'll be good practice for the beardlings,' said Arbrek with a grim smile. 'If they can catch themselves some thaggoraki, grobi will be no problem.'

'I'll talk to the other mining clans,' offered Tharonin. 'We'll split the job between us, send guides for those parties that don't know the workings out eastward. We'll delve into every tunnel, root them out.'

'Good,' said Barundin. 'Do what you must to keep safe, but find me proof of what's happening. It'll take more than a few rats in the dark to turn me from this path.'

* * *

A STRANGE ATMOSPHERE settled over Zhufbar as news of
the mysterious disappearances spread. Speculation was
rife, particularly amongst the older dwarfs, who cited
tales from their past, or their father's past, or their
grandfather's past. The old stories resurfaced – sagas of
ancient dwarf heroes who had fought the grobi and
thaggoraki.

In meticulous detail, the wisest oldbeards spoke of
Karak Eight Peaks, the hold that had fallen to both of
these vile forces. Surrounded by eight daunting mountains – Karag Zilfin, Karag Yar, Karag Mhonar, Karagril,
Karag Lhune, Karag Nar and Kvinn-wyr – the dwarfs of
the hold had thought they were protected by a natural
barrier as sure against attack as any wall. In its glory
days, Karak Eight Peaks was known as the Queen of the
Silver Depths, Vala-Azrilungol, and its glory and magnificence were surpassed only by the splendour of
Karaz-a-Karak, the capital.

But the earthquakes and volcanic eruptions that preceded the Time of the Goblin War rent the Eight Peaks
and threw down many of the walls and towers that had
been erected there by the dwarfs. For nearly a hundred
years, orcs and goblins attacked the hold from above.
The beleaguered dwarfs were already under threat from
below by the skaven, and gradually they were pushed
towards the centre of the hold, assaulted from above
and below.

The final, vile blow came when the skaven, arcane
engineers and manipulators of the raw stuff of Chaos,
warpstone, unleashed poisons and plagues onto the
besieged dwarfs. Sensing that their doom was nigh,
King Lunn ordered the treasuries and armouries locked
and buried, and led his clans from the hold, fighting
through the greenskins to the surface. To this day, short-
lived expeditions ventured into Karak Eight Peaks in

attempts to recover the treasures of King Lunn, but the warring night goblin tribes and skaven clans had destroyed or turned back any attempt to penetrate the hold's depths.

Such talk did nothing but darken the mood of Barundin. Though none had yet brought it up, he could sense the mood of the thanes was changing. They were preparing to dig in, as the dwarfs had always done, to fight off the skaven threat. It was a matter of days before the first real evidence that the skaven were close by in any numbers would be found, and then the thanes would suggest that the march against Dukankor Grobkaz-a-Gazan be postponed. They would have good reason, Barundin knew well, and he had his own doubts. His greatest fear, though, was that the impetus that had begun to stir the hold would be lost again.

Barundin was young in dwarf terms, less than one hundred and fifty, and older heads than his would call him impetuous, rash even. His growing dream of conquering the lost mines, avenging his father, and leading his hold boldly into the future would slowly wither away. His centuries, such as the ancestors granted him, would be bound to Zhufbar, watching the world outside fall into the grip of the orcs, his people afraid to venture forth over what were once their lands, their mountains.

These thoughts stirred a deep anger in Barundin, the latent ire that lay dormant within every dwarf. Where the greyhairs would wag their beards, growl into their cups and speak of the lost glories of the past, Barundin felt the need to seek reparation, to act rather than talk.

So it was that the King of Zhufbar waited with growing trepidation for every report from the mines. Tharonin Gungrik had assumed authority over the investigations, being the oldest and most respected of the mine-thanes. Each day, he would send a summary to Barundin, or report in person when his many duties allowed.

Each account made Barundin's heart sink. There were tales of strange smells in the depths, of fur and filth. The most experienced miners spoke of weird breezes from the deeps, odd odours that no dwarf-dug tunnel contained. With senses borne of generations of accumulated wisdom, the miners reported odd echoes, subtle reverberations that did not bear any relationship to the dwarfs' own digging. There were scratching noises at the edge of hearing, and odd susurrations that fell quiet as soon as one began listening for them.

Even more disturbing were the tales of peculiar shadows in the darkness, blacker patches in the gloom that disappeared in the light of a lantern. No dwarf could swear by it, but many thought they had half-glimpsed red eyes peering at them, and a growing sense of being watched pervaded the lower halls and galleries.

The disappearances were becoming more frequent too. Whole parties had gone missing, the only evidence of their abduction being their absence from the halls at mealtimes. Neither Tharonin, nor Barundin or any of the other council members could discern a pattern in the disappearances. The current mine workings covered many miles east, north and west, and the older mines covered several leagues.

IT WAS A disconcerted Tharonin that addressed Barundin's council when they were next gathered. The thane had come to the king's audience chamber directly from the mines, and he still wore a long shirt of grom-ril mail and his gold-chased helm. His beard was spotted with rock dust and his face grimy.

'It is bad news, very bad news,' said Tharonin before taking a deep gulp of ale. His face twisted into a sour expression, though whether this was because of the beer or the news that he bore was unclear.

'Tell me everything,' said Barundin. The king leaned forward with his elbows on the table, his bearded chin in his hands.

'There's new tunnels, without a doubt,' said Tharonin with a shake of the head.

'Skaven tunnels?' asked Harlgrim.

'For certain. They have the rat reek about them, and there's been spoor found. We've started finding bodies too, many of them, some of them little more than skeletons, picked clean by vermin.'

'How many tunnels?' asked Barundin.

'Seven so far,' said Tharonin. 'Seven that we've managed to find. There could be more. In fact, I'd wager there are definitely more that we don't know about yet.'

'Seven tunnels...' muttered Arbrek. He stirred the froth of his ale with a finger as he considered his words. He looked up, feeling the gazes of the others on him. 'Seven tunnels – this is no small number of foes.'

Barundin looked at the faces of the council members, wondering which of them was going to be the first to mention the planned war against the goblins. They looked back at him in silence, until Snorbi Threktrommi cleared his throat.

'Someone's got to say it,' said Snorbi. 'We can't march against the grobi while there's an enemy at our doorstep. We must move against the skaven before we can deal with the grobi.'

There was a chorus of grunted approvals, and Barundin could tell by the looks on their faces that they were expecting his reply and were ready with their arguments. Instead, he nodded slowly.

'Aye,' said the king. 'My saga will not begin with a tale of foolish stubbornness. Though it pains me beyond anything, I will postpone the war against Dukankor Grobkaz-a-Gazan. I will not be remembered as the king who reclaimed our distant realm and lost his hold in doing so. The throng that has been mustered for the march must be sent to the mines, and we shall root these vile creatures from our midst. Tomorrow morning, I want companies of warriors to go with the miners into the tunnels that have been found. We shall seek out their lair and destroy it.'

'It is a wise king that listens to counsel,' said Arbrek, patting Barundin on the arm.

Barundin looked over at Thagri, the loremaster, who was taking notes in his journal.

'Write this,' said the king. 'I said the war on the grobi was postponed, but I swear that when our halls are safe, the army will march forth to reclaim that which was taken from us.'

'You'll get no argument from me,' said Harlgrim, raising his tankard. There were similar words of affirmation from the others.

From the hall, word was passed around the hold to the thanes of the clans. In the morning they would assemble their throngs in the High Hall, to be addressed by the king. There was much more planning and wrangling to be done, which lasted past midnight. With even his considerable dwarf constitution waning, it was a weary Barundin who left the audience chamber and walked back to his bedchambers.

The king could feel the mood of the hold as he walked along the lantern-lit corridors. It was subdued and tense, and each little creak and scratch drew his attention, suspecting some vile thing to be hidden in the shadows. Like the ominous oppression before a

cave-in, Zhufbar was poised, laden with potential cata-
strophe. After the long weeks of preparation for war, the
tunnels and halls were eerily quiet and still.

Barundin reached his chambers and sat wearily on his
bed. He removed his crown and unlocked the chest
beside the bed, placing the crown into the padded velvet bag inside. One by one, he removed the seven
golden clasps in his beard, wrapped them and placed
them next to the crown. Taking a troll-bone comb from
his bedside table, he began to straighten his beard,
working out the knots that had gathered during his fid-
geting through the day. He untied his ponytail and
brushed his hair, before taking up three strands of thin
leather and tying his beard. He stripped off his robes
and folded them neatly into a pile on top of the chest,
and then grabbed his nightgown and cap from the bed
and donned them.

He stood and crossed the chamber to throw a shovel
of coal onto the dying fire in the grate at the foot of the
bed. As it caught, the flames grew and smoke billowed,
disappearing up the chimney, which was dug down
hundreds of feet from the mountainside above, barred
by mesh and grates to prevent anything entering, acci-
dentally or otherwise. He poured water from the ewer
beside his bed and washed behind his ears. Lastly, he
opened the window on the lantern above his bed and
blew out the candle, plunging the room into the ruddy
glow of the fire. His preparations complete, Barundin
flopped back on to the bed, too tired to crawl beneath
the covers.

Despite his fatigue, sleep did not come easily, and
Barundin lay fitfully on the bed, turning this way and
that. His mind was full of thoughts, of the discussions
of the day and the fell deeds that had to be done the
next. As his weariness finally overcame him, Barundin

sunk into a disturbing dream, filled with fanged, rat-like faces. He imagined himself surrounded by a swarm of vermin, scratching and biting, gnawing at his lifeless fingers. There were eyes in the shadows, staring at him with evil intent, waiting to pounce. Scratching echoed in the darkness around him.

Barundin woke and for a moment he was unsure where he was, the after-images of the dream lingering in his mind. He was alert, aware that something was not right. It was a few moments before he determined the cause of his unease. The chamber was pitch dark and silent. Not just the gloom of a cloudy night, but the utter dark beneath the world that holds terror for so many creatures. Even the dwarfs, at home in the subterranean depths, filled their holds with fires and torches and lanterns.

Straining his eyes and ears, Barundin sat up, his heart thudding in his chest. He felt as if he was being watched.

The fire was out, though it should have burned through the night.

Moving slowly, he began to slide his legs towards the edge of the bed, ready to stand. It was then that he heard the faintest of noises. It was little more than a tingling at the edge of hearing, but it was there, a scraping, wet noise. In the darkness to his right, beside the dead grate, he caught a flicker of something. It was a pale, sickly green glow, a sliver against the blackness. Looking out of the corner of his eye, he saw a tiny dot drop and hit the ground.

He heard rather than saw the figure move towards him: a fluttering of cloth, the scritch-scratch of claws on the stone floor. Unarmed, he grabbed the first thing to hand, a pillow, and flung it at the approaching shape.

Now, dwarfs are a hardy folk, and are not only able to withstand much discomfort, but take pride in the fact. They eschew the dainty comforts of other races, and their soft furnishings are anything but soft. So it was that the intruder was greeted with a starched canvas bag stuffed with a dozen pounds of finely ground gravel mixed with goat hair.

In the dark, Barundin saw the figure fling up an arm, but to little effect as the dwarf pillow thudded into its shoulder, knocking it backwards, its blade toppling from its grip and clanging to the floor. Barundin was off the bed and running full tilt by the time the foe recovered.

With a hiss, the creature leapt aside from Barundin's mad rush, springing against the wall and hurtling over his head. Barundin tried to turn, but his impetus slammed him shoulder-first into the wall. Underfoot, he felt something snap, and his bare foot stung with pain. With a grunt, he turned to see the assassin dart forward, a knife in one hand. It was fast, so fast that Barundin barely had time to raise a hand before the dagger plunged into his stomach. With a roar, Barundin swept a fist backwards, smashing it against the rat-like muzzle of the creature, knocking it backwards.

'Hammerers!' bellowed Barundin, backing away from the skaven assassin until his spine was against the wall. 'To your king! Hammerers to me!'

Barundin fended off another blow with his left arm, the knife blade scoring the flesh of his hand. He could feel blood soaking into the fabric of his nightshirt and running down onto his legs.

The door burst open, spilling in light from outside, momentarily blinding Barundin. As he squinted he saw Gudnam Stonetooth running into the room, followed by the other bodyguards of the king. The assassin spun on its heel and was met by a crunching blow to the ribs from Gudnam's warhammer, sending it sprawling backwards. In the light, Barundin could now see his attacker clearly.

It was shorter than a manling, though a little taller than a dwarf, hunched and alert, and clad in black rags. A furless, snake-like tail twitched back and forth in agitation, and its verminous face was curled in a snarl. Red eyes glared at the newly arrived dwarfs.

The creature bounded past Gudnam, heading towards the fireplace, but Barundin launched himself forward, snatching up a poker and bringing it down onto the skaven's back, snapping its spine with a crack. It gave a hideous mewl as it collapsed, legs twitching spasmodically. A hammerer, Kudrik Ironbeater, stepped forward and brought his weapon down onto the assassin's head, crushing its skull and snapping its neck.

'My king, you are hurt.' said Gudnam, rushing to Barundin's side.

Barundin pulled open the ragged tear in the nightshirt and revealed the gash across his stomach. It was long, but not deep, and had barely cut into the solid dwarf muscle beneath the skin. The wound on his arm was similarly minor, painful but not threatening.

Kudrik picked up the broken blade on the ground, gingerly holding it in his gauntleted fist. A thick ichor leaked from the rusted metal of the sword, gathering in dribbling streams along its edge. The poison shimmered with the disturbing un-light of ground warpstone.

'Weeping blade,' the hammerer spat. 'If this had wounded you, things would be more serious.'

'Aye,' said Barundin, glancing around the room. 'Bring me a lantern.'

One of the hammerers went into the antechamber and returned with a glass-cased candle, which he passed to the king. Barundin stooped into the grate and held up the lantern, illuminating the shaft of the chimney. He could see where the assassin had cut its way through the bars blocking the duct.

'There may be others,' said Gudnam, hefting his hammer over one shoulder.

'Send the rangers out to the surface,' said Barundin. 'Have them start with the waterwheels and forge chimneys. Check everything.'

'Yes, King Barundin,' said Gudnam with a nod to one of his warriors, who strode from the chamber. 'The apothecary should have a look at those wounds.'

As Barundin was about to reply, there came a sound from outside, distant but powerful. It was the low call of a horn, blowing long blasts, a mournful echo from the depths.

The king's eyes met the worried look of Gudnam. 'Warning horns from the deeps!' snarled Barundin. 'Find out where.'

'Your wounds?' said Gudnam.

'Grimnir's hairy arse to my wounds – we are under attack!' bellowed the king, causing Gudnam to flinch. 'Rouse the warriors. Sound the horns across Zhufbar. Our foe is upon us!'

THE TUNNEL RANG with the sound of clinking metal and the tramp of booted feet as Barundin and a force of warriors ran down through the hold towards the lower levels. He was still tightening the straps on the gromril plates of his armour and his hair was loosely packed under his crowned helm. Across his left arm, Barundin carried a circular shield of steel inlaid with gromril in the likeness of his great-great-great grandfather, King

Korgan, and in his right hand he carried Grobidrungek – the Goblinbeater – a single-bladed runeaxe that had been in his family for eleven generations. Around him, the dwarfs of Zhufbar readied axes and hammers, their bearded faces stern and resolute as they quickly advanced.

Above the din of the assembling throng, shouts and horn blasts from further down the mineshaft could be heard, growing louder as Barundin pounded forward. The low arched tunnel opened out into the Fourth Deeping Hall, the hub of a network of mines and tunnels that delved north of the main chambers of Zhufbar, which branched out from the chamber through open square archways. Here, Tharonin was waiting with the Gungrik clan, armed and armoured for battle. Thanes marched to and fro bellowing orders, assembling the battle line in the wide hall.

'Where?' demanded Barundin as he stepped up next to Tharonin.

'The seventh north tunnel, the eighth north-east passage and the second north passage,' the thane said breathlessly. His face was smeared with grime and sweat beneath his gold-rimmed miner's helm. The candle in the small lantern mounted on its brow guttered but still burned.

'How many?' asked Barundin, stepping aside as hand-gun-bearing thunderers jogged past, the silver and bronze standard in their midst displaying their allegiance to the Thronnson clan.

'No way of telling,' admitted Tharonin. He pointed to an archway to the left, opposite which the army was gathering. 'Most of them seem to be in the north passages. We've held them in the seventh tunnel for the moment. Perhaps it was just a diversionary attack, or maybe there's more to come.'

'Bugrit!' snapped Barundin, glancing around. There were about five hundred warriors in the hall now, and more were entering with every moment. 'Where're the engineers?'

'No word from them yet,' said Tharonin with a shake of his head that sent motes of dust cascading from his soiled beard.

The hall was roughly oval, seven hundred feet at its widest point and some three hundred feet deep, running east to west. Through a series of low stepped platforms, it sloped down nearly fifty feet to the north and the missile troops of the hold were gathering on the higher steps so that they could shoot over the heads of their kinsdwarfs assembling in shieldwalls halfway across the hall.

With clanking thuds, a traction locomotive puffed into sight from the eastern gateway, pulling with it three limbered war machines. Two were cannons, their polished barrels shining in the light of the hall's gigantic lanterns, suspended from the ceiling a dozen feet above the dwarfs' heads. The third was more archaic, consisting of a large central boiler-like body and flared muzzle, surrounded by intricate pipes and valves: a flame cannon.

Engineers clad in armoured aprons, carrying axes and tools, marched alongside the engine, their faces grim. A bass cheer went up upon their arrival. The engine grumbled to a halt and they began unlimbering their machines of destruction on the uppermost step.

'Hammerers, to me!' ordered Barundin, waving his axe towards the archway leading to the north passages. He turned to Tharonin. 'Care for a jaunt into the tunnels to have a look-see?'

Tharonin grinned and signalled to his bodyguards, the Gungrik Longbeards, who fell into step beside the king's hammerers. The two hundred warriors marched across the platforms and down the steps, winding between the gathering regiments. Above the dwarf army, now over a thousand strong, golden icons shone and embroidered pennants fluttered, and the murmuring of deep dwarf voices echoed around the hall.

Ahead the tunnel was dark and forbidding. Tharonin explained that they had extinguished the lanterns to prevent the retreating warriors from being silhouetted against the light from the hall. Barundin nodded approvingly and they paused for a few moments while warriors were sent to light torches and lanterns to carry into the darkness. Suitably illuminated, they continued forward.

The tunnel was nearly twenty feet wide and just over ten feet high, allowing the dwarfs to advance ten abreast, Tharonin at the front of a five-wide line of longbeards, Barundin leading his hammerers. The sounds of fighting grew even as the noise from the hall behind them receded into the distance. Side tunnels, some no bigger than two dwarfs side by side, branched off from the main passage, and as they reached a fork, Tharonin signalled to the left. The shouts and clash of weapons echoed from the walls in odd ways, sometimes seemingly behind the group, other times quiet and from one side or the other.

It soon became obvious that they were on the right course though, as they started to find dwarf bodies littering the ground. Their jerkins and mail coats were ragged and bloody, but there were piles of dead skaven too. The human-like rats were scabrous things, their fur mangy and matted, their faces balding and scarred. Those that wore any clothing at all were dressed in little more than rags and loincloths and their broken weapons were crude mauls and the occassional sharpened hunk of metal with wooden handles. Most seemed to have been killed as they ran away; vicious axe wounds cut across shoulders and spines, hammer blows marked into the backs of heads and shattered backbones.

'These are just slaves,' said Tharonin. 'Fodder for our weapons.'

Barundin did not reply immediately, but looked around. Skavenslaves were cowardly creatures, herded into battle by the goads and whips of their masters. He knew what little there was to know about the foe, having read several of the old journals of his predecessors and accounts from other holds. If the skaven had intended to break through into the upper reaches, slaves were a poor choice of vanguard, no matter how expendable they were.

Barundin stopped suddenly, the hammerer behind him cannoning into his back and causing him to stumble.

'Halt!' Barundin called out over the apologies of the bodyguard. The king turned to Tharonin with a scowl. 'They're drawing us out. The fools have followed them into the tunnels.'

Tharonin glanced over his shoulder with sudden concern, as if expecting a horde of ratmen to burst upon them from the rear. He tapped his hornblower on the shoulder.

'Sound the retreat,' he told the musician. 'Get them to fall back.'

The hornblower raised his instrument to his lips and blew three short blasts. He repeated the note three more times. After a few moments, it was answered by another call from ahead, repeating the order. Barundin gave a satisfied nod and ordered the small force to turn around and head back to the Fourth Deeping Hall.

* * *

As THEY PASSED back into the hall, Barundin peeled away from his hammerers and waved them on, stopping to admire the sight. The Fourth Deeping Hall was packed with dwarf warriors from each clan and family, standing shoulder to shoulder, gathered about their standards, drummers and hornblowers arrayed along the line. Fierce axe dwarfs of the Grogstoks with their golden dragon icon above them stood beside Okrhunk-haz clansdwarfs, their green shields emblazoned with silver runes. On and on, from one end of the hall to the other they stretched.

Beyond them waited ranks of thunderers with their handguns and quarreller regiments loading their crossbows. Five deep they stood along three steps of the hall, their weapons directed down towards the north arches.

Beyond them the engineers now had five cannons, and beside them the bulky, menacing shape of the flame cannon. To each flank, five-barrelled organ guns were set close to the walls, their crews tinkering with firing locks, inspecting the piles of cannonballs and stacking parchments bags of black powder charges.

Arbrek had arrived and now stood in the centre of the front line, where the hammerers and other battle-hardened fighters of the clans were assembled. Barundin walked over to the runelord, and as he crossed the gap between the passage and the dwarf line he saw the staffs of several lesser runesmiths amongst the throng.

The aged Arbrek stood stiff-backed, his iron and gold runestaff held in both hands across his thighs, his piercing eyes peering at the approaching king from under the brim of a battered helm glowing with flickering golden runes.

'Good to see you,' said Barundin, stopping beside Arbrek and turning to face the north passages.

'A damned unwelcome sight you are,' growled Arbrek. 'In the name of Valaya, what an uncivilised time for a battle. Truly, these creatures are vile beyond reckoning.'

'It's more than their manners that leaves a lot to be desired,' said Barundin. 'But it is truly shocking that they have no respect for your sleep.'

'Are you mocking me?' said Arbrek with a curled lip. 'I have laboured many long years and I have earned the right to a full night's sleep. I used to miss bed for a whole week when I was casting the Rune of Potency upon this staff. Your forefathers would wag their beards to hear such flippancy, Barundin.'

'No offence was meant,' said Barundin, quickly contrite.

'I should think not,' muttered Arbrek.

Barundin waited in silence, and a quiet descended upon the hall, broken by the shuffling of feet, the clink of armour, the rasp of a whetstone and scatters of conversation. Barundin began to fidget with the leather binding of his axe haft as he waited, teasing at stray threads. From his left, a deep voice started to sing. It was Thane Ungrik, descended from the ancient rulers of Karak Varn, and soon the hall was filled with the ancient dwarf verse resounding from the mouths of his clan.

Beneath a lonely mountain hold
There lay a wealth worth more than gold
In a land with no joy nor mirth
Far from welcome of the hearth

In the dark beneath the world
A place never before beheld
The wealth of kings awaited there
Only found by those that dared

Deep we dug and far we dove
Digging gromril by the drove
No light of star, no light of sun
Hard we toiled, sparing none

But came upon us, green-skinned foes
Our joys were ended, came our woes
No axe nor hammer turned them back
Their blood-stained lake and turned it black

King and thanes, a war we spoke
Upon our fists, their armies broke
But from the deep, a fear unspoken
Our fighting had now loudly woken

Up from darkness, our coming fall
A terror beneath us, killing all
With heavy hearts we left our dead
Our hope now broken, turned to dread

Driven from our halls and homes
Forced upon the hills to roam
Forever gone, a loss so dear
Left in the dark of fell Crag Mere

Even as the last verses echoed from the walls and ceiling, noises could be heard from the passage. There was a rush of feet and panicked shouting. Wracking coughs and wet screams could be heard, and an unsettled ripple of muttering spread across the dwarf throng.

A deep fog began to leak from the tunnel entrance, in thin wisps at first but growing in thickness. It was yellow and green, tinged with patches of rotten blackness; a low cloud that seeped across the floor, its edges dusted with flecks of glittering warpstone.

'Poison wind!' a voice cried out, and within moments the hall was filled with a cacophony of shouts, some of dismay, many of defiance.

Barundin could now see shapes in the sickly cloud, floundering shadows of dwarfs running and stumbling. Alone and in twos and threes they burst from the mist, hacking and coughing. Some fell, their bodies twitching, others clasped hands to their faces, howling with pain, falling to their knees and pounding their fists on the stone ground.

One beardling, his blond hair falling in clumps through his fingers as he clawed at his head, staggered forward and collapsed a few yards in front of Barundin. The king stepped forward and knelt, turning the lad over and resting his head against his knees. The king had to fight back the heaving of his stomach.

The dwarf's face was a wretched sight, blistered and red, his eyes bleeding. His lips and beard were stained with blood and vomit, and he flailed his arms blindly, clutching at Barundin's mailed shirt.

'Steady there,' said the king, and the beardling's floundering subsided.

'My king?' he croaked.

'Aye lad, it is,' said Barundin, dropping his shield to one side and laying a hand on the dwarf's head. Arbrek appeared next to them as other dwarfs rushed forward to help their fellows.

'We fought bravely,' the lad rasped. 'We heard the retreat, but did not want to run.'

'You did well, lad, you did well,' said Arbrek.

'They came upon us as our backs were turned,' the beardling said, his chest rising and falling unsteadily, every breath contorting his face with pain. 'We tried to fight, but we couldn't. I choked and ran...'

'You fought with honour,' said Barundin. 'Your ancestors will welcome you to their halls.'

'They will?' the lad said, his desperation replaced with
hope. 'What are the Halls of the Ancestors like?'

'They are the finest place in the world,' said Arbrek,
and as Barundin looked up at the runelord he saw that
his gaze was distant, drawn to some place that nobody
living had seen. 'The beer is the finest you will ever
taste, better even than Bugman's. There is roast fowl on
the tables, and the greatest hams you will ever see. And
the gold! Every type of gold under the mountains can
be found there. Golden cups and plates, and golden
knives and spoons. The greatest of us dwell there, and
you will hear their stories, of fell deeds and brave acts,
of foul foes and courageous warriors. Every dwarf lives
better than a king in the Halls of the Ancestors. You
shall want for nothing, and you can rest with no more
burden upon your shoulders.'

The beardling did not reply, and when Barundin
looked down he saw that he was dead. He hefted the
boy over his shoulder and picked up his shield. Carrying him back to the dwarf line, he handed the corpse
over to one of his warriors.

'See that they are interred with the honoured dead,'
said Barundin. 'All of them.'

As he turned back, Barundin saw that the poison
wind was dispersing into the hall. It stung his eyes and
caused his skin to itch and every breath felt heavy in his
chest, but it was thinning now and not so potent as it
had been in the confines of the mine tunnels.

Other figures appeared in the mist, hunched and
swift. As they came into sight, Barundin saw that they
were skaven, clad in robes of thick leather, their faces
covered with heavy masks pierced with dark goggles. As
they scuttled forward they threw glass orbs high into

the air, which shattered upon the ground, releasing new clouds of poison wind. As the dwarfs pushed and pulled at each other get away from this attack, more skaven marched through the dank cloud. Some succumbed to the poison and fell twitching to the ground, but those that survived pressed on without regard for their dead. They wore heavy armour, made from scraps of metal and rigid hide, painted with markings like claw scratches, and tattered triangular red banners were carried at their fore.

There was a bellowed shout from behind Barundin as one of the thanes gave an order, and a moment later the chamber rang with the thunder of handguns. Metal bullets whirred over the king's head, plucking the skaven from their feet, smashing through their armour.

The rippling salvo continued from east to west, punctuated by the twang and swish of crossbow bolts from the quarrellers. A hundred dead skaven littered the floor around the passage entrance and still they pressed forward. From behind them, a nightmarish host spread out into the hall, running swiftly.

The skaven swarm advanced, chittering and screeching, the rat warriors bounding forward with crude blades and clubs in their clawed hands. A cannon roar drowned out their noise for a moment and the iron ball, wreathed in magical blue flame, tore through them, smashing bodies asunder and hurling dismembered corpses into the air. As more cannonballs crashed into the press of bodies, the skaven advance slowed and some tried to turn back. Another solid fusillade of handgun fire tore a swathe through the swarming horde as some skaven attempted to retreat, others pushed forwards, and even more tried to advance out of the confines of the tunnel, clambering over the corpse-piles.

The crossfire of thunderers and quarrellers turned the mouth of the tunnel into a killing ground, forcing those skaven that managed to scuttle through the opening to dart to the left and right, circling around the devastation. Barundin watched warily as they began to gather in numbers again, clinging to the shadows in the northern corners of the Deeping Hall. From amongst them, weapon teams began to advance on the dwarf line, partially obscured from attack by the ranks of clanrat warriors around them.

Consisting of a gunner and a loader, the weapon teams sported a variety of arcane and obscene armaments. Hidden behind shield bearers, engineers fired long, wide-bored jezzails into the dwarf throng, their warpstone-laced bullets smashing through chainmail and steel plates with ease. The thundering fusillade smashed aside a rank of quarrellers on the third step, killing and wounding over a dozen dwarfs in one salvo.

Ahead of the jezzails, gun teams worked their way forward. One pair stopped just a couple dozen feet from Barundin. The gunner lowered a multi-barrelled gun towards the dwarf line and began to crank a handle on the side of the mechanism. A belt carried in a barrel on the back of the loader was dragged into the breach and a moment later the gun erupted with a torrent of flame and whizzing bullets, ripping into the hammerer. Small shells screamed and clattered around Barundin, and beside him Arbrek gave a grunt as a bullet buried itself in his left shoulder, knocking the runelord to one knee. Wisps of dark energy dribbled from the wound.

The skaven was turning the handle faster and faster with growing excitement, the rate of fire increasing as it did so. Green-tinged steam leaked from the heavy gun and oil spattered the creature's fur from the spinning gears, chains and belts.

With a detonation that flung green flames ten feet in every direction, the gun jammed and exploded, hurling chunks of scorched, furred flesh into the air and scything through the skaven with shrapnel and pieces of exploding ammunition. As they moved away from the explosion, the skaven strayed into range of the flame cannon on the east flank of the hall.

Helping Arbrek to his feet, Barundin watched as the engineers pumped bellows, wound gears, adjusted the elevations of the war machine and twirled with valves and nozzles to balance the pressure building inside the fire-thrower. At a signal from the master engineer standing on the footplate of the war machine, one of the apprentices threw down a lever and unleashed the might of the flame cannon.

A gout of burning oil and naphtha arced high over the heads of the dwarfs in front, dripping fiery rain onto them. Splashing like waves against a cliff, the flaming concoction burst over the nearest skaven, setting fur alight, searing flesh and seeping through armour. Doused in burning oil, the creatures wailed and flailed, rolling on the ground and setting their kin alight with their wild thrashing. Their panicked screams echoed around the hall, along with the cheers of the dwarfs.

Terrified by this attack, a swathe of skaven broke and fled, fearing another burst of deadly flame. Bullets and crossbow bolts followed them, punching into their backs, ripping at fur and flesh as they ran for the tunnel, accompanied by the jeers of the army of Zhufbar.

Despite this triumph, the fighting had become hand-to-hand in many places, the steel-clad dwarfs holding the line against a tide of viciously fanged and clawed furry beasts. With pockets of bitter combat breaking out across the hall, the war machines and guns of the skaven were finding fewer and fewer targets to attack,

and the sound of black powder igniting and the thwip
of crossbow quarrels was replaced with the ringing of
rusted iron on gromril and steel biting into flesh.

Barundin bellowed for the line to push forward in the
hope of forcing the skaven back into the tunnels where
their numbers would be no advantage. Inch by inch,
step by step, the dwarfs advanced, their axes and hammers rising and falling against the brown deluge
rushing upon them.

Barundin turned and cast a glance at the wound in
Arbrek's shoulder. Already the vile poison of the warpstone was hissing and melting the flesh and gromril
mail around the puckered hole in his flesh.

'You need to get that cleaned up and taken out,' the
king said.

'Later,' replied Arbrek, his teeth gritted. He pointed
towards the tunnel. 'I think I shall be needed here for
the moment.'

Barundin looked out across the hall, over the heads of
the dwarfs in front battling against the skaven horde. In
the gloom of the passage entrance he could see a glow:
the unearthly aura of warpstone. In that flickering, dis-
mal light he saw several skaven hunched beneath large
backpacks. Their faces were coiled with thick wires,
their arms pierced with nails and bolts.

'Warlocks,' the king murmured.

As the skaven spellcasters advanced, they gripped
long spear-like weapons, connected to the whirling
globes and hissing valves of their backpacks with thick,
sparking wires. Motes of energy played around the
jaggedly pronged tips of the warp-conductors, gathering
in tiny lightning storms of magical energy.

Their grimacing, twisted faces were thrown into stark
contrast as they unleashed the energies of their warp-
packs; bolts of green and black energy splayed across

dwarfs and skaven alike, charring flesh, exploding off
armour and burning hair. Arcs of warp-lightning leaped
from figure to figure, their smouldering corpses contorting with conducted energy, glowing faintly from
within, smoke billowing from blackened holes in skin
and ruined eye sockets.

Here and there, the magical assault was countered by
the runesmiths harmlessly grounding the arcs of devastating warp energy with their runestaffs. Beside
Barundin, Arbrek was muttering under his breath and
stroking a hand along his staff, the runes along its
length flaring into life at the caress of his gnarled hands.

Behind the advancing warlocks, another figure
appeared, swathed in robes, its hood thrown back to
reveal light grey fur and piercing red eyes. Twisted horns
curled around its ears as it turned its head from side to
side, surveying the carnage being wrought by both sides. A
nimbus of dark energy surrounded the Grey Seer as it drew
in magical power from the surrounding air and rocks.

It raised its crooked staff above its head, the bones
and skulls hanging from its tip swaying and clattering.
A shadow grew in the tunnel behind the skaven wizard
and Barundin strained his eyes to see what was within.
Brief lulls in the fighting brought a distant noise, a far-
off scratching and chittering that grew in volume,
echoing along the north passage.

In a cloud of teeth, claws and beady eyes, hundreds
upon hundreds of rats burst into the Deeping Hall,
pouring around the Grey Seer. In a packed mass of verminous filth, the rats spewed forth from the
passageway, scuttling across the ground and spilling
over the skaven. Onwards came the swarm until it
reached the dwarf line. Barundin's warriors struck out
with hammers and axes, but against the tide of creatures, there was little they could do.

Dwarfs flailed with dozens of rats scrabbling into their armour, biting and scratching, clawing at their faces, tangling in their beards, their claws and fangs lacerating and piercing tough dwarf skin. Though each bite was little more than a pinprick, more and more dwarfs began to fall to the sheer number of the rodents, their bites laced with vile poison.

Barundin took a step forward to join the fray but was stopped by Arbrek's hand on his shoulder. 'This is sorcery,' said the runelord, his face set. 'I shall deal with it.'

Chanting in khazalid, the runelord held his staff in front of him, its runes growing brighter and brighter. With a final roar, he thrust the tip of the staff towards the immense rat pack spilling up the steps, and white light flared out. As the magical glow spread and touched the rats, they burst into flames, ignited by the mystical energy unleashed from the runes. In a wave spreading out from Arbrek, the white fire blazed through the tide of vermin, driving them back, destroying those touched by its ghostly flames.

The counter-spell dissipated as the Grey Seer extended his own magical powers, but it was too late. The few dozen rats that remained were scurrying back into the darkness of the passageway. With a hiss and a wave of its staff, the Grey Seer urged its warriors on, and the skaven threw themselves once more against the dwarf line.

'Come on, time to fight!' Barundin called to his hammerers.

They marched forward as a solid block, driving into the skaven horde. Barundin led the charge, his axe chopping into furred flesh, the blades and mauls of the skaven bouncing harmlessly from his armour and shield. Around him, the hammerers gripped their mattocks tightly, crushing bones and flinging aside their foes with wide sweeping attacks. The king and his veterans pushed on through the melee, driving towards the Grey Seer.

More skaven were still emerging from the passageway in a seemingly unending stream. Barundin found himself facing a rag-tag band swathed in tattered, dirty robes, bearing wickedly spiked flails and serrated daggers. Their fur was balding in places, their skin pocked with buboes and lesions. The ratmen frothed at the mouth, their eyes rheumy yet manic, their ears twitching with frenzied energy, and launched themselves headlong at the dwarfs.

There were those amongst their number whirling large barbed censers around their heads, thick dribbles of warp-gas seeping from their weapons. As the choking cloud enveloped Barundin, he felt the poisonous vapours stinging his eyes and burning his throat. Coughing and blinking, through tear-filled eyes, he saw the rat-things leaping towards him and raised his shield barely in time to ward off a vicious blow from a flail.

Knocked sideways by the force of the jolt, Barundin only had time to steady his footing before another swipe rang against the side of his helm, stunning him for a moment. Ignoring the rushing of blood in his ears and the cloying smoke, the king struck out blindly with his axe, hewing left and right. He felt the blade bite on more than one occasion and gave a roar of satisfaction.

'Drive the filth back to their dirty holes!' he urged his fellow dwarfs, and could feel his hammerers pressing forward around him.

His eyes clearing slightly, Barundin continued his advance, surrounded by the swirl and cacophony of battle. He struck the head from a skaven that had launched itself at him with two daggers in its hands, its tongue lolling from its fanged mouth. Goblinbeater proved

equally good at killing skaven as again and again,
Barundin buried the axe's head into chests, lopped off
limbs and caved in skulls.

As he wrenched the runeaxe from the twitching
corpse of yet another dirt-encrusted invader, Barundin
felt a pause in the advance around him and caught a
murmur of dismay spreading through the warriors close
by. Battering aside another foe with the flat of his axe
blade, the king caught a glimpse of the passageway
ahead.

From the gloom loomed four massive shapes, each at
least thrice the height of a dwarf. Their bodies were distended and bulged with unnatural muscle, in places
bracketed with strips of rusted iron and pierced with
metal bolts. Tails tipped with blades lashed back and
forth as the creatures were driven on by the barbed
whips of their handlers.

One of the rat ogres, as they had been named in the
old journals, charged straight at Barundin. The skin and
flesh of its face hung off in places, revealing the bone
beneath, and its left hand had been sawn away and
replaced with a heavy blade nailed into the stump. In
its other hand the creature held a length of chain
attached to a manacle around its wrist, scything left and
right with the heavy links and scattering dwarfs all
around.

Barundin raised his shield and broke into a run,
countering the beast's impetus with his own charge. The
chain glanced off the king's shield in a shower of sparks,
and he ducked beneath a vicious swipe of the rat ogre's
blade. With a grunt, Barundin brought Goblinbeater
up, the blade biting into the inner thigh of the creature's leg.

It gave a howl and lashed out, its swipe crashing into
Barundin's shield with the force of a forge hammer,

hurling him backwards and forcing him to lose his grip on Goblinbeater. Pulling himself to his feet, Barundin ducked behind his shield once more as the chain whirled around the head of the rat ogre and crashed down, splintering the stone floor.

His short legs driving him forward, Barundin launched himself at the rat ogre and smashed the rim of his shield into its midriff, wincing as the impact jarred his shoulder. With the brief moments this desperate act bought him, Barundin snatched at the handle of Goblinbeater and ripped it free, dark blood spouting from the wound in the mutated monstrosity's leg.

With a backward slash, Barundin brought the blade of the runeaxe down and through the knee of the rat ogre, slicing through flesh and shattering bone. With a mournful yelp the rat ogre collapsed to the floor, lashing out with its blade-hand and scoring a groove across the chest plate of Barundin's armour. Using his shield to bat aside the return blow, the king stepped forward and hewed into the creature's chest with Goblinbeater, the blade slicing through wooden splints and pallid, fur-patched flesh.

Again and again, Barundin pulled the axe free and swung it home, until the rat ogre's thrashing subsided. Panting with the effort, Barundin glanced up to see the other beasts fighting against the embattled hammerers. More skaven were pouring from the tunnel and the dwarf line was buckling under the weight of the attack, being driven back simply by the numbers of the horde.

The crackle of gunfire and the boom of the occasional cannon shot echoed around the Fourth Deeping Hall. Flares of warp-lightning and the glow of runes highlighted bearded faces shouting battle oaths and ratmen features twisted in snarls. A horn blast joined the tumult and a silvery knot of dwarf warriors pushed through the tumult, their weapons cutting a swathe through the skaven mass.

Tharonin's Ironbreakers surged forward to the king, their rune-carved gromril armour glowing in the light of lanterns and magical energies. Virtually impervious to the attacks of their foes, the veteran tunnel-fighters tore into the skaven army like a pickaxe through stone, smashing aside their enemies and marching over their hewn corpses.

Heartened by this counter-attack, the dwarfs, Barundin amongst them, surged forward once more, ignoring their casualties, shrugging off their wounds to drive the skaven back into the tunnel. As he fought, Barundin saw that the Grey Seer was no longer in view, and could sense that victory was close. In growing numbers, the skaven began to break from the bloody combat, their nerve shattered. In their dozens and then their hundreds they bolted and fled, hacking at each other in their attempts to escape and reach the passageway.

GRUDGE FOUR
The Beer Grudge

UNLIKE THE NEAT, geometric construction and straight lines of the dwarf mines, the skaven tunnels were little more than animal holes dug through dirt and laboriously clawed through hard rock. Linking together natural caves, underground rivers and dark fissures, they extended down into the depths of the mountain in every direction.

The subterranean warren had no planning, no sense or reason behind its layout. Some tunnels would simply end, others double-backed frequently as they sought easier routes through the rock of the World's Edge Mountains. Some were broad and straight, others so small that even a dwarf was forced down to his hands and knees to navigate them.

The walls were slicked with the passing of the creatures, their oily, furry bodies wearing the rock smooth in places over many years. The stench of their musk was like a cloud that constantly hung over the hunting parties of Zhufbar as they tried to track down the skaven and map their lair. The task was all but impossible, made more difficult by the fear of ambush and the sporadic fighting that still broke out.

Most of the expeditions were led by detachments of Ironbreakers, whose skill and armour were invaluable in such close confines. As they descended into the dank maze of burrows, they took with them signalling lanterns, and left small sentry groups at junctions and corners. By keeping track of the beacon lights in this way, the various parties could communicate with each other, albeit over relatively short distances. The tunnels themselves made navigating by noise all but impossible, with odd echoes and breaks in the walls through unseen crevasses making any sound seem closer or further away than it was, or coming from a different direction.

The lantern-lines at least allowed the dwarfs to signal for help, to send warnings and sometimes simply to find their way back to the outer workings of the north Zhufbar mines.

Barundin was accompanying one of the delving bands, as they had come to be called, searching through the rat-infested caverns north-east of Zhufbar, several miles from the hold. There had been quite a lot of fighting in the area over the previous days, and the opinion of several of the team leaders was that they had broken a considerable concentration of the skaven in the region.

It was cold, depressing work: clambering over piles of scree, scraping through narrow bolt-holes, kicking the vermin from underfoot. These were the evil places of the mountainscape, crawling with beetles and maggots, writhing with rat swarms, and made all the more awful by the stench of the skaven and pockets of choking gas.

As far as Barundin could judge this far underground, it was the middle of the afternoon. They had laboured through the tunnels since an early breakfast that morning, and his back was almost bent from frequent stooping and crawling. They tried to move as quietly as possible so as not to alert any ratmen that might be nearby, but it was a vain effort. Dwarf mail chinked against every stone, their hobnailed boots and steel-shod toecaps clumping on rock and crunching through dirt and gravel.

'We're getting close to something,' whispered Grundin Stoutlegs, the leader of the group.

Grundin pointed to the ground and Barundin saw bones in the dirt and spoil of digging – bones picked clean of flesh. There were scraps of cloth and tufts of fur, as well as skaven droppings littering the floor. Grundin waved the group to a stop and they settled. Silence descended.

A strange mewling sound could be heard from ahead, distorted by the winding, uneven walls of the tunnel. There were other noises: scratching, chittering and a wet sucking sound. Now that they were still, Barundin could feel the ground throbbing gently through the thick soles of his boots, and he pulled off a gauntlet and touched his hand to the slimy wall, ignoring the wetness on his finger tips. He could definitely feel a pulsing vibration, and as they adjusted, his ears picked up a humming noise from ahead. Wiping the filth from his hand as best he could, he pulled his gauntlet back on with a grimace.

Grundin slipped his shield from his back and pulled his axe from his belt, and the other Ironbreakers followed his example and readied themselves. Barundin was carrying a single-handed hammer, stocky and heavy, ideal for tunnel-work, and he pulled his shield onto his left arm and nodded his readiness to Grundin.

They set off even more cautiously than before. Barundin could feel the bones and filth slipping and shifting underfoot, and he cursed silently to himself every time there was a scrape or clatter. Ahead, in a growing glow from some distant light, he could see the tunnel branching off through several low openings.

Reaching the junction, it was clear that the tunnels all led by different paths to some larger chamber ahead; the flickering light that could be seen in each of them was the same quality. Grundin split the group into three smaller bands, each about a dozen strong, sending one to the left, one to the right, and taking the centre group himself. Barundin found himself directed to the right by a nod from Grundin. The king took the order without a word. In the halls of Zhufbar he was beyond command, but in these grim environs he would not dare to question the grizzled tunnel fighter.

One of the Ironbreakers, recognisable as Lokrin Rammelsson only by the dragon-head crest moulded from the brow of his full face helm, gave Barundin a thumbs up and waved the king into the tunnel, following behind with several more of the Ironbreakers. Rats shrieked and fled down the passageway as the dwarfs advanced, following the tunnel as first it wound to the right and then banked back of itself, dropping down to the left. It widened rapidly and Barundin saw the group ahead gathering at the edge of whatever lay beyond. He pushed his way between two of them to see what had halted their advance, and then stopped.

THEY STOOD ON on the edge of a wide, oval-shaped cave, which sloped down away from them and arched high overhead. It was at least fifty feet high, the walls dotted with crude torches, bathing the scene in a fiery red glow. Other openings all around the chamber led off in every direction, some of them almost impossibly high up the walls, which could have only been reached by the most nimble of creatures were it not for the rickety gantries and scaffolds that ran haphazardly around the chamber, connected by bridges, ladders and swaying walkways. Here and there Barundin recognised scavenged pieces of dwarf-hewn timber or metalwork, bastardised into new purpose by the skaven.

The floor of the chamber was a writhing mass of life, filled with small bodies in constant motion, some pink and bald, others with patches of fur growing on them. Like a living carpet, the skavenspawn spread from one end of the cavern to the other, crawling over each other, fighting and gnawing, biting and clawing in heaving piles. Mewing and crying, they blindly slithered and scuttled to and fro, littering the floor with droppings and the corpses of the weakest runts.

Amongst them hurried naked slaves, their fur marked with burns from branding irons and the scores of whips. They pushed their way through the morass of wriggling flesh, picking out the largest offspring and taking them away. Several dozen guards dressed in crude armour stood watch with rusted blades, while pack masters cracked their whips on slaves and skavenspawn alike, chittering orders in their harsh language.

At the centre of the nightmarish heap were three pale, bloated shapes, many times larger than any of the other skaven. They lay on their sides, their tiny heads barely visible amongst the fleshy mass of their offspring and the arcane machineries they were connected to. The skavenspawn were all the more vicious here, biting and tearing in a frenzy to get at the food, the older ones feeding upon the dead runt corpses instead of the greenish-grey spew coursing from the distended, pulsating udders of the skaven females.

Barundin felt the contents of his stomach lurch and swallowed heavily to avoid vomiting. The stench was unbelievable: a mix of acrid urine, rotting flesh and sour milk. One of the Ironbreakers lifted his gold-chased mask, revealing the scarred face of Fengrim Dourscowl, one of Barundin's distant nephews.

'We've not found one of these for quite a while,' Fengrim said to Barundin.

'There must be hundreds of them,' said Barundin after a moment, still staring in disbelief. He had heard stories of these brood chambers, but nothing could have prepared him for this awful vision of sprawling, noxious life.

'Thousands,' spat Fengrim. 'We have to kill them all and seal the chamber.'

A sound from behind caused them to turn quickly, weapons raised, but it was another ironbreaker.

'Grundin has sent a signal to bring up the miners and engineers,' the Ironbreaker told them, his voice metallic from inside his helm. 'We have to secure the chamber for their arrival.'

Looking back out into the brood-chamber, Barundin saw two knots of dwarfs advancing from other entrances, crushing the skavenspawn underfoot. Slaves were shrieking in panic and fleeing while the guards, alerted to the attack, were gathering quickly under one of the soaring gantries.

'Come on then, let's be about it!' said Barundin, hefting his hammer and marching out of the tunnel mouth.

His footing was unsure as he waded through the carpet of skaven offspring, his heavy boots snapping bones and squashing flesh. He could not feel anything through the heavy armour he was wearing, but as he looked down at his feet he saw the skavenspawn squirming and clawing, scraping ineffectually at the gromril plates or pulling themselves sluggishly away. With a snarl, he brought his foot down onto the back of one particularly loathsome specimen, its beady eyes flecked with bloodspots, snapping its spine.

Advanced upon from three directions, and realising they were outnumbered, the guards quickly fled without a fight, stampeding over the bodies of their own children in an effort to escape the advancing, vengeful dwarfs.

Barundin kicked and battered his way through the filth, sometimes thigh-deep in writhing skavenspawn, caving in heads with the edge of his shield, smashing small bodies against the rock with his hammer. Eventually he stood a short way from one of the broodmothers. Its eyes were almost lifeless with no flicker of intelligence or recognition and its artificially fattened bulk several times his height. Its entire body was riddled with blue veins and coarse with spots and blisters. The feeding spawn did not even react to his presence, so intent was it on its unwholesome nourishment.

'This is axe work, my king,' said Fengrim, who had followed Barundin to the nearest female.

Raising his axe, Fengrim brought the blade up and over his head and then into a downward stroke, as one might chop wood. The razor-sharp blade sliced through bloated flesh, peeling away the skin and revealing a thick layer of fat beneath. Another stroke opened the wound to the flesh and bone, spilling dark blood and globules of fatty tissue onto the crawling carpet of skavenspawn.

A wave of stench hit Barundin and he turned away, gagging heavily. Although he could no longer see it, he still felt sickened by the wet chopping noise of Fengrim's bloody work. A spouting wave of fluids splashed over the king's legs; deep red and pale green life fluids stained the once-polished gromril of his greaves.

Barundin raised his hammer and began sweeping it through the morass of squirming creatures around him, the slaughter of the vile skavenkin distracting him from the noisome sounds and smells of the broodmother's grisly execution.

THE SKAVEN ATTACKED the brood chamber twice over the next day, but the dwarfs had moved up in strength and the ratmen were easily pushed back. Barundin agreed with Grundin that it seemed the skaven's strength in the area had been thoroughly broken. With their breeding grounds taken, they would not be a threat from this quarter for many years.

Engineers with casks of oil and kegs of black powder were brought in, and aided by dwarf miners prepared for the demolition of the many tunnels leading from the brood chamber. Already a pyre of burning skaven bodies was piled in the centre of the cavern, the oily smoke from the flaming carcasses filling the air with a choking fume.

Miners dug holes into the sides of the access tunnels for charges to be placed, while the engineers measured and drew up plans, arguing about where to place the explosives, where to dig out the tunnels and burn away supports to bring the roofs down. As teams of dwarfs dismantled the ramshackle walkways and towers of the skaven, reclaiming what had been taken from them, Barundin toiled alongside them, cutting through planks and ropes, smashing apart timbers and poles to fuel the demolition work.

Amongst the debris, Barundin found a stone ancestor face, looted from one of the miners' halls. It was Grungni, ancestor god of mining, his beard chipped and mould-covered, his horned helm cut with crude skaven marks. Wiping away the filth with his fingers, Barundin realised that it had been seventeen long years since the battle of the Fourth Deeping Hall.

Since their first victory, the dwarfs had been hard-pressed for many years, losing many of the mine-workings to the innumerable skaven assaults. Time and again they had been driven back, sometimes within sight of the central hold itself. Always Barundin's resolution had held firm, and he would not give an inch of ground to the invaders without a fight. It would have been easy to abandon the northern passages and mines, to seal the gates and bar them with steel and runes, but Barundin, like all his kind, was stubborn and loathe to retreat.

Losing the war of attrition, outnumbered by many thousands of ratmen, Barundin and his council had devised a plan. New workings had been dug to the east, where the skaven seemed fewer, perhaps wary of the goblins of Mount Gunbad that lay in that direction. Using these new tunnels, Barundin and his warriors had sallied forth several times, trapping the skaven between them and armies issuing from Zhufbar itself.

Month by month, year by year, the skaven had been pushed back once more, into the Second Deep, then the Third and the Fourth. Six years ago, the Fourth Deeping Hall had been reclaimed and Barundin had allowed a month's respite to celebrate the victory and for his host to rest and regain its strength. Young beardlings were now hardened warriors, and hundreds of new tombs had been dug in the clan chambers across the hold to house the dead the bitter fighting had claimed.

Three years ago they had been able to first venture into the skaven tunnels, bringing death and fire to cleanse the verminous creatures from the mountain depths around Zhufbar. For the last year, the fighting had been sporadic and little more than skirmishes. Barundin was in no doubt that the skaven would gather their numbers again and return, but not for many years. Just as it had been over a century since the last skaven assault of Zhufbar, the king hoped that it would be decades before they came again.

For three more days the dwarfs toiled, preparing for the destruction of the brood chamber. When it was done, slow fuses hanging from supports in the walls, fires flickering in cracks and holes dug into the tunnels walls, the engineers ordered the other dwarfs to return to Zhufbar. Barundin was allowed to watch, and was even given the privilege of lighting one of the touch-fuses.

The dwarf mines shook with the detonations which rumbled on for many hours as caves and tunnels collapsed. There was no cheering, no celebration from the dwarfs. Seventeen years of desperate war had left them ruing the evils of the world and feeling sombre for the fallen.

It was the first time Barundin truly understood himself and his people; the long march of centuries eroded their lives and culture. There could be little joy in the victory, not only for its cost, but for the fact that it was nothing more than a respite, a pause of breath in the unending saga of bloodshed that had become the lot of the dwarfs for four thousand years.

The golden age of the ancestor-kings had passed, the silver-age of the mountain realm had been swallowed by the earthquakes and the greenskins. Now Barundin and his people clung to their existence, their hold half-filled and full of empty halls, the ghostly silence of their ancestors' shades wandering the corridors and galleries, mourning for the glories of the past.

But though he understood better the plight of his race, Barundin was not without hope. While those older and greyer than he were content to grumble into their beer and sigh at the merest mention of the old times, Barundin knew that there was still much that could be done.

First and foremost, he resolved as he lay that night in his chambers, he would lead Zhufbar to the conquest of Dukankor Grobkaz-a-Gazan, destroying the grobi as they had vanquished the skaven. It would take a while to rebuild, but within twenty years, perhaps thirty, the halls of Grungankor Stokril would again be filled with good, honest dwarf lights, and the gruff laughter of his people.

IT WAS WITH some surprise that Barundin received a message from the Engineers Guild the next day. He had not yet sent word to them to continue on their war production so that the army might be rebuilt for the invasion of Dukankor Grobkaz-a-Gazan. He was, the message told him, politely invited to attend a meeting of the Engineers Guild High Council that night. It was worded as a request, as befitted the king, but not even the king refused the Engineers Guild in Zhufbar. He ruled, if not by their consent, then at least by their acceptance. Larger than any of the clans, and essential to the running of the hold, the Engineers Guild wielded its power lightly, but it wielded it nonetheless.

Barundin spent the day overseeing the withdrawal of warriors from the north passages, and spent much time with Tharonin, discussing the reopening of the mine workings so that ore and coal could be sent to the smelters again, which had run low on many supplies during periods of fighting with the skaven.

So it was armed with this good news, and a light heart, that Barundin dressed that evening. A guild meeting was a formal occasion, part committee meeting, part celebration dedicated to Grungni and the other ancestor gods. Barundin decided to leave his armour upon its stand. This was perhaps only the third or fourth time he had not worn it in seventeen years. It would be a good sign to his people, their king walking through Zhufbar unarmed, safe in his own hold.

He dressed in dark blue leggings and a padded jerkin of purple, tied with a wide belt. To say that the years of war had made him lean would have not been entirely true, for all dwarfs have considerable girth even when starved, but his belt was certainly a few notches tighter than it had been when he had taken to the throne of Zhufbar. His beard was longer and now hung to his belt, a source of private pride for the king. He knew that he was young for his position, too young in the eyes of some of his advisors, he suspected, but soon he would be able to use belt-clasps to secure his beard, a sure sign of growing age and wisdom. By the time the grobi of Dukankor Grobkaz-a-Gazan had been sent running back to their holes in Mount Gunbad, he would have the respect of them all.

Warriors from the guild, bearing shields with the anvil motif of the Master Engineers, came for Barundin in the early evening, to provide escort. He knew the way, of course, but the formality of the invitation had to be respected, and due ceremony observed.

They led him down to the forges powered by Zhufbar's waterwheels, which had continued their slow turns all through the fighting, never once stopping, the lights of the furnaces never dimming. It was a credit to the engineers that they had done so much with so little for those seventeen years, and Barundin decided to make a point of complimenting them to this effect. He was about to ask them for just as much effort for another potentially long war, and a little flattery would never harm his cause.

Having passed through the foundries they came to the workshops, hall upon hall of benches and machinery, from the finest clockwork mechanism to the mighty casting cranes of the cannon-makers. Even at this hour, it was alive with activity – the clinking of hammers, the buzz of heated conversations, the whirr and grind of whetstones and lathes.

At the far end of the workshops was a small stone door, no taller than a dwarf and wide enough for two to enter abreast. The lintel stone above it was heavy and carved with shallow runes in the secret language of the engineers. A brass boar's-head knocker was set into the stone of the door; below it was a metal plate worn thin with centuries of use. One of Barundin's guides took the knocker in his hand and rapped it onto the plate in a succession of rapid knocks. Answering taps resounded from the other side, to which the engineer replied with more raps of his own.

A few moments passed and then, with a grinding sound from within the walls, the door slid to one side, dark and forbidding. The dwarf guards gestured for Barundin to enter and he did so with a nod, stepping through into the smoky gloom beyond. Another guard on the far side of the door nodded in welcome as the portal closed, rolling back into place on hidden gears.

He was in the antechamber to the guildhall and could hear raised voices from the closed double doors ahead of him. A few small candles did little to light the darkness, but his eyes soon adjusted and he could make out the wheel-gears of the door locks mounted into the walls around him. Like all the work of the engineers, it was not only functional but a piece of artistic beauty. The gears were chased with golden knotwork and a thick bolt decorated with an ancestor head pinioned each cog. The chains glistened in the candlelight with oil and polish.

'They're ready for you,' said the dwarf, walking across the room and laying his hands upon the door handles, giving Barundin a moment to collect himself. The king straightened his jerkin, smoothed the plaits of his beard across his chest and belly and gave the guard a thumbs up.

Thrusting open the doors, the guard strode into the room. 'Barundin, Son of Throndin, King of Zhufbar!' bellowed the guard turned herald.

Barundin walked past him into the great Guild Hall and stopped while the doors were closed behind him. The engineers were not so proud that they would try to outshine their king, and so their guild hall was smaller than Barundin's own audience chamber, though not by much. No pillars supported the rock above their heads. Instead the ceiling was vaulted with thick girders crossing each other in intricate patterns, their foundations set within the walls of the hall itself. Gold-headed rivets sparkled in the glow of hundreds of lanterns, though the size of the hall meant that the furthest reaches were still swathed in shadow.

In an island of light in the centre of the vast hall, around a fire pit blazing with flames, was the guild table. It was circular, and large enough for two dozen dwarfs to sit in comfort, although only half that number were now there; they were the twelve thanes of the guild clans, twelve of the most powerful dwarfs in Zhufbar. Each held office as the high engineer for five years, although this was regarded as a position of first amongst equals, a spokesman, not a ruler, hence the circular meeting table.

The current incumbent was Darbran Rikbolg, whose clan in times past had been granted the title kingmakers for their efforts in supporting Barundin's ancestors' accession to the throne of Zhufbar. Before him was a large sceptre of steel, its head shaped like a spanner, holding a bolt carved from a sapphire as big as two clasped fists. The guildmasters, as the thanes were known, were dressed in identical robes of deep blue, trimmed with chainmail and fur. Their beards were splendidly trimmed and knotted, clasped with steel designs and imbedded with sapphires.

'Welcome, Barundin, welcome,' said Darbran, standing up. His smile seemed genuine enough.

Barundin crossed the hall, the guildmasters' eyes upon him, and shook hands with the high engineer. Darbran gestured to a seat at his right that stood empty, and Barundin sat down, exchanging nods with the guildmasters. The remains of a meal lay scattered about the table, as did several half-full flagons of ale.

Catching the king's gaze, Darbran grinned. 'Please, help yourself. There's plenty to go around, right?' he said, grabbing a spare cup and emptying a flagon into it, handing the frothing ale to the king.

'Aye, plenty of ale for all,' echoed Borin Brassbreeks, thane of the Gundersson clan. 'The guild would not have it said we offer a poor welcome to the king, would we?'

There was much naying and shaking of heads, and Barundin realised that the aging dwarfs were already well into their cups. He wasn't sure whether this was a bad thing; as when dwarfs get more drunk they are more susceptible to flattery and bribery, but their stubborn streak widens considerably and their ears tend to close. All in all, the king considered, what he was going to propose was more likely to fall better on drunk ears than sober ones.

'It's no secret the war with the skaven is all but over,' said Darbran, sitting down heavily. He raised his tankard, spilling beer onto the stone floor. 'Well done, Barundin, well done!'

There was a chorus of hurrahs and a few of the thanes slapped the table with calloused hands in appreciation.

'Thank you, thank you very much,' said Barundin. He was about to continue but he was interrupted.

'We showed 'em, didn't we?' laughed Borin.

'Yes, we showed them,' said Barundin, taking a gulp of ale. It was a little too bitter for his liking, but not altogether unpleasant.

'Now that we've got all of this nasty business out of the way, things can get back to normal around here,' said another of the thanes, Garrek Silverweaver. He wore a pair of thick spectacles that had slipped down to the end of his pointed nose, making it look as if he had four eyes.

'Aye, back to normal,' said one of the other thanes.

Barundin gulped another mouthful of ale and smiled weakly. Darbran noticed his expression and scowled.

'The war is won, isn't it?' asked the engineer.

'Oh yes, well as much as it will ever be against that loathsome filth,' said Barundin. 'They'll not trouble us again for many a year.'

'Then why wear a face that would spike a wheel?' asked Darbran. 'You look troubled, my friend.'

'The war with the skaven is over, that is true,' said Barundin slowly. He had been rehearsing this for the whole day between his talks with Tharonin, but now the words jarred in his throat. 'There is, however, the issue of the goblins still to be resolved.'

'The goblins?' said Borin. 'What goblins?'

'You know, Dukankor Grobkaz-a-Gazan,' said the engineer sitting next to Borin, ramming an elbow into his ribs as if this would act as a reminder. 'Barundin's father's dying grudge!'

Barundin was pleased that they had remembered, but his hopes were dashed by Borin's reply.

'Yes, but we decided we can't be having any of that, didn't we?' the old dwarf said. 'That's what we were just saying, wasn't it?'

Barundin turned his inquisitive glare to Darbran, who, to his credit, looked genuinely guilty and nonplussed. 'We knew you would want to discuss this, and so made it one of our items of business for today's meeting,' explained Darbran. 'We can't support another war, not now.'

'No, not now, not ever,' growled Borin, who had only recently handed over the role of high engineer and was quite clearly not out of the habit. 'For Grungni's sake, there's barely an ounce of iron or steel left. We can't forge from the bones of dead ratmen, can we? It's out of the question!'

'The mines are reopened even as we speak,' said Barundin, leaning forward and looking at the assembled guildmasters. 'I have spoken to Tharonin and he assures me there will be ore aplenty within a few weeks. We'll not let your furnaces grow cold.'

'We know about your talks with Tharonin,' said Darbran. 'He might have promised his own mines, but there's no guarantee the other clans will be back to work straight away. They've been fighting those bloody skaven for seventeen years, lad. That's a fair time in anybody's book. You don't run from one war into another.'

Barundin turned to the others, mouth open, but it was Gundaban Redbeard, youngest of the guildmasters at just over three hundred years old, who spoke first.

'We know you have to fulfil your father's dying grudge before you can go after that toad Vessal,' said Redbeard.

'But wait awhile. Let everyone catch their breath, so to speak. The clans are tired. We're tired.'

'Vessal's a manling, he'll not live forever,' snapped Barundin, earning him scowls from the eldest members of the guild council. 'Next year or a hundred years, the war with the grobi is going to be hard and long. Sooner started, sooner finished, isn't that right? If we stop now, it will take us years to get going again.'

His plea was met by blank expressions. They were not going to cooperate. Barundin took a deep breath and another swig of beer. He had hoped it wouldn't come to this, but he had one last bargaining chip.

'You're right, you're right,' said Barundin, sitting back in his chair. He waited a moment, then raised his tankard and said, almost conversationally, 'How's work on the brewery?'

There was much angry muttering and shaking of beards.

'We're far behind schedule,' admitted Darbran with a grimace. 'Behind schedule! Can you imagine? I tell you, some proper ale would soon give the clans some backbone again.'

'Curse that Wanazaki,' grumbled Borin. 'Him and his new-fangled ideas.'

'Look, Borin, we agreed,' said Redbeard. 'He was stupid not to have tested his automatic kegger, but the principles were sound. He just got his pressures mixed up.'

'Yes, but he burned all of his notes, didn't he?' said Barundin, and the engineers turned as one and glared at him.

'The coward,' said Borin. 'Running away like that. Showed a lot of promise that lad, but then to go and flit off like some manling…'

'I can get him back,' said Barundin. His statement was met with blank stares. 'I'll organise an expedition, to go and find him and bring him back.'

'What makes you think we want that oath-breaker back?' snarled Darbran.

'Well, to bring him to book, at the very least,' said Barundin. 'Surely he has to make account for himself. Besides which, if you can get him back, there's a chance he'll repent and try to make good.'

'If we wanted him, what makes you think we couldn't go and get him ourselves?' asked Redbeard.

'We all know he would make another run as soon as he saw a flag or sigil of the guild,' said Barundin. 'He's in terror of what punishment might be meted out on him.'

'And why do you think he'll stay around for you?' asked Darbran.

'I've already met him once,' said Barundin. 'When my father marched out to meet Vessal, remember? He didn't seem at all coy then.'

The engineers looked at each other and then at Barundin.

'We'll table the topic for a meeting,' said Darbran. 'We need to talk it over.'

'Of course you do,' said Barundin.

'We'll let you know our decision as soon as it's made,' the high engineer assured him.

'I'm sure you will,' said the king, standing. He downed the dregs of his ale. 'In fact, why don't I leave you learned folk to continue your meeting without me? I am weary, and I am sure you still have many other things to talk about, my proposition notwithstanding.'

'Aye, many things,' said Borin, his eyebrows waggling furiously.

'Then I bid you good night,' said Barundin.

He could feel their anxious stares on his back as he turned and walked away, and had to suppress a smile. Yes, he thought contentedly, he had given them plenty to talk about. A knock on the doors opened them and as the warden closed them behind him, he could already hear the guildmasters' voices rising.

THE LAST CHILLS of winter still lingered over the mountain, and the sky above was clear and blue. Barundin had spent those winter months preparing for the expedition, knowing that the snows would make any travelling almost impossible before the first spring thaws. While the mountain passes had remained navigable, he had sent rangers south and west, seeking for some news of Wanazaki. As the snows had closed in, a few brave bands had used the underway towards Karak Varn, though in places it was flooded and collapsed. Though none had found the mentally unstable engineer, there were several sightings of his gyrocopter in the lands to the south.

So it was that Barundin found himself leading a party of twenty dwarfs around the shore of Karak Varn. Both Tharonin and Arbrek had argued against the king accompanying the expedition, saying that it was too dangerous. Barundin had ignored their council, much to the older dwarfs' annoyance, and enlisted the services of Dran the Reckoner, one of the less respectable thanes of Zhufbar. Dran had a good reputation with the rangers, and knew the lands between Karak Varn and the Black Mountains, where Wanazaki was now reputedly living.

Barundin was in a fair mood. Though the heart of every dwarf is for solid stone and deep tunnels, there was also something about a crisp morning on a mountainside that stirred his soul. They had skirted west of Blackwater the night before and camped in a small hollow not far from the lake. Now, as they looked across the dark, still waters, the peaks of the mountains beyond could clearly be seen. Highest amongst them was Karaz Brindal, atop whose summit was one of the greatest watch towers of the dwarf realm, though now abandoned and infested with stone trolls. It was said that a dwarf upon Karaz Brindal could see all the way to Mount Gunbad, and that when the city had fallen, the sentries of the keep had bricked up the eastern windows so that they did not have to look upon the sight of their ancient hold despoiled by goblins.

On a ridged shoulder of Karaz Brindal was the sprawling open mine of the Naggrundzorn, now also flooded by the same waters that had burst open Karak Varn. It was there that Barundin's great-great-great-great-great grandfather had met his doom, fighting wolf riders from Mount Gunbad whilst protecting an ore caravan taking tribute to the high king at Karaz-a-Karak. A king's ransom it was called at the time, although perhaps in these years it would have been half the wealth of all Zhufbar. The days when the Silver Road to Mount Silverspear had been decorated with real silver had long passed, and the pillaging of the dwarfs' wealth for four millennia was just one more reason to berate the world for its shortcomings.

Snow still lay far down the mountain slopes, and Barundin wore a heavy woollen cloak over his chainmail and gromril armour. He wore a new pair of stout walking boots, which still needed breaking in, and his left heel was badly blistered from the march of the day before. Ignoring the pain, he pulled on his boots, as Dran filled his canteen from a thin rill of water running off the lake and down the mountainside.

'How far to Karak Varn?' asked Barundin.

The ranger looked over his shoulder at the king and grinned. The expression twisted the scar that ran from his chin to his right eye, leaving a bald slash through Dran's beard. Nobody knew how he had got the scar, and the dispossessed thane certainly wasn't telling.

'We'll be there by midday tomorrow,' said Dran, stoppering his water bottle as he walked back. 'From there it's three, maybe four, days to Black Fire Pass.'

'How can you be sure that Wanazaki has headed towards the Black Mountains?' asked the king, standing up and grabbing his pack. 'He might have headed south-east.'

'Towards Karaz-a-Karak?' said Dran with a snort. 'Not a chance. The guild will have sent word to their members there. Wanazaki knows that. No, he'll not go within a dozen leagues of Karaz-a-Karak.'

'I don't intend to walk all the way to Karak Hirn, only to find there's no sign of him,' said Barundin, shouldering his pack.

Dran tapped his nose. 'I make my money doing this, your highness,' said the Reckoner. 'I know how to find folk, and Wanazaki's no different. Mark my words, he doesn't know much, but he's clever enough to stick to the old North Road.'

'It's been nearly twenty years since I last saw him,' said Barundin as Dran waved to the other rangers to assemble. 'He could be in Nuln by now.'

'Well, you've got a choice then, haven't you?' said Dran. 'Turn back now before we've walked too far, and forget about Dukankor Grobkaz-a-Gazan and Vessal, or we can get going.'

'Lead on,' said the king.

THE GATES OF Karak Varn were a pitiable sight. Gaping into the darkness beyond, the great portal was thrown open, half sunk in the water. The ancient faces of the kings of Karak Varn carved into the stone had been worn away, leaving only the faintest of marks, which could barely be seen from the shore.

The entire lakeside around the area was littered with the spoor of grobi and other creatures, though none of it recent by the estimate of Dran. Just like most living things, even greenskins preferred not to venture too far abroad in the winter, and they would be in the dark places of the fallen hold away from the harsh light.

The dwarfs turned away from the depressing view, skirting the hold to the west, looking down upon the foothills of the World's Edge Mountains. To the west these rugged, rock-strewn hills gave way to the meadows and pastures of the Empire, and on the edge of vision at the horizon the dark swathe of the forests that swept across most of the manling realm.

South and west they travelled, leaving behind the bleak shores of Blackwater, passing the desolate, ruined towers that had once been the outlying settlements of Karak Varn. Now they were overgrown and barely visible; they were the dens of wolves and bears, and other, more wicked, creatures.

The mountains shallowed as they neared the Black Fire Pass, though their route took them across steep ridges and amongst the broad shoulders of the World's Edge Mountains, as if cutting across the grain of the mountain range. Dran led them on without pause or doubt, finding caves and hollows when the weather turned foul, which it did often. Usually they pressed on even into the last flurries of snow and the gales that howled up the valleys from the Border Princes and Badlands to the south.

On the seventeenth day after leaving Zhufbar, having covered some two hundred and twenty miles as the crow flies, they came upon the mountainside of Karag Kazak. Below them, the slope fell steeply to the floor of the pass, dotted with pines and large boulders. Though it was just before noon and there were many hours left in the day, Dran made camp. By the light of the noon sun, he led them a short way from the dell where their packs were left. Storm clouds glowered in the eastern sky, dark and menacing, coming towards them on a strong wind.

The Reckoner took them to a shoulder of rock which jutted from Karag Kazak for a half a mile. Barundin was astounded, for the area was littered with cairns, each adorned by an ancient oathstone, so time-worn many were little more than hillocks identified only by the rings of bronze occasionally spied amongst the tufts of hardy grass and heaps of soil. There were dozens of them, perhaps hundreds; the last resting places of a great many fallen dwarf warriors who chose to stand and die in the pass rather than retreat.

Further down the slope there was a large gathering of manlings: men, women and children were clustered around a tall statue of a large, bearded man holding a hammer aloft. Some were dressed in little more than rags, while others wore the pale robes Barundin had seen worn by manling priests.

'This is where they fought, isn't it?' said the king.

'Aye,' said Dran with a solemn nod. 'Here was arrayed the host of High King Kurgan, and down there Sigmar and his warlords made their stand.'

'Who are these manlings?' asked one of the rangers.

'Pilgrims,' said Dran. 'They consider it a sacred site, and travel for months even to tread upon the same ground where Sigmar fought alongside us. Some come here to pray to him, others to give thanks.'

'Are they not afraid of the greenskins?' asked Barundin. 'I see no garrison, no soldiers.'

'Even the orcs remember this place,' said Dran. 'Don't ask me how, but they do. They know that thousands of their kind were slaughtered here, upon these rocks, and most give it a wide berth. Of course, warbands still pass along here, and the odd army, but the manlings have a small keep away to the east beyond that ridge, and a much larger castle at the western end. Warning can be sent and the pilgrims can find refuge in plenty of time if there are greenskins on the move.'

'We could ask them if they have heard news of a dwarf engineer around these parts,' said Barundin.

'Aye, that was my purpose,' said Dran. 'As well as letting you see this, of course. I'll go down to their camp this evening. It's probably best that they not know one of our kings is abroad.'

'Why so?' asked Barundin.

'Some of them are a little, let's say, unhinged,' said Dran with a look of distaste. 'Dwarf worshippers.'

'Dwarf worshippers?' said Barundin, looking with sudden suspicion at the gathering below them.

'Sigmar's alliance and all that,' said Dran. 'It was very important to them, the battle here, and they see our part in it as almost divine. Crazy, the lot of them.'

They did not speak as they made their way back up the slope, out of sight of the manling pilgrims. Barundin mused upon Dran's words, and the strange beliefs of the manlings. The Battle of Black Fire Pass had been important to the dwarfs too, and the alliance with the fledgling Empire of Sigmar no less significant at the time. It had signalled the end of the Time of the Goblin Wars, when a great host of orcs and grobi had been crushed along this pass, having been driven from the west and down out of the mountains by men and dwarfs. Not for many centuries had the greenskins returned in any numbers, and never again in the numberless hordes that had ravaged the lands since the fall of Karak Ungor some fifteen hundred years before.

Barundin passed the afternoon reading his father's journal which he had brought with him. He had read it many times since the old king's death, trying to find inspiration and meaning in his father's words. At times the runic script was heavy and clumsy and his language more colourful. Barundin guessed these to be the nights on which he had gotten drunk with the loremaster, Ongrik. Time and again he felt himself drawn to the pages on which Throndin had scrawled his dying grudge, and the two signatures beneath it. The page was almost falling out, the edges well thumbed.

Never once had it crossed Barundin's mind that it was too much to ask. He had never contemplated abandoning the grudge against Baron Vessal, no matter what obstacles were in his path. It was not in his nature to accept defeat, just as it was not in the nature of the whole dwarf race to accept that their time as a power in the world had long since passed.

Barundin would take his people through war and fire to avenge his father, for the death of a king was beyond any counting of value, worth more than any amount of effort. Not only did his father expect nothing less from Barundin, but also all his ancestors, back to Grimnir, Grungni and Valaya themselves. Not once did the burden feel too heavy, though, for from those same ancestors he knew he had the strength and the will he needed to persevere and to triumph. To countenance anything other than success was unthinkable to the king.

Dran returned from the manling gathering after dark, having spent several hours amongst them. He had a certain self-satisfaction about him that told Barundin the

Reckoner had been right. Indeed, Dran confirmed, the half-mad engineer had taken employment in a manling town not far from the western approach to the pass. It would be two days' travel, three if the weather turned foul, as it seemed it would. The news bolstered Barundin's confidence further, knowing that Wanazaki's return would bring the Engineers Guild into his camp, and with that the hold would be willing to embark on another war, this time against the grobi of Dukankor Grobkaz-a-Gazan.

'DWARF-BUILT FOR sure,' said Barundin, looking down at the keep at the foot of the pass. 'Oh, the manlings have put all sorts of nonsense on top, like those roofs, but that's dwarf masonry down at the bottom.'

'Yes, our forefathers helped build this place,' said Dran, leading them down a track that wound between thin trees and scattered boulders. 'If you'd travelled as much as I have, you'd have seen the cut of dwarf chisel all across the Empire. The manlings might have driven out the orcs, but their castles and cities were built with dwarf hands.'

'And Wanazaki is in there?' said Fundbin, a ranger swathed in a deep red cloak, little more than his beard and the tip of his nose protruding from the hood. The bitter wind blowing from the east along Black Fire Pass had chilled even the hardy dwarfs.

'Oh, he's here all right,' said Dran.

Dran pointed to a tower on the north wall, a thick chimney protruding from its stones. Its iron-crowned tip belched grey smoke that gathered in clouds, shrouding the mountainside. Looking down over the walls from the slope of the pass, they could see two massive pistons moving up and down near the base of the tower, though their purpose was unclear. Part of the wall next to the tower had been extended over the courtyard with a wooden gantry and steel platform, and atop the platform sat a gyrocopter, its blades taken off and stacked neatly next to the flying machine.

There were few people on the road as they reached the floor of the pass. Scattered groups of travellers, most walking, a few with horse and wagon, gave them long looks as they passed. Some stared openly in disbelief at the large group of dwarfs, and some had a look of awe that sent a nervous shiver through Barundin. Dran's talk of dwarf worshippers had unsettled him considerably.

It was late afternoon and the shadow of the tall castle lay long across the road. A ravine, nearly two hundred feet deep and thirty feet wide, was dug around the base of the castle on three sides, which was itself built out of the rock of the pass itself, its foundations were the feet of the World's Edge Mountains. The walls were some fifty feet high, studded with two gate towers and protected by blocky fortifications at each corner.

The dwarfs passed over a wooden bridge laid across the ravine, and noted the heavy chains and gear mechanisms that would allow the bridge to be toppled into the chasm with the pull of a couple of levers. The only way to storm the castle was from the mountainside itself, and looking up the slope Barundin could see entrenchments and revetments dug into the rock. They were empty now, and the dwarf king could see few soldiers on the walls. He wondered if perhaps the watch of the manlings had grown lax in the recent years of peace and prosperity they had enjoyed since the Great War.

There was a cluster of guards at the gate, over a dozen, and their captain approached the party as they came off the bridge. He was dressed in the same black and yellow livery as his men, his slashed doublet obscured by a steel breastplate wrought with a rear griffon holding a sword. His sallet helm sported two plumed feathers, both red, and he held a demi-halberd across his chest as he walked toward the dwarfs. His expression was friendly, a slight smile upon his lips.

'Welcome to Siggurdfort,' the manling said, stopping just in front of Dran, who stood ahead of Barundin. 'At first I thought I had misheard when news came of twenty-one dwarfs travelling the pass, but now I see the truth of it. Please, enter and enjoy what comforts we have to offer.'

'I'm Dran the Reckoner,' said Dran, speaking fluently in the mannish tongue. 'It's not our custom to accept invitation from unnamed strangers.'

'Of course, my apologies,' said the manling. 'I am Captain Dewircht, commander of the garrison, soldier of the Count of Averland. We have someone who might be very pleased to meet you, one of your own.'

'We know,' said Dran, his voice betraying no hint of the dwarfs' intent. 'We want to see him, if you could send word.'

'He is fixing the ovens in the kitchen at the moment,' said Dewircht. 'I say fixing, but actually he's fitting a new redraft chimney, which he tells us means we'll have to burn only half as much wood. I'll send him word to meet you in the main hall.'

Dewircht stood aside and the dwarfs passed into the shadow of the gatehouse, feeling the stares of the guards upon them. Inside the castle, the courtyard was filled with small huts and wooden structures, with roofs made of hides and slate. The ground was little more than packed dirt, potholed and muddy, and the dwarfs hurried through the ramshackle buildings, ignoring the dogs and cats running stray and the pockets of whispering people.

Smoke from cooking fires was blown by gusts of wind into eddies, and the sounds of clattering pans and muffled conversation could be heard from within the huts as the folk of the keep readied their evening meals.

Coming to the rear of the castle, they found the main hall. It was built into the foundations of the wall and from the same huge stone blocks. It was roofed with red-painted tiles, chipped and worn and slicked with moss. A great double door stood open at the near end, the gloomy firelight of the inside barely visible within. Laughter and singing could be heard.

Entering, they found that the hall was much longer than it appeared, burrowing under the wall and into the roots of the mountain beyond. Along the length of the walls were four huge fireplaces, two on each side, the smoke from the fires disappearing up flues that had been dug through the wall and the mountain slope. The room was full of tables and benches, and there were several dozen people inside, many in the uniforms of the garrison, some dressed in the manner of the pilgrims the dwarfs had seen in the pass the last two days.

There was an empty bench near the far end, close to one of the fires, and a stone counter that ran nearly the whole width of the hall. Small grates were built into the counter, over which pots boiled and shanks of meat on spits roasted gently. The aroma made Barundin's mouth water and he realised that it had been a while since he had really filled his stomach, having had nothing more than trail rations and what game the rangers had caught whilst on the journey south.

'Hungry?' said Dran.

Barundin nodded enthusiastically. 'And some beer!' the king said, and there were grunts of agreement from the other dwarfs. 'We'll need plenty of it, I bet. Manling beer is little more than coloured water.'

'We need to pay,' said Dran, with a pointed look at the king.

'I'll come with you,' Barundin agreed with a sigh.

As the rangers took places around the table, looking slightly ridiculous on the manling benches, their feet dangling above the ground, Dran and Barundin walked to the counter. There were a man and a woman behind it, arguing. The woman saw the two dwarfs approach and broke off the conversation.

'You'll be wanting a hearty meal after your travels, I'll warrant,' she said. 'I'm Bertha Felbren, and if there's anything you'll be wanting, just shout for me. Or my lazy oaf of a husband, Viktor, if you can't find me.'

'We have twenty-one hungry stomachs to fill,' said Dran with a nod to the table full of dwarfs. 'Bread, meat, broth, whatever you have, we'll take.'

'And your best ale,' added Barundin. 'Lots of it, and often!'

'We'll bring it over,' said Bertha. 'If you're wanting rooms, I'll ask around for you. Most folk that come through here camp in the pass, but we'll be able to find enough beds if you wish.'

'That would be grand,' said Dran. The Reckoner looked at Barundin and gestured with his head towards Bertha. Barundin didn't responded and Dran repeated the gesture, this time with a scowl.

'Oh,' said Barundin with a sheepish grin. 'You'll want paying.'

Sweeping back his cloak, Barundin lifted up the chainmail sleeve of his armour and slipped the gold torque from around his upper arm. He took a small chisel from his belt, carried for just such a purpose, and chipped off three silvers of shining metal. He pushed them across the counter to Bertha, who looked at the dwarf with wide-eyed surprise.

'Not enough?' said Barundin, turning to Dran for guidance. 'How much?'

'I think you've just paid them enough for a week,' said Dran with a grin.

Barundin fought the urge to grab the gold back, his fingers twitching as Bertha swept up the shards of precious metal, quickly depositing them out of sight.

'Yes, whatever you want, just give Bertha a shout, any time, day or night,' she said breathlessly, turning away. 'Viktor, you worthless donkey, get out the Bugman's for these guests.'

'Bugman's?' said Dran and Barundin together, looking at each other in amazement.

'You have Bugman's ale here?' said Barundin.

'Aye, we do,' said Viktor, walking over to the counter, wiping his hands on a cloth. 'Not much, perhaps a tankard each, I'm afraid.'

'It's not Bugman XXXXXX, is it?' asked Dran, his voice dropping to a reverential whisper.

'No, no,' laughed Viktor. 'Do you think I'd be stuck out here with this hag of a wife if I had a barrel of XXXXXX? It's not even Troll Brew, I'm sorry to say. It's Beardling's Best Effort. Nothing fancy for you folk, I'm sure, but much more to your taste than our own brew.'

'Beardling's Best Effort?' said Barundin. 'Never heard of it. Are you sure it's Bugman's?'

'You can inspect the cask yourself, if you don't believe me,' said Viktor. 'I'll bring it to the table with some mugs for you.'

'Aye, thanks,' said Dran, nudging Barundin in the side and signalling for them to return to the table.

THE MEAL WAS pleasant enough, consisting of tough stewed goat's meat broth, roast lamb and boiled potatoes. There was plenty of bread and goat's cheese with which the dwarfs could vanquish the last vestiges of their appetites, in anticipation of the ale to come.

Although it was by no means the quality associated with most of the beer from the Bugman brewery, it was certainly finer than the manlings' own brew. Having been starved of proper dwarf beer even at home for nearly twenty years, the dwarfs supped the Beardling's Best Effort in a cautious manner. Each mouthful was greeted with much contented umming and aahing.

In the convivial atmosphere, the dwarfs began to relax. As night fell outside, Bertha built up the fires and lit more candles, and the hall was awash with a warm glow and the gentle hubbub of voices as more folk of the castle, soldiers and visitors, entered. Maids came in, young lasses from the soldiers' families, to serve the growing crowd, and in one corner a minstrel broke out a fiddle and began to play quietly to himself. The dwarfs were left to their own devices for the most part, disturbed only by the enquiries of Bertha and Viktor checking that they were well served.

Barundin was nudged by Dran, tearing him away from the silent contemplation of his pint, and he looked up to see the gathered patrons parting to allow Rimbal Wanazaki to pass through. The engineer looked much the same as he had when Barundin saw him in the foothills west of Black Water; his beard was longer, his eyes red-rimmed through the grime and soot that stained his tanned skin. He held a lump hammer in one hand and an oil can in the other.

'Evening, lads, nice of…' The engineer's voice trailed off as he caught sight of Barundin, sitting with a stern expression on his face, his arms crossed tightly. 'Well, blow me!'

'Sit down, Rimbal,' said Dran, standing up on the bench to reach for the tankard of ale they had kept aside for the engineer. 'Have yourself a drink.'

Wanazaki cautiously wormed his way between the Reckoner and Barundin, and took the ale with a grin.

'You're not here to check on my health, are you?' said Wanazaki, and Barundin noticed that his tic was very pronounced now, his whole body twitching occasionally. 'You'd think that after all that happened, you'd be the last people I'd want to see, but bless my mail, you are a welcome sight! These manlings are fine enough folk once you know them, but they're so difficult to get to know, so flighty. One year they're a youngster you can bob up and down on your knee, a few years later, they're married and leaving. There's no time to enjoy their company. They're always in such a rush to get things done.'

'You're coming back with us,' said Dran, laying a hand on Wanazaki's shoulder. 'Plenty of good company back in Zhufbar.'

A panicked expression fixed on the engineer's face and he shrugged off Dran's hand and stood up, backing away from the group. 'Well, it's nice of you to visit me and everything, but I don't think that's a good idea,' said Wanazaki, his voice rising in volume with the level of his fear. 'The guild... I can't... I'm not going back!'

This last was a shout in the Reikspiel of the manlings, which turned the heads of the others in the hall. There were angry murmurings and a crowd began to gather around the dwarfs.

Captain Dewircht pushed his way through the growing group and stood at the end of the table, his demi-halberd gripped in his right hand.

'What's the commotion here?' he demanded. 'What's going on?'

'Rimbal is coming back with us to Zhufbar,' said Dran, his voice emotionless.

'It seems that he isn't so keen on the idea,' said Dewircht as a knot of soldiers closed around him, more forcing their way through the crowd. 'Maybe you should think about returning without him.'

'Yeah!' said another man, faceless in the throng. 'Old Rimbal here doesn't need to be going nowhere. He's good enough right here.'

'He must return to Zhufbar to account for himself,' said Dran. 'I am the Reckoner, and I do not come back empty-handed.'

'He lives in lands that are free to him, to do as he pleases,' said Dewircht. 'It is his choice whether he comes or goes, not yours.'

'No, it is mine,' growled Barundin. 'He is my vassal, oath-sworn and honoured, and I command him.'

'And who would you be?' said Dewircht. 'Who would dare issue commands in a fortress of the Emperor, in from the wilds and nameless?'

Barundin stood up and jumped onto the table, unclasping his cloak and tossing it aside to reveal his silver and gold inlaid armour, glowing subtly with rune power. He pulled forth his axe and held it in front of him. Awe and surprise swept across the hall.

'Who am I?' he roared. 'I am Barundin, son of Throndin, King of Zhufbar. Do not tell me of rights! What right have you to deny me, who sit and feast in a hall hewn from the rock by dwarfish hands? What right have you to deny me, who stand guard upon walls laid by dwarfish masons? What right have you to deny me, who keep these lands only by the unseen might of dwarf axes, whose lands were once those ruled over by my ancestors?'

'A king?' laughed Dewircht, astounded. 'A king of the dwarfs comes here? And if we still deny you, what then? Will you declare war on the whole Empire?'

At their captain's words, a few soldiers drew their weapons and some raised crossbows, pointing at Barundin. Quicker than one would expect from a dwarf, Dran was stood on the bench, a throwing axe in one hand. He stared at Dewircht and the soldiers.

'Your captain dies the moment one of you moves against my king,' the Reckoner warned, his scarred face crumpled in a menacing scowl.

Barundin looked at Dewircht then lowered his axe and hung it on his belt again. 'There will be no fighting here, today,' said the dwarf king. 'No, it would not be so simple for you. If you do not surrender up the renegade engineer to me, I shall return to Zhufbar. There I shall call for the loremaster to bring forth our book of grudges. Within its many pages shall be recorded the place of Siggurdfort, and the name of Captain Dewircht.'

The king turned on the rest of the crowd, his eyes ablaze with anger. 'With an army I shall return,' said Barundin. 'While you protect Wanazaki from his judgement, the grudge will stand. We shall tear down the walls that we built, and we shall kill every man inside, and we shall take your watery beer and pour it into the dirt, and we shall burn down the wooden hovels you have spoiled our stones with, and we shall take your gold as recompense for our trouble, and the engineer will still return with us. And if not I, then my heir, or his heir, until the lives of your grandfathers have passed, your names shall still be written in that book, the wrong you do us unavenged. Do not treat the ire of the dwarfs lightly, for there may come a day when your people again look to us as allies, and we might then open our books and see the account you have made for yourselves. In this place, upon the very slopes where our ancestors fought and died together in an age past, you would deny me for the sake of this rogue?'

The speech was followed by a deep, still silence across the hall. Dewircht looked between Barundin and Dran, and then his gaze fell upon Rimbal Wanazaki.

The engineer looked worried, and glanced up at the king. He walked forward and stood in front of the captain. 'Put down your weapons,' said Rimbal. 'He is right, everything he says.' He turned to the king. 'I do not want this, but even more I do not want what you will surely do. I shall fetch my things. What of my gyrocopter?'

'If you give me your word to stay with me until Zhufbar, then you may fly it back,' said Barundin.

'My word?' said Wanazaki. 'You would take the word of an oathbreaker?'

'You are not yet oathbreaker, Rimbal,' said Barundin, his expression softening. 'You never were, and I do not think you will be one now. Come home, Rimbal. Come back to your people.'

Rimbal nodded and turned back to Captain Dewircht. He shook the manling's free hand with a nod, and the people in the hall parted again to allow him to leave, his head held proudly, his steps brisk and firm.

GRUDGE FIVE
The Goblin Grudge

STEAM AND SMOKE billowed from the chimneys of the brewery, swiftly appearing from gold-edged flues and out into the mountain sky. The great oast towers glistened in the light of the morning sun, and miles of glinting copper piping sprouted from the stone walls and coiled about each other.

The brewery had been built on top of the foundations of the original site, extending out from the southern side of the hold, high up the mountain overlooking Black Water. From the cavernous interior of Zhufbar the building spilled across the mountainside, a massive edifice of grey stone, red brick and metalwork. A narrow, fast torrent of water spilled down from the mountainside above, disappearing into the depths of the brewery, for the dwarfs only used the freshest spring water in their beer-making.

As the construction had neared completion, the master brewers and their clans had read their old recipe books and orders for the finest ingredients had been sent to the other holds and the lands of the empire. The vast storehouses of the brewery were now brimming with barrels of different malts and barleys, yeast and honey, and sundry other ingredients, some of them clan secrets for many generations.

Barundin stood atop a stage made from empty barrels, a great host of dwarfs around him, in front of the brewery entrance. Beside him stood the brewmasters and the engineers, Wanazaki amongst them. The itinerant dwarf had renewed his oaths with the Guild and, in and act of clemency, they had spared him the humiliation of the Trouser Leg Ritual and banishment. Instead he had agreed to work on the rebuilding of the brewery for free, and act that would quell the act of even the most rebellious dwarfs. With Wanazaki's aid, work had progressed apace and now, only three years since his return, the brewery was finished.

In his hand the king held grains of barley, which he scrunched nervously in his palm as he waited for the crowd to settle. The sun was warm on his face, even this early in the morning, and he was sweating heavily. As quiet descended, Barundin cleared his throat.

'Today is a great day for Zhufbar,' the king began. 'A proud day. It is a day when we can once again make a claim to our ancestral heritage.'

Barundin held up his hand and allowed the grains to dribble through his fingers, pattering against the wooden barrel beneath his feet.

'A simple seed, some might think,' he continued, gazing up above the crowd to the mountains beyond. 'But not us, not those that know the real secrets of beer-making. These simple seeds contain within them the essence of beer, and in that the essence of ourselves. It is in beer that we might judge our finest qualities, for it requires knowledge, skill and patience. Beer is more than a drink, more than something to quench a thirst. It is our right, its making passed down to us from our oldest ancestors. It is the lifeblood of our people, our hold. The ale that we shall drink will have been long in the making, tested for its qualities, proven in the taverns.'

Barundin flicked the last few grains from his hand and turned his gaze to the assembled dwarfs, his expression fierce.

'And just as an ale must pass the test for it to prove its qualities, so to must our warriors,' Barundin told them. 'The skaven have been crushed, their menace to us passed. Our brewery is rebuilt and this very day the first pints of fine ale shall begin their lives. These tasks are done, but there is one great task that yet remains unfulfilled, an oath yet to be met.'

Barundin turned to the east and waved his hand across the view, his gesture encompassing the rising peaks of the World's Edge mountains and the clear blue sky.

'These are my lands,' he said, his voice rising. 'These are your lands! From ages past we have lived upon and within these peaks, and unto the ending of the world itself, here we shall remain, as steady as the mountains from which our spirits were hewn. But we shall never know peace again, not while there is a vile taint upon our lands that we dare not face. East of here, the vile, disgusting grobi have plundered our mines, stolen our halls, desecrated our tunnels with their presence. For a score of generations they have been interlopers upon our realms, their stench filling the taverns and drinking dens of our forefathers, their black throats breathing the air once breathed by our kin.'

Again Barundin turned his gaze back to the throng, who were murmuring loudly now, the anger roused by his words.

'No more!' bellowed Barundin. 'No more will we stand idly by while these pieces of filth live and breed in our homes. No more shall we whisper the name of Dukankor Grobkaz-a-Gazan. No more shall we stare into our ale and ignore the creatures that knock upon our door. No more will the grobi feel themselves safe from our wrath.'

'Kill the grobi!' someone shouted from the crowd, and the chant was taken up by many dozens of throats.

'Yes!' shouted Barundin. 'We shall march forth and slay them in their lair. Once more we shall build Grungankor Stokril, and it will be filled with the light of our lanterns, not the darkness of the grobi; it will resound to the hearty laughs of our warriors and not the snickering cackles of greenskins.'

Barundin began to pace up and down the stage, spittle flying from his lips as he ranted. He pointed south across across Black Water.

'Within two days' march of here, they lie in their rags and filth,' he said. 'Karak Varn, taken by them scant years after Karak Ungor fell to the wicked-eyed thieves. Then, to the east, Mount Gunbad was taken, and from there came the creatures that invaded our lands. There they looted the wonderful brynduraz from Gunbad and spoiled it with their pawing hands, destroying most beautiful stones to be found beneath the world. Not content, they assailed Mount Silverspear, and it is now a dark place filled with their grime, a toilet for grobi! Where once a king sat, a hateful greenskin now squats! In this way, the east was taken from us.'

Barundin's roaring now could be barely heard above the tumult of the throng, their angry chanting resounding from the mountainside.

'South, far south, the greenskins came for our gold,' he continued. 'In Karak Eight Peaks, they slew our kin, in wretched alliance with the ratmen. Not content, their invasions continued, until Karak Azgal and and Karak Drazh were swarming with their litters. They even tried to beat upon the gates of Karaz-a-Karak!

'Well, no more! Now only seven holds remain. Seven fortresses against this horde. But we shall make them know that there is still strength left in the arms of the dwarfs. Though we might not reclaim the holds of our ancestors from their clutches, we can yet show them that our lands are our own still, and that trespassers are not welcome. The grobi may have forgotten to fear dwarf steel and gromril, but they shall come to dread it again. We shall drive them forth, cleanse the old tunnels of their disgusting spoor, and hound them back to the halls of Gunbad itself. Though it might take a generation, I swear upon my father's tomb and upon the spirits of my ancestors that I shall not rest while one greenskins still treads upon the flagstones of Grungankor Stokril!'

Barundin stormed to the front of the stage and raised his hands above his head, his fists trembling mightily.

'Who shall swear with me?' he called out.

The bellow from the crowd was such that the clanking of the waterwheels, the hissing of the brewery pipes and even the steam hammers of the forges were drowned out by the wall of noise.

'We swear!'

THE TRAMPING OF feet, hornblows and drums kept a steady rhythm as the Zhufbar army marched eastwards. The steel-clad host passed out through the eastern deep gates into the mighty underground highway that once led eastwards to Mount Gunbad. Part of the Ungdrim Ankor, the massive network of tunnels that once linked all the dwarf holds together, the highway was wide

enough for ten dwarfs to march abreast. Above the
clinking of mail and the clump of boots, Barundin led
the several thousands warriors in a marching song, their
deep voices echoing ahead of them along the tunnel.

Let no warrior mine now refuse
To march out and reclaim his dues,
For now he's one of mine to pay
Under the Hills and far away.

Under the Hills and o'er the moor,
To Azul, Gunbad and bright Ungor,
The king commands and we'll obey
Under the hills and far away.

I shall keep more happy tracks
With gleaming armour and shining axe
That cut and cleave both night and day
Under the Hills and far away.

Under the Hills and o'er the moor,
To Azul, Gunbad and bright Ungor,
The king commands and we'll obey
Under the hills and far away.

Courage, lads, 'tis one to a tun,
But we'll stay the fight til it is done
All warriors bold on every day,
Under the Hills and far away.

Under the Hills and o'er the moor,
To Azul, Gunbad and bright Ungor,
The king commands and we'll obey
Under the hills and far away.

In the vanguard of the host marched the Ironbreakers, whose regular duties included patrolling the Ungdrin to hunt down interloping grobi and other creatures. The going was slow at times, for the walls and sometimes the ceiling had collapsed in places. Teams of miners worked hard to clear piles of debris, toiling ceaselessly for hours on end until there was room to pass. In this way, their hundreds of lanterns lighting the ancient flagstones and statues that lined the highway, the dwarfs travelled eastwards towards their long-lost outpost.

It was after two days of travel and much backbreaking labour by the caravan that they came upon the tunnels beneath Grungankor Stokril. There was grobi-sign everywhere. Old stairwells were choked with filth and debris, bones littered amongst them and dried dung piled in heaps.

Barundin felt his ire rising once more as he looked upon the scars left by the goblins. Statues of the ancestors lay ruined and defaced with blood and grime, and the ornate mosaics that had once decorated the walls had been torn down in many places, the bright ssquares of stone taken as baubles by the greenskins. Here and there they found the body of a dwarf; ages-dead carcasses that were little more than piles of dust and rust, identified only by the odd scrap of cloth. Anything of value had been looted long ago and not a shred of steel, silver or gold remained. Barundin ordered these remains to be gathered up in sealed boxes and sent back to Zhufbar for a proper burial.

Though it was dark both night and day, it was in the shadow-shrouded early hours of one morning, when the dwarfs had doused most of their lanterns to get some sleep, that the first grobi foray attacked. The assault was short-lived, for the Ironbreakers were swift in their response and the sentries wary so close to the lair of the enemy. Shrieking and crying, the grobi were sent fleeing back into the depths.

The next morning, Barundin met with many of the thanes and his best advisors. They decided to launch an expeditionary attack into the south vaults, a series of mines and halls less than a mile from where they were camped. In an effort to establish some form of presence in the tunnels away from the Ungdrin, Barundin would lead half the army south and try to take one of the larger halls. From here he could make more raids on the grobi holes, while Hengrid Dragonfoe would lead a third of the army north the next day and attempt to cut the grobi off from the much larger settlement of Mount Gunbad, which lay some two hundred miles to the east. Hengrid, once gatewarden and leader of the hammerers, had proved himself an able general in the fighting against the skaven and, upon the death of his uncle had become Thane of his clan. They were counted amongst the fiercest fighters in the hold now, and if anyone would be able to stop more grobi coming from the east it would be Hengrid and his warriors.

The remaining part of the force was to stay in the Ungdrin to act as a rearguard or a reserve as necessary. The youngest and quickest warriors were designated as runners, and they spent several hours with the Ironbreakers, learning the quickest routes around the Ungdrin and nearby tunnels. It would be dangerous work, travelling alone and in the dark, but Barundin gave the beardlings a stirring speech to bolster their courage, and impressed upon them the necessity of the messengers' task; the dwarfs were massively outnumbered, and if they were to prevail they would need to be disciplined, resolute and, most of all, coordinated.

The plan thus devised, Barundin gave the command for the army to march forth just before noon. Afraid of the bright light of the sun, the night goblins would be in their holes during the day, which had earned them the name of night goblins over the many centuries of enmity between their kind and the dwarfs. Barundin hoped that by attacking during daylight hours he would have a better idea of the enemy's numbers. With luck, he chuckled to his hammerers, many of them would be asleep and easy targets.

THE INITIAL ADVANCE went well, with the Ironbreakers in the fore leading the way and meeting little resistance. As the army wound its way up a large staircase into the halls above, the grobi were waking to the threat. Gongs and bells began to clamour, echoing down to the dwarfs. Here and there, small bands of greenskins were trying to organise themselves, but they were little match for the stout dwarf warriors that fell upon the, and most of the grobi fled deeper into their lair.

Splitting his force into three, Barundin spread out his army, herding the grobi eastwards and southwards. Through the corridors, the dwarfs pushed on. In the close confines the diminutive greenskins were outclassed by the skill and weapons of the dwarfs, and unable to bring their numbers to bear.

After three hours of fighting, Barundin was on the second level of the mine-workings, only one level down from the main hall of the south vaults. He was taking a brief rest and wiping the dark goblin blood from the blade of his axe. He stared with contempt at the pile of bodies that littered the floor. The grobi were scrawny creatures, a head shorter than a dwarf and far skinnier. They wore ragged robes of black and dark blue, trimmed with stones and bits of bone, and with long hoods to shield themselves from the light that occasionally trickled through the millennia-old grime that stained the high windows of their lair.

The green of their skin was pallid and sickly, even lighter along their pointed ears and thin, grasping fingers. Shards of sharp, small fangs and broken claws were scattered across the bodies from the blows of Barundin's hammerers, stained and filthy. Barundin kicked at one of the corpses, smashing it against the wall, feeling that death was not near enough punishment for the thieving little fiends that had despoiled the fine halls of his ancestors.

Giving a satisfied grunt, he turned to his hammerers, who were resting further along the corridor, some munching on food they had brought with them and swigging from their flasks. Barundin saw Durak, once stonebearer to the dead king and now the new gatekeeper. The weathered face of Durak looked back at him and the veteran gave his king a thumbs up. Barundin nodded in return.

'Been a while, eh?' said Durak, reaching into his belt and pulling out a pipe.

'Since what?' asked Barundin, declining the gatekeeper's offer of pipe weed with a shake of his head.

'Since I carried your father's stone to the battle where he fell,' said Durak. 'Who could have guessed then that it would lead us here, eh?'

'Aye,' said Barundin. 'It's been a while, for sure.'

'Worth it, though, I reckon,' said Durak. 'All the fighting, I mean. Always feels good to smash a grobi skull, eh?'

'Let's smash some more, shall we?' suggested Barundin.

'Aye, let's,' said Durak with a grin.

* * *

ONWARDS THE DWARF host advanced, until they reached a wide stairway leading up to the gates of the Great South Hall. From the end of the tunnel the steps fanned outwards onto a wide platform, easily large enough for several hundred dwarfs to stand upon at the same time. Dirt and mould slicked the stairs, obscuring the veins of the marble with filth. The huge gates themselves had been torn off their hinges long ago and the remains lay across the upper steps. The great bands of iron were rusted and looted in places, the nails torn from the thick oak beams that made up the doors. Scraps of torn cloth were caught on rusted rivets, and the goblin spoor was heaped around the gateway in piles taller than a dwarf. The stench that wafted from the hall beyond stuck in Barundin's throat.

'By Grimnir's tattooed arse, they'll pay for this,' the king muttered.

'Bring up the firepots,' shouted Durak, waving to some of the engineers that accompanied the army. 'We'll burn them out.'

'Wait!' said Barundin, holding up a hand to halt the dwarfs pushing their way to the front of the line. 'Enough destruction has been heaped upon our ancient homes here. First we'll drive them out with axe and hammer, and then we'll burn the filth.'

A horde of greenskins awaited them on the stairs, more and more pouring through the ruined doorway as the dwarfs advanced. Barundin led the charge with his hammerers, flanked by Ironbreakers and miners. Like a mailed fist crashing into soft flesh, the dwarf warriors battered into the goblins, scattering them quickly and driving them back into the hall.

Caught up in the fighting, Barundin hewed left and right with his axe, felling a score of goblins before gaining the gateway. Here he paused to catch a breath, as the

goblins retreated from his wrathful attack. He stopped
in his stride, eyes narrowing in anger as he saw what
had become of the Great South Hall.

The large chamber had once been the focal point
of the mine workings, the audience chamber and
throne room of the clan that had delved for ore
beneath the mountain. Though not as grand as the
halls of Zhufbar proper, it was still a large space.
Columns as thick as tree trunks supported the
vaulted roof, and to Barundin's right a large area,
where once the thane's throne had sat, was raised up
a dozen feet above the rest of the chamber, reached
by a sweeping stair.

The detritus of the grobi was everywhere. Glowing
fungal growths sprawled across the floor and walls, with
towering toadstools erupting from the fronds and spore
clouds. The statues that had once formed a colonnade
leading towards the throne had been toppled, daubed
in disgusting glyphs with unidentifiable filth. Small
fires blazed everywhere, filling the chamber with acrid
smoke and a ruddy glow.

The place was crawling with night goblins, hastily
grouping together around crude standards of beaten
copper shaped like stars and moons, the shrieking
bawls of their masters attempting to instil order upon
the chaos. Strange creatures, little more than round,
fanged faces with legs, gibbered and screeched amongst
the throng, held in check with whips and barbed
prongs.

Here and there leaders bedecked in more ornate robes
moved to and fro, carrying wickedly serrated blades or
leaning upon staffs hung with bones and fetishes. Upon
the dais several rickety war machines had been hastily
drawn up; bolt throwers and rock lobbers capable of
skewering and crushing a dozen dwarfs at a time.

As Barundin led his army through the gateway, the goblins responded, streaming forward in a dark wave. Clouds of black-feathered arrows sailed above the onrushing horde, loosed from the short, crude bows of the night goblins. As Barundin and his hammerers worked their way to the right, allowing more dwarfs through the gate, they raised their shields to ward away the iron-tipped volley falling towards them. Thin arrows splintered and ricocheted of the steel wall of shields, although an unlucky dwarf fell, the shaft of an arrow protruding from his exposed cheek, blood spilling into his beard.

Ahead of Barundin, night goblin herders goaded their charges forward, unleashing a drove of betoothed monstrosities that bounded forward, gnashing and growling. Barundin knew the creatures well: cave squigs. The tanned hide of the creatures worked well as rough bindings, and their guts, suitably treated, made for hardwearing laces.

From amongst the orange-skinned beasts, riders emerged, haphazardly mounted atop several of the strange creatures, clinging on with little control over their outlandish steeds. Waving spiked clubs and short swords, the riders were carried forwards by the springing hops of their beasts, and one leaped high into the air, over the front of the shieldwall raised by the hammerers.

The rider brought his club down atop the helmet of a dwarf with a resounding clang, while the squig snapped its massive jaws shut around the poor hammerer's arm, ripping it from the shoulder. Another beast launched itself straight at the row of shields, it's unnaturally powerful legs smashing it through the wall of metal and hurling a handful of dwarfs to the ground. It scratched and bit at the fallen until driven away in another bounding leap by the attacks of the other hammerers.

Several hundred dwarfs had now made it into the hall and a line formed and began to slowly advance towards the approaching grobi. Spears with barbed tips were launched across the cavern from the two bolt throwers atop the dais, one arcing high over the dwarfs' heads to smash uselessly against the wall. The other found its mark, however, punching through armour and flesh and scything through the dwarf ranks, leaving a line of dead and maimed warriors in its trail.

Barundin watched with apprehension as the goblins pulled back the arm of a mighty catapult and loaded its sling with a large rock. As the crew hastily backed away, their captain pulled a lever. Nothing happened. The crew cautiously returned to their machine, prodding and poking, shouting at each other. Suddenly the strands of one of the ropes holding the machine together parted, and with a crack that could be heard over the cacophony of the goblins horde, the arm snapped forward. In a shower of rusted nails and splintered rotten wood, the catapult disintegrated, shards of metal and chunks of rock exploding outwards, cutting down the goblins in a cloud of dust, tattered rags and dark blood. Barundin noticed the crews of the other machines pointing and laughing at the remains of their unfortunate comrades.

Barundin bellowed to his quarrellers, who turned their crossbows towards the war machines. With a steady staggered volley, the quarrellers loosed a storm of bolts at the engines, most of the missiles missing or breaking harmless against the machines themselves. However, a few robed bodies, pinned with crossbow bolts, littered the bloodstained stones after the salvo.

With the war machine crews reloading their engines, the goblins surged forwards again under another storm of arrows. To Barundin's right, the hammerers were still fighting against a swarm of cave squigs, and many of their number lay dead amongst the corpses of the savage beasts heaped in front of their line.

The goblins advanced as a sea of spiteful green faces poking from beneath their black hoods, spitting and snarling. The horde advanced haphazardly as fights broke out amongst the ranks of unruly fighters; their chiefs cracked heads together and shouted shrill commands to keep the tide of grobi moving. The light from dozens of fires glinted cruelly from serrated short swords and barbed speartips, a constellation of fiery stars in the fumes and shadows.

Bursts of green energy erupted from the advancing line as cavorting shamans gathered their magical powers and unleashed them, spewing forth vomits of destruction and blasts from their staffs. Axe and hammer-wielding warriors to Barundin's left were hurled from their feet by the sorcerous attacks, green flames licking up from their shattered bodies.

A particularly ostentatious-looking shaman stood near the centre of the approaching horde, his tall hood bedecked with bones and crudely shapes precious stones, delved a hand into a pouch hung from his crude rope belt and pulled forth a fistful of luminous fungus. Devouring these, he began to hop from one foot to the other, cackling and yelping, swinging his staff around his head. Sickly green tendrils of energy began to leak from his mouth and from under his hood, rising up like a mist around the grobi. Green sparks leaped from hood tip to hood tip, until a mass of warriors in front of the shaman were swathed in a flowing green cloud of energy. Invigorated by these conjurations, the goblins surged forwards ever more quickly, the tramping of their feet echoing from the high walls.

A detonation to Barundin's right attracted the dwarf king's attention and he turned just in time to see a shaman bursting from the ranks, bathed in crackling green force. With manic energy, the shaman fell to the ground, flailing madly, legs and arms jerking spasmodically. The creature began to glow from within and then, after a few moments, exploded in a cloud of green-tinged arcs of lightning, striking down a handful of his fellows stood too close.

'Brace yourselves!' bellowed Barundin, setting his shield and getting a firm grip on his axe.

The foremost goblins were now less than two dozen yards away and charging fast. As they closed the gap, their ranks parted to unleash a new terror. Frothing at the mouth, their eyes glazed, goblins wielding immense balls on lengths of chain burst from the goblin horde. Intoxicated by strange mushrooms and toadstools, imbued with narcotic strength, the fanatics began to spin madly, their heavy weapons whirling around with deadly speed. Some careened off dizzily, smashing into one another in bloody tangles of metal, while others spun back into the grobi army, cutting a devastating swathe through the night goblins, who advanced onwards, unconcerned with their losses.

Several of the fanatics fell or tripped before they reached the dwarf line, crushing their own heads and bodies with their heavy iron balls, but a handful made it as far as the dwarfs. The carnage was instant, shields and mail no protection against the crushing blows of the twirling lunatics. A score of dwarfs were reduced to bloody pulps by the first impact, and as the fanatics bounced back and forth, ricocheting from one dwarf to another they left a trail of mangled bodies in their wake.

A great groan rose up from the dwarf line and they began to edge away from the fanatics, pushing and shoving at each other to get away from the demented goblins. Even as the line buckled under the onslaught the goblin charge hit home.

Their shieldwall broken in places by the fanatics, the dwarfs were unprepared for the grobi and many fell to jabbing swords and wild spear thrusts as they attempted to reform the line. As they weathered the initial assault, the dwarfs locked their shields together and pushed back, hewing down the goblins with their axes and hammers, smashing helmeted heads into the faces of their foes and breaking bones with their steel shields.

A score of centuries of hatred boiled up from within the dwarf army and they lashed out vengefully. The explosion of violent anger erupted along the dwarf line, engulfing Barundin, who threw himself forward, axe raised.

'For Zhufbar!' he shouted, bringing his axe down into the hooded head of a goblin, shearing through its skull with a single blow. 'For Grimnir!'

Hacking to his right, he chopped through the upraised arm of another foe, and the return blow sheared the head from the shoulders of another. The rune axe blazed with power, trailing droplets of dark grobi blood that spattered into the king's beard. He did not notice it, for the battle rage was upon him. As the goblins closed in on him, Barundin's rune armour and shield rang with blows, although the gromril plates remained true and he felt nothing. Another wide swing of his axe tore down another two goblins, a bloody furrow carved across their chests, their tattered robes flung into the air.

Growling and panting, Barundin slashed again and again, his arm strengthening with every corpse hurled to the ground. All around him was bedlam as dwarf weapons cut through flesh and bone and goblin spears and swords broke upon dwarf-forged steel. The clattering of metal and wood, the bellowing of dwarf curses and the panicked shrieks of the grobi filled the cavern, resounding back off the walls, growing in volume.

Step-by-step, the dwarfs advanced into the hall, trampling over countless bodies of the goblins they had slain, spitting vengeful oaths at their hated foes. Their beards and armour doused with goblin blood, they were a horrific sight, their eyes fixed with the madness that only millennia of enmity can create. With every axe blow, with every hammer strike, the dwarfs repaid the goblins for each and every dwarf death at their hands, for every mine they had taken, for each hold they had overrun.

There was a purity in Barundin's fury; he felt a keen sense of satisfaction with each goblin death. The righteousness of his anger filled him with purpose and he easily ignored the soft, clumsy blows of his enemies, his axe hewing death all around him.

He was broken from his destructive reverie by panicked shouts to his left. Cutting down another handful of goblins, he broke free from the knot of grobi that had surrounded him and saw the cause of his kinsmen's dismay.

Towering above both dwarfs and grobi, eight gigantic trolls strode through the goblins' line, pushing and kicking aside their small masters. Each three times the height of a man, the stone trolls were lanky, their limbs taut with whipcord muscle, their fat bellies gawky and distended. As the trolls lumbered forward their blunt faces regarded the dwarfs stupidly, and they scratched idly at their ragged, pointed ears and swollen bellies, or dug clawed fingers into their bulbous noses. Their greyish-blue skin was thick and nobbled, and had a cracked appearance like old granite. One of the trolls stopped and looked around in dazed confusion, moaning loudly into the air, the goblins around it trying to urge it forwards with shouts and the hafts of their spears. The other trolls loped forward and broke into a long-strided run that covered the ground with surprising speed, dragging rocks and crude wooden clubs behind them.

As it reached the dwarf line, the foremost troll raised a massive fist above its head and brought it down upon the helm of one of the dwarfs, crushing it with a single blow and snapping the warrior's back. A backhanded smash crumpled the shield of another, driving shards of steel into the bearer's ribs. Another troll, a rock gripped between its hands, flattened another dwarf with its improvised weapon, and then stopped and bent over to peer dumbly at the twitching corpse.

Their momentum suddenly halted by the stone trolls, the dwarfs found themselves on the back foot. More and more goblins were swarming forwards, circling left and right, avoiding the left of the dwarf line where the trolls were wreaking horrendous damage on the dwarfs around them.

'My king!' called Durak, pounding his hammer into the chest of a goblin and pushing past the falling corpse. The gatekeeper turned and pointed behind him.

Turning to look, Barundin daw that the dwarfs had advanced away from the doorway into the hall, and there was a growing number of goblins gathering behind them.

'We'll be cut off,' said Durak.

'Not if we're victorious!' Barundin replied, catching a sword on his shield and then swinging his axe to decapitate the greenskin attacker.

'There's too many of them,' Durak yelled as a handful of goblins rushed forward to attack him.

Barundin grunted as he cut down another goblin, and risked a glance around. The fanatics and trolls had carved a bloody hole in the left flank of his host, and the warriors and quarrellers holding that side were in danger of being surrounded. His hammerers held the right and the cave squigs had all been slain, but they were being hard-pressed by the sheer numbers of the grobi. Every fibre in his body and soul urged him to keep fighting, but he mastered his natural hatred and realised that it would be folly to stay. Nothing would be achieved if they were cut off from their route back to the Ungdrin. He spied a hornblower not far away and hacked his way through half a dozen goblins to reach the dwarf's side.

'Sound the retreat,' Barundin said, spitting out the words with distaste.

'My king?' replied the hornblower, eyes widening.

'I said sound the retreat,' snarled Barundin.

As the king fended off more goblins, the hornblower raised his instrument to his lips and blew the notes. The horn blast echoed dully over the clash of weapons, the angry shouts of the dwarfs, the low moaning of the trolls and the screeches of dying goblins. It was picked up by other musicians along the line, and soon the dwarf army was reluctantly stepping back.

In a fighting withdrawal, falling back in small groups of a dozen or so warriors, the dwarfs made their way back to the edge of the hall and their line reformed into a semi-circle around the doorway. Barundin and his hammerers held the apex of the arc, the Ironbreakers to his left and right, as the other dwarf warriors retreated back down the steps.

With a shout full of wrath and disappointment, Barundin sheared his axe through the gut of a troll, spilling out the noxious guts, the air filled with the acrid reek of its powerful stomach juices. As the goblins backed away from the spray of filth, Barundin and his rearguard broke from the fighting, quickly backing away through the gateway and onto the steps.

'Keep going!' he roared over his shoulder as he saw some of his warriors hesitating, thinking of turning back to aid their king. 'Secure the tunnels back to the Ungdrin!'

AS STEADILY AND methodically as they had advanced, the dwarfs withdrew from the Great South Hall. At junctions and stairways the Ironbreakers and hammerers paused, holding the corridors and chambers against the goblin attacks while the rest of the army fell back towards the underway, taking up positions to defend. Covered by volleys from the quarrellers and thunderers, the king and his elite fighters broke away from the goblins and trolls.

For several more hours the dwarfs fought on, making the goblins pay a heavy price for their pursuit. In places, the tunnels were literally filled with the dead, as the dwarfs heaped the bodies of the grobi to make barricades to defend, or set fire to piles of corpses to block the goblins' advance. The two engineers that had accompanied Barundin made small charges of black powder and rigged traps that triggered rock falls and cave-ins on the heads of the following goblin horde, sealing off tunnels or choking them with the slain.

With the black-feathered arrows of the goblins skittering off the walls and ceiling around them, Barundin and his hammerers were the last to set foot on the stairwell winding back down to the Ungdrin. Barundin gave a last, sour look at the realm of Dukankor Grobkaz-a-Gazan, before turning and running down the steps.

He could hear the thundering of hundreds of feet not far behind him as the goblins poured down the stairs after the retreating dwarfs. Their harsh cackles and the flickering flames of their torches followed him.

Bursting out onto the highway from under the wide arched stairwell, Barundin was pleased to see that his host had organised themselves into something resembling an army, and stood waiting not far from the entranceway.

In particular, he saw the four barrels of an organ gun to his right, pointed directly at the stairway. Behind it he saw Garrek Silverweaver, one of the thane-engineers, holding a long lanyward. The engineer gave him a thumbs up as the king marched across the flags to take up a position near the centre of the line that stretched out, awaiting the goblins.

The first grobi burst into view, hurried on by their fellow goblins from behind. They were met by a hail of crossbow bolts and died to a goblin. More followed quickly and were greeted by a thunderous volley of handgun fire that tore them to shreds. Still not aware of the danger awaiting them, more goblins stormed into sight, almost tripping over themselves in their excitement.

'Skoff 'em!' Garrek shouted as he pulled the lanyard of the organ gun.

The war machine belched fire and smoke as the barrels fired in quick succession, hurling four fist-sized cannonballs at the mass of goblins. Packed into the confines of the stair entrance, there was no way to avoid the fusillade and the heavy iron balls ripped through the grobi, smashing heads, punching through chests and ripping off limbs. A tangled ruin of green flesh, dark blood and black robes littered the steps.

Aware that they would not catch their prey unprepared, the goblins halted out of sight, although a few came tumbling down the steps, followed by the childish cackling of the goblins that had pushed them. A lull began, and the dwarfs stood in silence, listening to the grating, high-pitched voices of the goblins as they argued amongst themselves about what to do. Now and then a poor volunteer came stumbling down the steps and would have only time to give a panicked shriek before being picked off by a bolt or bullet.

After more than an hour, amid much laughing and shouting, the goblins finally began to withdraw back up the steps. Barundin ordered the Ironbreakers to follow a little way behind and ensure that the goblins were not making a false retreat, and to set guards at the top of the long stairway. With that done, he ordered his warriors to get some rest and food.

As the dwarfs broke out water, cheese, cold meats and stonebread from their packs, Barundin sought out Baldrin Gurnisson, the Thane that had been left in charge of the reserve. He saw the elderly dwarf in conversation with one of the runners.

'What news from Hengrid?' the king asked as he walked towards the pair.

Both thane and runner turned towards Barundin, their expressions sorrowful.

'Come on, tell me!' snapped Barundin, who was in no mood for niceties. 'How fares Hengrid Dragonfoe and his army?'

'We don't know, my king,' said Baldrin, wringing a gnarled hand through the long braids of his beard.

'I couldn't find them,' explained the runner, the beardling's face a mask of worry. 'I looked and looked, and asked the others, but no one has seen or heard from them since they set out.'

'I did not know whether to march to their aid or not,' said Baldrin, shaking his head woefully. 'I can still go now, if you command it.'

Barundin took off his helmet and dragged his fingers through his matted, sweaty hair. His face was covered in grime and blood, his beard tangled and knotted. His armour was scratched and dented, stained with goblin blood and splashed with troll guts. He dropped his helmet, and in the quiet the clang of its falling rang along the Ungdrin like a death knell.

'No,' the king finally said. 'No, we must accept that they are probably lost to us now.'

'What are we to do?' asked the beardling, his eyes fearful.

Barundin turned away from them and looked at his army, which had lost over a tenth of its number that day. Many were already asleep, using their packs as pillows, while others sat in small groups, silent or talking in hushed whispers. A good number of them turned and looked at Barundin as they noticed the gaze of their king sweeping over them.

'What do we do now?' he said, his voice steadily rising. 'We do what we always do. We keep fighting!'

GRUDGE SIX
Barundin's Grudge

THE EMPTY HALL was disquieting to Barundin. Now scoured of the last of the grobi desecration, it was at least an imitation of its former glory, if not a replica. He stood upon the thane's platform, resting a hand on the arm of the newly carved throne that had been set there. A diamond the size of his fist pierced the top of the back of the chair, glinting in the light of the dwarf lanterns.

Voices echoed from beyond the hall's portal, once again hung with two mighty doors hewed from the thickest oak, and Barundin looked up to see Arbrek. The runelord leaned heavily on his staff, his flowing grey beard knotted to his belt to stop him tripping on it. With him were several of the thanes, Tharonin Grungrik amongst them, and Loremaster Thagri. The small group crossed the hall and walked up the steps. They stopped just before reaching the dais, except for Tharonin who strode up and stood before the king. Thagri had a book and writing chisel in his hands, and sat down upon the seat. He dipped the chisel in his inkwell and looked up at the king expectantly.

'Hail, Tharonin Grungrik, thane of Grungankor Stokril,' said Barundin, his voice stiff with formality.

Tharonin glanced over his shoulder at the other thanes and then looked back at Barundin.

'Some might say usurper,' he said with a wink. There was a tut from Arbrek at the thane's flippancy.

Barundin pressed on. 'Let it be now recorded that I, King Barundin of Zhufbar, hereby and forthwith bestow the halls, corridors, chambers, mineworkings and all associated lands and properties of Grungankor Stokril to the stewardship of Thane Tharonin Grungrik,' said Barundin. 'In recognition for the valorous acts of his clan in the reclaiming of these lands, this deed to him shall be passed on to his descendants forever, or until such time as the thane of the Grungriks breaks oath with the king of Zhufbar.'

'I, Thane Tharonin Grungrik, do solemnly accept the stewardship of the halls, corridors, chambers, mineworkings and all associated lands and properties of Grungankor Stokril,' replied Tharonin. 'I hereby renew my oath of fealty to the King of Zhufbar, Barundin, and that of my clan. These halls we will protect with our lives. These mines we shall work diligently and with due care, and give over not less than one tenth of any such ores, precious metals and valuable stones derived thereof to the king of Zhufbar, in repayment for his protection and patronage.'

Tharonin stood beside the king as Thagri pushed himself to his feet and walked up the steps. He held out the pen chisel to Barundin, who took it and signed his mark underneath the new entry in the Book of Realms. Tharonin did likewise, and then the book was passed around the six other thanes, who each signed witness to the pledges. Finally Arbrek and Thagri countersigned the agreement, and the deal was sealed.

'Thank you, my friend,' said Barundin, laying a hand on Tharonin's shoulder. 'Without you, I don't know if I would have had the strength to keep going.'

'Pah!' snorted Tharonin. 'The blood of our kings is thick in your veins, Barundin. You have a gut of stone, and no mistake.'

The clumping of iron-shod boots and voices raised in laughter echoed around the hall as a group of iron-breakers entered from the western doorway. At their front was Hengrid Dragonfoe, a goblin head in each hand. Droplets of blood dribbled from the creature's severed necks.

'Hoy there, we've just had the floor cleaned!' snapped Tharonin. 'Show some manners!'

'Well, that's gratitude for you,' said Hengrid with a grin, handing the heads to one of his comrades and marching quickly across the dark stone flags to the foot of the steps. 'Here's you accepting your new realm, while I'm out there protecting it for you. And if you don't want your inauguration presents, I'll keep them myself. My cousin, Korri, he's a dab hand at taxidermy. Reckon them two would look good flanking my mantel.'

'Has anybody told you that you're a bloodthirsty thug?' said Tharonin, smiling as he walked down the steps.

Clapping a hand to Tharonin's shoulder, Hengrid walked up the steps, shaking hands and nodded in greeting to the other thanes. He gave a respectful bow to Arbrek, who merely glowered back, and then stepped up in front of Barundin.

'Are the halls of Grungankor Stokril now safe?' the king asked.

'I swear by my grandfather's metal eyeball, there's not a grobi within two days of where we stand,' said Hengrid. 'It's been a long time coming, but I think we can safely say that you can add conqueror of Dukankor Grobkaz-a-Gazan to your list of achievements.'

'They will come again,' warned Arbrek, glaring at Tharonin. 'Keep a sharp watch and a sharper axe close by, lest that name not be consigned to history.'

'It will be a lifetime before the grobi dare come within sight of these halls,' said Barundin. 'As I swore, they have learned to fear us again.'

'A lifetime, aye, it will be,' said Hengrid. He leaned forward and pointed at Barundin's beard. 'Is that a grey hair I see? Have these past forty-two years of war aged the youthful king?'

'It is not age, it is worry,' growled Barundin. 'You could have been the death of me, disappearing for months, years at a time! Retaking the north gate and besieged by goblins for three years – what were you thinking?'

'I got carried away, that's all,' laughed Hengrid. 'Are you going to keep mentioning that every time I see you? It's been forty years, for Grimnir's sake. Let it go.'

'It'll be forty more years before I forgive you,' said Barundin. 'And forty more after that before I can forget the voice of your wife in my ear, accusing me of abandoning you every day for three years. I shudder in my sleep when I think about it.'

'I can't stand around here gossiping, there's preparations to be made,' grumbled Arbrek, turning away.

'Preparations?' asked Hengrid, darting an inquiring glance at the thanes. They shuffled nervously, looking pointedly at the king.

Hengrid shrugged and turned back to Barundin, a look of mock innocence on his face. 'Is there something important happening?'

'You know very well that it is my hundred and seven-tieth birthday tomorrow,' said Barundin. 'And you better bring something better than a couple of grobi heads. This will be a celebration of your victories as much as my birthday, so make sure you wash that blood from your beard before you come. I hope you have a speech ready.'

'A speech?' said Tharonin with a gasp. 'Grungni's beard, I knew I'd forgotten something!'

They watched as the ageing thane hurried down the steps and disappeared from the hall.

Barundin laid an arm across Hengrid's shoulders and walked him down the steps. 'And you're not to get drunk and sing that damnable song again,' he warned.

HENGRID SWAYED FROM side to side in beat to the clap-ping and the thumping of tankards on tables. As he walked along the table he stumbled over ale jugs and plates covered with bones and others remains of the feast. Beer swilled from the mug in his hand, spilling down the front of his jerkin and sticking in his beard. With a roar, he upended the tankard over his face, and then spluttered for a moment before his voice boomed out in song. Barundin covered his face and looked away.

A lusty young lad at his anvil stood beating,
Lathered in sweat and all covered in mucket.
When in came a rough lass, all smiles and good greeting,
And asked if he could see to her rusty old bucket.

'I can,' cried the lad, and they went off together,
Along to the lass's halls they did go.
He stripped off his apron, 'twas hot work in thick leather,
The fire was kindled and he soon had to blow.

Her fellow, she said, was no good for such banging,
His hammer and his arms were spent long ago.
The lad said, 'Well mine now, we won't leave you hang-
ing,
As I'm sure you'll no doubt all very soon know.'

Many times did his mallet, by vigorous heating,
Grow too soft to work on such an old pail,
But when it was cooled he kept on a-beating,
And he worked on it quickly, his strength not to fail.

When the lad was all done, the lass was all tearful:
'Oh, what would I give could my fellow do so.
Good lad with your hammer, I'm ever so fearful,
I ask could you use it once more ere you go?'

Even Barundin was laughing uproariously by the time
Hengrid had finished, and laughed even more heartily
when the thane, on attempting to clamber down from
the table, slipped and fell headlong to the floor with a
crash and a curse. Still chuckling, Barundin pulled himself up on to the table and raised his hands. Quiet
descended, of a sort, punctuated by snorts and belches,
the glug of beer taps and numerous other sounds made
by any group of drunken dwarfs.

'My wonderful friends and kin!' he began, to an
uproarious shout of approval. 'My people of wonderful
Zhufbar, you have my thanks. There is no prouder day
for a king to be amongst such wonderful company. We
have wonderful beer to drink in plentiful amounts,
wonderful food and wonderful song.'

His face took on a sincere expression and he looked
down sternly at the still-prostrate form of Hengrid.

'Well, perhaps not such wonderful song,' he said, to
much clapping and laughter. 'There have been many

speeches, fine oratory from my great friends and allies, but there is one more that you must listen to.'

There were groans from some of the younger members of the crowd, and cheers from the older ones.

In the short silence before Barundin spoke, the distinctive sound of snoring could be heard, and Barundin turned to look in its direction. Arbrek was at the foot of the table, his head against his chest. With a snort, the runelord jerked awake, and sensing the king's gaze stood up and raised his tankard.

'Bravo!' he cried. 'Hail to King Barundin!'

'King Barundin!' the crowd echoed enthusiastically. Arbrek slumped down and his head began to nod toward his chest once more.

'As I was saying,' said Barundin, pacing up the table. 'We are here to celebrate my one hundred and seventieth birthday.'

There was much cheering, and cries of, 'Good Old Barundin', and, 'Just a beardling!'

'I was little over a hundred years old when I became king,' said Barundin, his voice solemn, his sudden serious mood quieting the boisterous feasters. 'My father was cut down in battle, betrayed by a weak manling. For nearly seventy years I have toiled and fought, and for nearly seventy years you have toiled and fought beside me. It has been for one reason, and one reason alone, that we have endured these hardships: retribution! My father now walks the Halls of the Ancestors, but he cannot find peace while his betrayers still have not been brought to book. As I declared that day, so now do I renew my oath, and declare the right of grudge against the Vessals of Stirland. Before the year is out, we will demand apology and recompense for the wrongs they have done against us. My brave and vigorous people, who have kept faith with me through these hard times, what say you now?'

'Avenge King Throndin!' came one shout.

'Grudge!' bellowed a dwarf from the back of the hall. 'Grudge!'

'We'll be with you!' came another cry.

'Sing us a song!' came a slurred voice from behind Barundin, and he turned to see Hengrid slouched across the bench, a full mug of ale in his hand again.

'A song!' demanded a chorus of voices from all over the hall.

'A song about what?' asked Barundin with a grin.

'Grudges!'

'Gold!'

'Beer!'

Barundin thought for a moment, and then bent down and grabbed the shoulder of Hengrid's jerkin, dragging him back to the tabletop.

'Here's one you should all know,' said Barundin. He began to beat out a rhythm with a stamping foot, and soon the hall was shuddering again.

Well it's all for me grog, me jolly, jolly grog
It's all for me beer and tobacco
For I spent all me gold on good maps of old
But me future's looking no better.

Where are me boots, me noggin', noggin' boots?
They're all gone for beer and tobacco
For the heels are worn out and the toes kicked about
And the soles are looking no better.

Where's me shirt, me noggin', noggin' shirt?
It's all gone for beer and tobacco
For the collar's so thin, and the sleeves are done in
And the pockets are looking no better.

Where's me bed, me noggin', noggin' bed?
It's all gone for beer and tobacco
No pillows for a start and now the sheet's torn apart
And the springs are looking no better.

Where's me wench, me noggin', noggin' wench?
She's all gone for beer and tobacco
She's healthy, no doubt, and her bosom's got clout
But her face is looking no better!

THE CELEBRATIONS LASTED for several more days, during which Tharonin finally delivered his speech, thanking Barundin for his kingship and volunteering to act as messenger to the Vessals. After his sterling work in tracking down Wanazaki, Dran the Reckoner was brought in by Barundin to assist Tharonin in his expedition. Dran earned his keep by settling old debts and grudges, but for Barundin's missions, he volunteered his services free of charge.

When pressed by Barundin about this uncharacteristically generous offer, Dran was at first reluctant to discuss his reasons. However, the king's persistent inquiries finally forced the Reckoner to share his motives. They were sitting in the king's chambers, sharing a pitcher of ale by the fireside, and had been discussing Dran's plan to bring the Vessals to justice.

'Proper form must be observed,' insisted Barundin. 'They must be left in no doubt as to the consequences of failing to comply with my demands for restitution.'

'I know how to handle these matters,' Dran assured him. 'I will serve notice to the Vessals, and will warn them of your resolve. What exactly are your demands?'

'A full apology, for a start,' said Barundin. 'The current holder of the barony is to abdicate his position and take exile from his lands. We will take custody of the body

of Baron Silas Vessal and dispose of it in a way fitting to
such a traitor. Lastly, for the death of a king, there can
be no price too high, but I will settle for a full one-half
of the wealth of the Vessals and their lands.'

'And if they do not agree to your terms?' asked Dran,
taking notes on a small piece of parchment.

'Then I shall be forced to violent resolution,' said
Barundin with a scowl. 'I will unseat them from their
position, destroy their castle and scatter them. Look,
just make them realise I'm in no mood to be bargained
with. These manlings will try to get out of it, but they
can't. Vessal's despicable behaviour must be atoned for,
and if they can't move themselves to make that atone-
ment, I will make them regret it.'

'Seems pretty reasonable,' said Dran with a nod. 'I will
have Thagri write a formal declaration of this intent,
and Tharonin and I will deliver it to those dogs in Uderstir.'

'They have forty days to reply,' added Barundin. 'I
want them to know that I'm not messing about. Forty
days, and then they'll have the army of Zhufbar at their
gate.'

'It's my job to make sure it doesn't come to that,' said
Dran, folding the parchment into a small packet and
placing it in a pouch at his belt. 'But if it does, I'll be
standing there beside you.'

'Yes, and for no gain as far as I can tell,' said Barundin,
offering more ale. 'What's in this for you?'

'Why does there have to be something for me in the
deal?' asked Dran, proffering his mug. 'Can't I offer my
services to a just cause?'

'You?' snorted Barundin. 'You would ask for gold just
to visit your grandmother. Tell me, why are you helping
with this? If you don't answer, consider your services
not needed.'

Dran did not reply for a while, but sat in silence, sipping his beer. Barundin continued to stare intently at the Reckoner, until finally Dran put his mug down with a sigh and looked at the king.

'I've amassed a good deal of gold over the years,' said Dran. 'More even than most folk think I have. But I'm getting older, and I'm tiring of the road. I want to take a wife and raise a family.'

'You want to settle down?' said Barundin. 'A great wanderer like you?'

'I started because I wanted to see justice done,' said Dran. 'Then I did it for the money. Nowadays? Nowadays, I don't know why I do it. There's easier ways to earn gold. Perhaps have some sons and teach them my craft, who knows?'

'What's that got to do with the Vessals and my grudge?' asked Barundin. 'It's not like you're after a single last payoff to set yourself up.'

'I want a good wife,' said Dran, staring down into his cup. 'For all my success, I'm not that widely regarded. Being a Reckoner doesn't get you many friends, or much recognition. I'll be moving on, perhaps to Karak Norn or Karak Hirn. But for all my wealth, I don't have much to offer for a wife, and that's where you come in.'

'Go on,' said Barundin, filling his own mug and taking a gulp of frothy ale.

'I want to be a thane,' said Dran, looking deep into the king's eyes. 'If I arrive as Thane Dran of Zhufbar to go with my chests of gold, I'll be beating them off with a hammer.'

'Why didn't you mention this before?' asked Barundin.

'I didn't want to do it this way,' said Dran with a shrug. 'I hoped that if I helped you with this, and perhaps if you wanted to show a mark of your gratitude, I could ask for it then. I didn't want it to sound like naming a price by different means.'

'Well, I'm sorry then that I forced you to answer,' said Barundin. 'Don't worry too much about it. I remember that you were the first on his feet to protect me when we found Wanazaki, and a king's memory does not fade quickly. Do your job well with this matter, and I'll think of some way to reward you.'

Barundin raised his mug and held it towards Dran. The Reckoner hesitated for a moment and then raised his own cup and clinked it against the king's.

'Here's to a good king,' said Dran.

'Here's to justice,' replied Barundin.

IT WAS SEVERAL more days before Tharonin and Dran set out, the formalities of the grudge and reparations having been arranged with Thagri, and preparations for the expedition made. The aim of the journey was not war, so Tharonin took only his personal guard, some hundred and twenty longbeards, whose axes had made much fell work during the wars against the skaven and grobi. Dran mustered a few dozen rangers to act as his entourage, more for company than any other reason.

It was a solemn occasion as the group set out. Barundin bade them farewell from the main gate of Zhufbar, and watched for several hours until they were out of sight. He returned to his chambers, where he found Arbrek waiting for him.

The runelord was napping in a deep armchair near the fire, snoring loudly. Barundin sat down next to Arbrek, and was deep in thought for a long time, not wishing to waken the runelord from his rest.

Barundin pondered what might happen over the coming days. There was a chance, albeit slim to his mind that, Tharonin's expedition would come under attack from the Vessals and their warriors. If that happened, he would march straight away to Uderstir and raze their keep to the ground. More likely would be refusal. The thought of waging war against men of the Empire genuinely pained him, for they and the dwarfs had a long history together, and few conflicts. Despite the ancestral bonds between his kind and the Empire, Barundin knew he would not balk at doing his duty.

Eventually Arbrek roused himself with a snort, and spent a moment gazing around the room in slight confusion. Finally, his eyes focussed on Barundin, their harsh glare not at all dulled by his age.

'Ah, there you are,' said the runelord, straightening in the chair. 'I've been waiting for you. Where have you been?'

Barundin bit back his first retort, remembering not to be disrespectful of the aged runelord. 'I was seeing Tharonin off,' he explained. 'Nobody sent word that you wanted to see me, or I would have come quicker.'

'Nobody sent word, because I gave no word to send,' said Arbrek. The runelord leaned forward, resting his elbows on his knees. 'I'm getting old.'

'There's still years left in your boiler,' said Barundin, the reply made without hesitation.

'No,' said Arbrek, shaking his head. 'No, there is not.'

'What are you saying?' said Barundin, concerned.

'You have been a fine king,' said Arbrek. 'Your forefathers will be proud. Your mother will be proud.'

'Thank you,' said Barundin, not sure what else to say to such unexpected praise. Arbrek was as traditional as they got, and so expected anyone younger than him to be unsteady and somewhat worthless.

'I mean it,' said the runelord. 'You've a heart and a wisdom beyond your years. You've led your people on a dangerous path, taken them into war. If, for a moment, I thought this vain ambition on your part, I would have spoken out, turned the council against you.'

'Well, I'm glad I had your support,' said Barundin. 'Without it, I think many more of the thanes would have been difficult to win over to my cause.'

'I did not do it for you,' said Arbrek, sitting up. 'I did it for the same reasons you did. It was for your father, not for you.'

'Of course,' said Barundin. 'These long years, it has always been for my father, to settle the grudge I declared the day that he died.'

'And now that is almost over,' said Arbrek. 'Soon you will have settled it.'

'Yes,' said Barundin with a smile. 'Within weeks, the grudge will be no more, one way or another,'

'And then what will you do?' asked Arbrek, studying the king's face intently.

'What do you mean?' said Barundin, standing. 'Beer?'

Arbrek nodded and did not speak while Barundin walked to the door and called to his servants for a small cask of ale. As he sat down again, he glanced at the runelord. His penetrating gaze had not wavered.

'I don't understand. What do you mean,' said Barundin. 'What will I do?'

'This grudge of yours, it has been everything to you,' said Arbrek. 'As much as you were dedicated, devoted to your father in life, avenging his death has become your driving force, the steam within the engine of your heart. What will drive you when it is done? What will you do now?'

'I hadn't really thought about it,' said Barundin, scratching at his beard. 'It has been so long… I sometimes thought there would never be a time without the grudge.'

'And that is what concerns me,' said Arbrek. 'You have done well as king until now. The true test of your reign, though, will be what you do next.'

'I will rule my people as best I can,' said Barundin, confused by the intent of Arbrek's questioning. 'With luck, in peace.'

'Peace?' said Barundin. 'Pah! Our people have not known peace for thousands of years. Perhaps you are not as wise as you seem.'

'Surely a king does not court war and strife for his people?' said Barundin.

'No, he does not.' replied Arbrek.

He paused as one of the king's servants entered, carrying a silver tray with two tankards upon it. He was followed by one of the maids from the brewery, carrying a small keg. She set it on the table and then left.

Barundin took a tankard and leaned over to put it under the tap. Arbrek laid a hand on his arm and stopped him.

'Why so hasty?' said the runelord. 'Let it settle awhile. There is no rush.'

Barundin sat back, toying with the tankard, turning it over in his fingers, looking at the way the firelight glimmered off the gold thread inlaid into the thick clay cup. He risked a glance at Arbrek, who was contemplating the keg. Barundin knew better than to speak; to do so would risk the runelord's ire for hastiness.

'You are shrewd, and you have a good fighting arm,' Arbrek said eventually, still looking at the firkin. 'Your people admire and respect you. Do not let peace lull you into idleness, for it will dull your mind as much as battle dulls a poor blade. Do not seek war, you are right, but do not run from it. Hard times are not always of our own making.'

Barundin said nothing, but simply nodded. With an unusually spry push, Arbrek was on his feet. He took a step towards the door, and then looked back. He smiled at Barundin's perplexed expression.

'I have made a decision,' said Arbrek.

'You have?' said Barundin. 'What about?'

'Come with me. There is something I want you to see,' said Arbrek. There was a twinkle in the runelord's eye that excited Barundin and he stood swiftly and followed him out the door.

Arbrek led Barundin through the hold, taking him through the chambers and halls towards his smithy which lay within the highest levels. In all his years, Barundin had never been in this part of the hold, for it was the domain of the runesmiths. It did not seem any different from most of the rest of Zhufbar, although the sound of hammering echoed more loudly from behind the closed doors.

At the end of a particular corridor, the king found himself in a dead end. He was about to ask Arbrek what he was up to, but before he could the runelord had raised a finger to his lips with a wink. With careful ceremony, Arbrek reached into his robes and pulled a small silver key from its depths. Barundin looked around but could see no lock.

'If dwarf locks were so easy to find, they would not be secret, would they?' said Arbrek with a chuckle. 'Watch carefully, for very few of our folk have ever seen this.'

The runelord held the key just in front of his lips, and appeared to be blowing on it. However, as Barundin looked on, he saw that Arbrek was whispering, ever so softly. For several minutes he spoke to the key, occasionally running a loving finger along its length. In the silver, the king saw thin lines appear, narrower than a hair. They glowed with a soft blue light, just enough to highlight the runelord's features in azure tints.

Barundin realised that he had been concentrating so hard on the key, that he had not noticed anything else. With a start, he snapped his attention away from the runelord and glanced around. They were still in a dead-end tunnel, but where the end had been to his left a moment ago, it was now to his right. The walls emitted a golden aura and he saw that there were no lanterns, but more of the thin traceries of runes that had been on the key, covering the walls and providing the illumination.

'These chambers were built by the greatest of the runelords of Zhufbar,' said Arbrek, closing a gnarled hand around the key and deftly hiding it within the folds of his cloak. He took the king by the arm and started to lead him along the corridor. 'They were first dug under the instructions of Durlok Ringbinder, in the days when the mountains were still young, and Valaya herself was said to have taught him the secrets he used. During the Time of the Goblin Wars, they were sealed for centuries, and it was thought that all knowledge of them was lost, for no runelord had ever committed their secrets to written lore. But it was not so, for in distant Karaz-a-Karak, the runelord Skargim lived, but he had not been born there. He was born and raised in Zhufbar, and upon being released from his duties by the high king, he returned and unearthed these chambers. He was the grandfather of my tutor, Fengil Silverbeard.'

'They're beautiful,' said Barundin, gazing around.

'Yes they are,' said Arbrek with a smile. 'But these are just tunnels. Wait until you see my workshop.'

The room to which Barundin was led was not large, although the ceiling was quite high, three times his height. It was simply furnished, with a grate, an armchair and small workbench. Upon the bench was a miniature anvil, no larger than a fist, and small mallets, pincers and other tools. By the fire was a clockwork bellows and many pails of coal. The wall opposite was decorated with a breath-taking mural of the mountains swathed in clouds.

And then movement caught Barundin's eye. One of the clouds in the painting had definitely moved. He staggered, amazed, across the room, Arbrek following close behind. As he stood a few paces from the wall, he could see downwards, along the mountainside of Zhufbar itself. Hesitantly, he stretched out an arm, and felt nothing. He felt dizzy and started to topple forward. Arbrek grabbed his belt and hauled him back.

'It's a window,' said Barundin, dazed by the magnificence of the sight.

'More than a window,' said Arbrek. 'And yet, oddly, less. It's just a hole, cut through the hard rock. There are runes carved into the ground outside that we cannot see from here. They ward away the elements, surer than any glass.'

'It is a wonderful sight,' said Barundin, gathering himself. From this high in the mountain, he could see far out across Black Water, the lake itself hidden by mist, and the mountains beyond. 'Thank you for showing it to me.'

'This isn't what I wanted to show you,' said Arbrek with a scowl. 'No, the view is nice enough, but a good view does not make a good king.'

The runelord walked to the corner of his room and took a bundle wrapped in dark sack cloth. 'This is what I wanted you to see,' he said, handing the package to Barundin. 'Open it, have a look.'

Barundin took the sacking, and there was almost no weight to it at all. He pulled away the cloth, revealing a metal haft, and then a single-bladed axe head. Tossing the sacking aside, he hefted the axe in one hand. His arm moved as freely as if it were carrying nothing more than a feather. There were several runes etched into the blade of the axe, which glittered with the same magical light as the tunnels outside.

'My last and finest work,' said Arbrek. 'Your father commissioned it from me the day that you were born.'

'One hundred and seventy years?' said Barundin. 'You've kept it that long?'

'No, no, no,' said Arbrek, taking the axe from Barundin. 'I have only just finished it! It has my own master rune upon it, the only weapon in the world. That alone took me twenty years to devise and another fifty before it was finished. These other runes are not easy to craft either: the Rune of Swift Slaying, the Rune of Severing, and particularly the Rune of Ice.'

'It is a wondrous gift,' said Barundin. 'I cannot thank you enough.'

'Thank your father, he paid for it,' said Arbrek gruffly, handing the axe back to Barundin. 'And thank me by wielding it well when you need to.'

'Does it have a name?' asked Barundin, stroking a hand across the flat of the polished blade.

'No,' said Arbrek, looking away and gazing out across the mountains. 'I thought I would leave that to you.'

'I have never had to name anything before,' said Barundin.

'Then do not try to do it quickly,' said Arbrek. 'Think on it, and the right name will come. A name that will last for generations.'

IT WAS SEVERAL days later when Tharonin and Dran returned. They had travelled to Uderstir and delivered the king's demands. Silas Vessal had been dead for over a hundred and fifty years and his great-grandson, Obious Vessal, was now baron, and an old man himself. He had pleaded with Dran to send his profuse apologies to the king for his forefather's damnable actions. However, upon the matter of his great-grandfather's body and the monies to be paid, he had given no answer.

It was the opinion of Dran that the new baron would renege on any deal that he struck, and that he could not be trusted. Tharonin, although he agreed in part with the Reckoner's view, urged Barundin to give the baron every chance to make recompense. For a manling, he had seemed sincere, or if not sincere, then suitably afraid of the consequences of inaction.

'Forty days I give him,' said Barundin to his council of advisors. 'Forty days I said, and forty days he shall have.'

Troubling news came only a few days later. There were shortages in the furnace rooms. The timber that was usually sent each month by ancient trade agreement from the Empire town of Konlach had not arrived. Although there was still coal aplenty, many of the engineers regarded using coal as a waste for many of their projects, since there were usually so many spare trees to cut down instead.

It was Godri Ongurbazum who had the most concerns. It was his clan that was responsible for the agreement, one that had been nearly unbroken for centuries, incomplete only during the dark times of the Great War against Chaos. There was no good reason, as far as Godri could discern, for the men of Konlach to break faith.

In one council meeting the thane of the Ongurbazumi argued against Barundin setting off with the army to remonstrate with Obious Vessal. He brought the argument that the trouble with Konlach was more urgent, for if no other supply of timber could be secured, the forges might have to stand cold for want of fuel.

Barundin would have none of it. When the forty days were up, the army of Zhufbar would go and take by force what the king was owed. The debate raged for several nights, with Godri and his allies arguing that after so long, an extra month or two would not be amiss. Barundin countered that it was because it had taken so long to resolve the grudge that he wanted to act as swiftly as possible and have it done with.

In the end, Barundin, losing his temper completely with the trade clan's leader, shouted him out of the audience chamber, and then dismissed the rest of the council. For three days he sat upon his throne and fumed. On the fourth day, he called them back.

'I will have no more argument against my course of action,' Barundin told the assembled thanes.

Arbrek arrived, mumbling about lack of sleep, but Barundin assured him that what he had to say was worth the runelord being disturbed. He drew out the rune axe that had been given to him, much to the awe and interest of the thanes. They looked at the craftsmanship of the blade, passing it amongst themselves, cooing delightedly and praising Arbrek.

'Fie to timber contracts!' said Barundin. 'Skaven and grobi have not stood in our way, and I'll not let a few damn trees halt us now. I have gathered you here to witness the naming of my new axe, and to assure you that if they do not comply with my demands, the first enemies to taste its wrath will be the Vessals of Uderstir.'

He took back the enchanted weapon and held it out in front of him. The lantern light shimmered in the aura surrounding the blade.

'I name it Grudgesettler.'

THERE WAS NO improvement in the timber situation and for the forty days until the Vessals' deadline, Barundin was under constant pressure from the trading clans and the engineers to put his grudge on hold once more to resolve the issue with Konlach. Although he was always polite about the matter, he made it clear that he would brook no more delays and no more disagreement.

On the eve before the ultimatum expired, Barundin addressed the warriors of the hold. He explained to them that the hour of their vengeance was almost at hand. He warned that they might be called upon to perform fell deeds in the name of his father, and to this they responded with a roar of approval. Many of them had fought beside King Throndin when he fell, or lost clan members to the orcs when Silas Vessal had quit the field without fighting. They were as eager as Barundin to make the noble family of the Empire atone for their forefather's cowardice.

It was a cold morning that saw the dwarf army setting out, heading westwards into Stirland. Autumn was fast approaching, and in the high peaks snow was gathering, frosting the highest reaches of the scattered pine woods that dotted the mountains around Zhufbar

They made swift progress, but did not force the march. Barundin wanted his army to arrive eager and full of strength. With them came a chugging locomotive of the Engineers Guild, towing three cannons behind it. Where once the machine had been a source of wonder and awe to the soldiers of Uderstir, it would become a symbol of dread should they choose to resist Barundin's demands again.

On the fourth day they arrived at the castle, the tops of its walls visible over a line of low hills some miles in the distance. It was not a large fortress, barely a keep with a low curtain wall. A green banner adorned with a griffon holding an axe fluttered madly from the flag pole of the central tower.

Smoke filled the air, and occasionally there was a distant reverberating thump, as of a cannon firing. As the head of the dwarf army crossed the crest of the line of hills, Barundin and the others were greeted by an unexpected sight.

An army encircled Uderstir. Under banners of green, yellow and black, regiments of halberdiers and spearmen stood behind makeshift siege workings, avoiding the desultory fire of handguns and crossbows from the castle walls. The noise had indeed been a cannon, ensconced in a revetment built of mud and reinforced with gabions made from woven wood and filled with rocks. The nearest tower was heavily damaged, its upper parts having fallen away under the bombardment, leaving a pile of debris at the base of the wall. Bowmen unleashed tired volleys against the walls whenever a head appeared, their arrows clattering uselessly from the old, moss-covered stones.

Several dozen horses were corralled out of range of the walls, and the armoured figures of knights could be seen walking about the camp or sitting in groups around the fires. It was immediately obvious that the siege had been going on for some time now, and that dreary routine had become the norm. Whoever was leading the attacking army was in no hurry to assault the strong walls of Uderstir.

Barundin gave the order for his army to form up from their column of march, even as the dwarfs were spied and the camp below was suddenly filled with furious activity. As the war machines of the dwarfs were unlimbered and brought forward, a group of five riders mounted up and rode quickly in their direction.

Barundin marched forward with his hammerers, flanked to the left by Arbrek and to the right by Hengrid Dragonfoe, who held aloft the ornate silver and gold standard of Zhufbar. They stopped just as the slope away down the hill began to grow steeper, and awaited the riders. To their left, Dran and the hold's rangers began to make their way down the slope, following the channel of a narrow stream, out of sight of the enemy camp.

The riders came up at a gallop, riding beneath a banner that was split with horizontal lines of green and black, with a lion rampant picked out in gold, standing atop a bridge. On an embroidered scroll beneath the device was the name 'Konlach'.

The riders stopped a little way off, perhaps fifty yards, and eyed the dwarfs suspiciously, their horses trotting back and forth. Barundin could see that they carried long spears, and carried heavy pistols in holsters upon their belts, in their boots and on their saddles.

'Who approaches King Barundin of Zhufbar?' shouted Hengrid, planting the standard firmly in the ground and pulling his single-bladed axe from its sheath.

One of the riders came forward to within a spear's throw of the king. He was dressed in a heavy coat, with puffed and slashed sleeves, showing green material beneath its black leather. He wore a helmet decorated with two feathers, one green and one black, and its visor was pulled down, shaped in the snarling face of a lion. He raised a hand and lifted his visor, revealing a surprisingly young face.

'I am Theoland, herald to Baron Gerhadricht of Konlach,' he said, his voice clear and loud. 'Are you friend to Uderstir? Have you come to lift our siege?'

'I most certainly am not a friend of Uderstir!' bellowed Barundin, stepping forward. 'Those thieves and cowards are my enemies through and through.'

'Then you are friend with Baron Gerhadricht,' Theoland said. He waved a hand to a large green and yellow pavilion at the centre of the camp. 'Please, come with me. My lord awaits you in his tent. He offers his word that no harm will come to you.'

'The words of manlings are meaningless,' said Hengrid, brandishing his axe fiercely. 'That is why we are here!'

Theoland did not flinch. 'If you would but come with me, this can all be settled quickly, I am sure,' said the herald, turning his horse. He looked over his shoulder at the dwarfs. 'Bring as many retainers as you feel comfortable with. You will not find our hospitality lacking.'

As the riders cantered away, Barundin looked to Hengrid and Arbrek. The old runelord simply shrugged and grunted.

Hengrid gave a nod towards the camp. 'They'll not try anything daft with another army arrayed on their flank,' said the thane. 'I'll come with you if you like.'

'No, I want you to stay and keep command of the army should I not return,' said Barundin. 'I'll go alone. Let's not show these manlings too much respect.'

'Fair enough,' said Hengrid.

Barundin took a deep breath and walked down the hill, following in the hoof prints left by the riders. He ignored the stares of the soldiers and peasants as he strode purposefully through the camp, his gilded armour gleaming in the autumn sun, which peeked occasionally from behind the low clouds.

He came to the tent of the baron and found Theoland and his guard of honour waiting outside. The baron's flag fluttered from a pole next to the pavilion. Without a word, Theoland bowed and held open the tent flap for Barundin to enter.

The material of the tent was thick and did not allow much light inside. Instead, two braziers, fuming and sputtering, illuminated the interior. The floor was covered with scattered rugs, hides and furs, and low chairs were arranged in a circle around the near end of the pavilion. The remainder was hidden behind heavy velvet drapes.

The tent was empty except for Barundin and a solitary man, wizened with age, who sat crooked upon one of the chairs, his eyes peering at the newly arrived dwarf. He raised a palsied hand and gestured to a small table to one side, on which stood a ewer and some crystal glasses.

'Wine?' said the man.

'No thanks, I'm not staying long,' said Barundin.

The man nodded slowly, and seemed to drift away again.

'Are you Baron Gerhadricht?' asked Barundin, walking forward and standing in the middle of the rugs.

'I am,' replied the baron. 'What business does a dwarf king seek in Uderstir?'

'Well, first off, I've a matter to bring to you,' said Barundin. 'You're from Konlach, right?'

'I am the Baron of Konlach, that is correct,' said Gerhadricht.

'Then where's our timber?' said Barundin, crossing his arms.

'You've come all this way with an army for some timber?' said the baron with a laugh. 'Timber? Can't you see we've got a war to fight? We don't have any spare timber!'

'We have an agreement,' insisted Barundin. 'I don't care about your wars. We have a contract between us.'

'Once Uderstir is mine, we shall make up the deficit, I assure you,' said the baron. 'Now, is that all?'

'One does not dismiss a dwarf king so easily!' snarled Barundin. 'I'm not here for your timber. I'm here for those bloody cowards, the Vessals. I mean to storm Uderstir and take what is mine by right of grudge.'

'What is yours?' said Gerhadricht with a hiss. 'What claim do you have to Uderstir? Mine goes back many generations, to the alignment of Konlach and Uderstir by my great-great-great uncle. Uderstir is mine by right, usurped by Silas Vessal with bribery and murder.'

The tent flap opened and Theoland entered. 'I heard raised voices,' he said, looking between the baron and Barundin. 'What are you arguing about?'

'Your inheritance, dear boy,' said Gerhadricht. He looked at Barundin. 'My youngest nephew, Theoland. My only surviving kin. Can you believe that?'

'He looks a fine enough lad for a manling,' said Barundin, eyeing up the baron's herald. 'So you think you have a claim to Uderstir?'

'My great-great-great grandfather was once baron here,' said Theoland. 'It is mine by right of inheritance through my uncle and his marriage.'

'Well, you can have whatever's left of Uderstir once I'm through with the Vessals,' said Barundin. 'I have declared right of grudge, and that's far more important than your manling titles and inheritances. Baron Silas Vessal betrayed my father, leaving him on the field of battle to be killed by orcs. I demand recompense and recompense I shall get!'

'Grudge?' said the baron with scorn. 'What about rights of law? You are a dwarf, and you are in the lands of the Empire. Your wishes are of no concern to me. If you agree to assist me in the shortening of this siege, I will gladly hand over the Vessals to your justice.'

'And one half of the coffers of Uderstir,' said Barundin.

'Ridiculous!' snapped Gerhadricht. 'You would have my nephew be a pauper baron, like one of those scrabbling wretches of the Border Princes or Estalia? Ridiculous!'

'Uncle, perhaps...' started Theoland, but he was cut off by the baron.

'There will be no more bargaining,' said Gerhadricht. 'That's my best offer.'

Barundin bristled and looked at Theoland, who shrugged helplessly. Baron Gerhadricht appeared to be contemplating the worn designs of one of the rugs.

'I intend to assault Uderstir, baron,' said Barundin, and his voice was low and calm, on the far edge of anger that is the icy cold of genuine ire rather than the tantrum that most people mistake for rage. 'Your army can stand aside, or stand betwixt me and my foe. It would not go well for you, should you be in my road.'

Without waiting for a reply, Barundin turned on his heel and marched out of the tent.

Footsteps behind him caused him to turn, and he saw Theoland striding after him.

'King Barundin!' the herald called out, and the king stopped, bristling with anger, his hands pale fists by his side. 'Please, let me talk to my uncle.'

'My attack begins as soon as I get back to my army,' growled Barundin. 'You have that long to convince him of his folly.'

'Please, I don't want more blood shed than is necessary,' said Theoland, stooping to one knee in front of the king.

'Remind your uncle that he has broken oath with us on the trade agreement,' said Barundin. 'Remind him that he will be lucky to have half the coffers of Uderstir for your inheritance. And remind him that should he attempt to stand in my way, it will not be just the lives of his men that are forfeit, but also his own.'

With nothing more to say, Barundin stepped around the distraught young noble and marched up the hill.

The dwarf army was now lined up in front of him, flanked to the north by two cannons, and by the third cannon to the south. The clans were gathered around their hornblowers and standard bearers: a row of grim-faced hammer- and axe-wielding warriors that stretched for nearly three hundred yards.

As he approached the army, Barundin pulled forth Grudgesettler and held the weapon aloft. The air shimmered as weapons were raised in return, glinting with the pale sunlight, and a throaty grumbling began to reverberate across the army.

Loremaster Thagri stood ready with the Zhufbar book of grudges open in his hands. Barundin took it from him and addressed his army, reading from the open page.

'Let it be known that I, King Barundin of Zhufbar, record this grudge in front of my people,' Barundin said, his voice loud and belligerent now that the time of reckoning was at hand. 'I name myself grudgesworn against Baron Silas Vessal of Uderstir, a traitor, a weakling and a coward. By his treacherous act, Baron Vessal did endanger the army of Zhufbar, and through his actions brought about the death of King Throndin of Zhufbar, my father. Recompense must be in blood, for death can only be met with death. No gold, no apology can atone for this betrayal. Before the thanes of Zhufbar and with Grungni as my witness, I swear this oath!

'I declare grudge upon the Vessals of Uderstir. Leave no stone upon another while they still cower from justice! Leave no man between us and vengeance! Let none that resist us be punished other than by death! Kazak un uzkul!'

Kazak un uzkul: battle and death. The dwarfs took up the cry, and the horns sounded long and hard from the hilltop.

'Kazak un uzkul! Kazak un uzkul! Kazak un uzkul! Kazak un uzkul! Kazak un uzkul!! Kazak un uzkul!'

The hills resounded with the war cry and all eyes in the shallow valley below were turned to them as the dwarfs began to march forward, beating their weapons on their shields, their armoured boots making the ground shake as they advanced.

The boom of the cannons accompanied the advance, hurling their shot high over the heads of the approaching dwarf army. Although smaller than the great cannons of the Empire, the cannons of Zhufbar were inscribed with magical runes by the runesmiths, their ammunition carved with dire symbols of penetrating and destruction. The cannonballs trailed magical fire and smoke, hissing with mystical energy.

The salvo struck the already-weakened tower, shattering it with three mighty blasts that shook the ground. A fountain of ruptured stone was flung high into the air, raining down blocks of rock and pulverised dust. The walls beside the now ruined tower, unsupported by its strength, buckled and began to crumble. Shouts of alarm and wails of pain echoed from within the walls.

Barundin aimed straight for the growing breach, some two hundred yards away, advancing steadily over the broken ground. The odd whine of a bullet and the hiss of an arrow went past, but the fire from the castle was lacklustre in the extreme and not a single dwarf fell.

The men of Konlach parted in front of the dwarf throng like wheat to a scythe, pushing and hurrying each other in their eagerness to be out of the line of march. Grunting and puffing, the dwarfs pulled themselves over the siege defences created by Baron Gerhadricht's men and poured through the gaps in the earth walls and shallow trenches, reforming on the other side.

Another salvo from the cannons roared out, and the south wall cracked and shuddered, toppling stones the size of men onto the ground, making the battlements jagged like the broken teeth of an impoverished vagrant.

Now only a hundred yards away, the dwarfs raised their shields in front of them, as arrows and bullets came at them with greater frequency and accuracy. Most of the missiles bounced harmlessly away from the shields and armour of the dwarfs, but here and there along the line a dwarf faltered, dead or wounded.

To the left, the gate opened and a troop of several dozen knights sallied forth. They quickly formed their line, lances levelled for the charge. Hengrid left Barundin's side and commanded several of the hand-gun-armed Thunderer regiments to wheel to the left, facing this new threat. The king forged onward, now only fifty yards from the walls, as another cannonball struck the castle, its cataclysmic impact tearing a hole several yards wide to the foundations of the wall. The king saw spearmen gathering in the breach, preparing to defend the gaping hole.

The thundering of hooves to the left announced the cavalry charge, met with the crackle of handgun fire. Barundin glanced in their direction and saw the knights bearing down on the Thunderers, who had not bothered to reload, but instead drew hammers and axes ready for the attack.

It never came.

On the flank of the knights emerged Dran and his rangers, stepping out from the reeds and scattered bushes of the stream's bank. With crossbows levelled, they formed a hasty line and fired, unable to miss at such close range. A quarter of the knights were toppled by the volley, and others fell as their horses tripped on falling bodies and crashed into each other.

Without pause, the rangers slung their crossbows, drew large double-handed hunting axes and stormed forwards. Their charge disrupted, their impetus lost, the knights tried to wheel to face this threat, but they were too disorganised and few of them had their lances at full tilt or were moving at any speed when the dwarf rangers hit. With Hengrid leading them, the Thunderers shouldered their weapons and moved forward to join the melee.

Barundin was the first into the breach, bellowing and swinging his axe. Spear points glanced harmlessly off his rune-encrusted gromril armour, their points sheared away by a sweep of Grudgesettler. As the hammerers pressed in beside him, he leapt forward from the tangle of rock and wood within the breach, crashing like a metal comet into the ranks of the spearmen, knocking them over. Grudgesettler blazed as limbs and heads were severed by a mighty swing from the dwarf king, and as the Hammerers pressed forward, their deadly war-mattocks smashing and crushing, the spearmen's nerve broke and they fled the vengeful dwarfs.

Once inside the castle, the dwarfs made short work of the fighting. Dozens of manlings had been slain by the collapse of the tower and wall, and those who remained were shocked and no match for the heavily armoured, angry host that poured through the gap in the wall. Many threw up their hands and dropped their weapons in surrender, but the dwarfs showed no mercy. This was not war, this was grudge killing, and no quarter would be given.

Hengrid breached the gates with Dran, having routed the knights, and the defenders gave themselves up in greater numbers. Swarms of women and children huddled in the crude huts inside the walls, shrieking and praying to Sigmar for deliverance. The dwarf army surrounded them, weapons drawn. Barundin was about to give the signal for the execution to begin when a shout rang out from the broken gateway.

'Hold your arms!' the voice commanded, and Barundin turned to see Theoland mounted upon his warhorse, a pistol in each hand, his visor lowered. 'The battle is won, put up your weapons!'

'You dare command King Barundin of Zhufbar?' bellowed Barundin, forcing his way through the dwarf throng towards the young noble.

Theoland aimed a pistol at the approaching king, his arm as steady as a rock. 'The body of Baron Obius Vessal lies outside these walls,' he said. 'These are my people now, my subjects to protect.'

'Stand against me and your life is forfeit,' snarled Barundin, hefting Grudgesettler, whose blade was slicked with blood, the runes inscribed in the metal smoking and hissing.

'If I do not, then my honour is forfeit,' said Theoland. 'What leader of men would I be, to allow the slaughter of women and children? I would rather die than stand by and allow such base murder.'

Barundin was about to reply, but there was something in the boy's voice that caused him to pause. There was pride, but it was tinged with doubt and fear. Despite the steadiness of his aim, Barundin could tell that Theoland was frightened, terrified in fact. The lad's courage struck Barundin heavily, and he glanced back to see the wailing women and children, huddled under the shadow of the north wall, the bodies of their fathers and husbands around them. In that moment, his anger drained away.

'You are a brave manling, Theoland,' said Barundin. 'But you are not yet commander of the armies of Konlach. You stand alone and yet you would confound me.'

'I am Baron of Konlach,' replied Theoland. 'My uncle lies dead, slain by my sword.'

'You would kill your own kin?' said Barundin, his anger beginning to rise again. There were few crimes more serious to the dwarfs.

'He was going to command the army to attack you,' explained Theoland. 'He wanted to destroy you once you had breached Uderstir. I said it would be folly and the death of us all, but he would not listen. We struggled and I drew my sword and cut him down. He was not a good ruler.'

Barundin did not know how to reply. That he owed the lad a debt now, for saving dwarf lives, was beyond question, but he was an enemy and a kin-slayer. Mixed emotion played across the king's face. Eventually he lowered Grudgesettler and glared up at the young baron.

'You would honour the debt of the Vessals?' the king asked. 'One half of the contents of the coffers, and the body of Silas Vessal to be turned over to me?'

Theoland holstered his pistols and dismounted. He flicked up the visor of his lion helm and extended a hand.

'I would honour their debt, as you would honour the people you can spare,' said Theoland.

Barundin gave the order for the army to allow the women and children to leave the castle, and they did so quickly, crying and screaming, pointing at fallen loved ones, some running to give one last hug or kiss to a dead father, son or brother. Soon the castle was empty but for the dwarfs and Theoland.

Another rider came in, bearing a corpse across the saddle of his horse. He flung it down at Barundin's feet.

'Obious Vessal,' said Theoland, kicking the body onto its back. The man was middle-aged, his black hair peppered with grey. His chest plate had been torn nearly in half by an axe blow, exposing shattered ribs and torn lungs. 'Silas Vessal will be in a tomb in the vaults beneath the keep. There too, we will find the treasury, and your precious gold.'

'Take me to it,' ordered Barundin.

The two of them entered a side gate of the keep, and taking a torch from the wall, Theoland led the dwarf king down a winding flight of stairs into the bowels of the castle, passing wine cellars and armouries. This was his ancestral home, denied his family for many generations, and he knew its secrets well. He located the hidden door to the treasury, clumsily hidden to Barundin's eye; he had seen the weaker joins in the stone walls immediately upon entering the arched cellar.

The treasury itself was small and barely high enough for Barundin to stand up in. In the light of the torch, half a dozen chests could be seen. Barundin dragged one out into the open, and sheared through the lock with the blade of Grudgesettler. Wrenching the lid open, he saw silver, but there were also gold coins, marked with the Stirland crown. He picked up a coin and smelled it, then gave it a taste with the tip of his tongue. There was no mistaking, this was dwarf gold, the same as had entranced his father so long ago. He picked up a handful of the coins and let them run through his fingers, a smile upon his lips.

GRUDGE SEVEN
The Gold Grudge

A SINGLE LANTERN illuminated the chamber, its yellow glow reflecting off the contents of Barundin's treasure store. Mail coats and gromril breastplates hung from the wall, shining with silver and dull grey. The gold-embossed axes and hammers, belt buckles and helms glimmered with rich warmth, bathing the king in an aura of wealth.

He sat at his counting desk, ticking off the contents of the fifteenth chest of treasure owned by the king. He picked up a coin and sniffed it, luxuriating in the scent of the gold. He remembered these coins well. Though they now bore the rune of the king, they had once been Imperial crowns, taken from the coffers of the Vessals of Uderstir. Re-smelted and purified by the goldsmiths of Zhufbar, they were now Barundin's favourites amongst all his vast wealth. They were a reminder of the heavy price paid for the betrayal of his father, and a token of his victory and the settling of the grudge.

He twirled the coin expertly through his fingers, enjoying its weight, the grooves around its edge, every little detail. It was intoxicating, the presence of so much gold in one place, and the thought of it made Barundin giddy with joy.

Like all dwarfs, his desire for gold went beyond mere avarice; it was a holy metal to his people, dug from the deepest mines, given to the dwarfs by the Ancestor God Grungni. No single dwarf knew all of the names for the different kinds of gold, for there were many types. It was a common pastime in the drinking halls to name as many different kinds of gold as possible, or even invent new words, and the dwarf that could name the most would win. Such competitions could last for hours, depending on the age, memory and inventiveness of the dwarfs in question.

This gold Barundin had dubbed dammazgromthiumgigalaz, which meant gold that he found particularly pleasing and beautiful because it was from the man grudge. He kept it all in a single chest, bound with many steel bands and made from the heaviest iron. In other chests he kept his lucky gold, his reddish gold, his moonlit and sort of silvery gold, his watergold – taken from beneath Black Water – and many others besides. A shiver of pleasure travelled down the dwarf king's spine as he placed the coin on the pile to his left and ticked it off the long list in front of him.

He took the next coin and ran a loving finger around its circumference, his light touch detecting a slight nick. This had been the last coin minted from the Vessals' gold, and he had scored it ever so slightly with the edge of Grudgesettler, as part of the ceremony during which he had crossed out the Vessals' name from the book of grudges.

To the manlings, the affair would be just a distant memory, but to Barundin it felt as if it had only happened yesterday, though over a hundred years had passed. Arbrek had still been alive then, and it had been before Tharonin's disappearance in the mines of Grungankor Stokril. He wondered idly what had become of Theoland. He had last seen him in his middle years, lord of two baronies and becoming an important member of the Count of Stirland's court. But then time had passed by and old age had claimed him before Barundin had the chance to visit him again. Such was the trouble with making friendships with manlings; they lasted such a short time, it was almost not worth the effort.

The memories continued, of Dran's wedding to Thrudmila of Karak Norn, when Barundin had sent the old Reckoner a silver letter-opener in the shape of Dran's favourite axe, with a reminder to keep in touch. Dran was now at the ripe old age of five hundred, and had fathered two daughters. From his last letter, he was apparently trying hard for a son, and enjoying being pestered by the women in his life.

Barundin smiled wryly. His mother had died not long after he had been born, and he had been raised by the other dwarf lords, amongst them his older brother, Dorthin, and the Runelord Arbrek. Now the closest thing to family that Barundin had was Hengrid Dragonfoe, who he spent much time with, drinking and reminiscing about the skaven and grobi wars.

A melancholy settled upon Barundin that even his gold could not cheer, and he packed away the remaining coins, uncounted. As he used his seven secret keys to lock the door to his vault, he came to a decision. Emerging from the hidden passage leading to his treasury, he called for a servant to send word to the thanes.

He would be holding a dinner that night in honour of the fiftieth anniversary of Arbrek's death, and they were all to attend, for he had an important announcement to make.

THE AUDIENCE HALL blazed with hundreds of candles and lanterns, illuminating the platters of sizzling pork and trestled troughs creaking with chickens, bowls filled with mountains of roasted, boiled and mashed potatoes, and all manner of other solid but tasty fare that the dwarfs liked to banquet on. The beer had been flowing well, but not recklessly, for the dwarfs present knew that they were gathered for a solemn occasion. Barundin wore a likeness of Arbrek – an ancestor badge – on a gold chain around his neck as a mark of respect and memory. Many others were also wearing his badge, on necklaces and brooches or hanging from their belts or as beard clasps.

When news of the king's banquet had gone through the hold, it had been accompanied by much rumour and gossip, for he had not thrown such a feast for many years, not since his two hundred and eightieth birthday. Some thought that perhaps he was going to announce a new war, as had been his custom in the past, or that a new grudge had arisen. Others said that the king was past such foolish displays, and would not risk the relative peace that they had enjoyed for the best part of a century.

Still, the dark mutterings persisted, even as the cooks and serving wenches of the royal kitchens grumbled about such short notice, and the trade clans rubbed their hands and negotiated with the king's agents for the best prices for their meat, bread and other produce they made or bought from the manlings.

They claimed that the grobi were returning, that Grungankor Stokril had been attacked in recent months. Word came less regularly from the distant mines and the disappearance of Tharonin had caused a stir for several weeks. His clan had denied that he was dead, and were not at all keen to discuss the matter, and so the idle speculation continued.

Others, who claimed to be better informed, said that armies had been gathering in the north: the dark armies of Chaos. There was said to be an evil host assembling, the likes of which had not been seen since the Great War against Kislev, and their alliance with Emperor Magnus. News from the distant hold in Norsca, Kraka Drak, seemed to confirm this, for the Norse were on the move in large numbers, and gathering their war parties.

Such murmurings were commonplace in a dwarf hold, but when there started to come tales from the east, those who would normally ignore such prattling began to take notice. Manling warriors, fierce and courageous, had been seen fighting amongst themselves across the frozen, desolate lands of Zorn Uzkul, east of the High Pass; some claimed to select their strongest leaders for a coming invasion.

The greatest fuel to the fires of rumour, though, were accounts from Zharr Naggrund, the barren plains far across the Dark Lands, where the Zharri–dum dwelt. Their furnaces were said to be filling the sky with a great pall of smoke, day after day, month after month. Such news was greeted with dismay by young and old alike, for it had been many years since the dwarfs had fought against their distant, twisted kin.

It was with some expectation, then, that the dwarf thanes gathered in the audience chamber and feasted on roast duck and grilled venison, quaffing tankards of ale and swapping their theories concerning Barundin's announcement.

The king let all of the idle chatter wash over him as he sat at the high table, surrounded by his closest advisors. Dromki Quickbeard, the new runelord, sat on one side of him, Hengrid on the other. Rimbal Wanazaki was there also, now one of the advisors to the Engineers Guild steam engine council. Thagri sat a little way down the table, with two of the more important thanes between him and the king, and the rest of the table was filled with various cousins and nephews. All except one chair, which stood empty. Barundin looked at the chair with a heavy heart, ignoring the chatter around him. Filling his tankard, he stood, and the hall hushed quietly, the hubbub of feasting replaced with the occasional murmur and whisper of expectancy.

'My friends and kin,' began Barundin, holding up his tankard. 'I thank you all for coming this day, and on such short notice. We are gathered here to pay respects to the spirit of Arbrek Silverfingers. He dwells now in the Halls of the Ancestors, where I am sure his advice is as pointed and appreciated as it was here.'

Barundin cleared his throat and lowered his mug to his chest, clasping it in both hands. Those around the table stifled their groans, for they knew this was Barundin's 'speaking pose', and it was a sign that he was likely to talk for quite some time.

'As you know, Arbrek was like a second father to me,' said Barundin. 'And after my father's death, perhaps the closest thing I had to family. Over the years that I knew him, and they were too few, he was never shy of correcting me or disagreeing with my opinion. Like any proper dwarf, he spoke little, but spoke his mind. Every word from his lips was as crafted and considered as the runes that he created, and certainly just as valuable.

'And though the worth of a life such as his cannot be easily measured, I would say that his greatest gift to me was my axe, Grudgesettler. It was forged with purpose over a great many years. So to did Arbrek forge my purpose for all the years that I knew him. Without his firm guidance, his looks of disapproval, and those odd moments of praise, I might have never succeeded as king. Though my companions and advisors are a comfort to me, and their wisdom always heeded, it is the words of Arbrek Silverfingers that I now greatly miss.

'And so I ask you, the leaders of Zhufbar, to raise your cups in thanks to Arbrek and his deeds in life, and to his memory now that he has passed on.'

There were no raucous cheers, no grandiose declarations. The company rose to their feet, lifting their tankards above their heads, and as one, they declared:

'To Arbrek!'

Barundin took a gulp of his ale, as much to fortify himself as to toast the memory of the dead runelord. While the other dwarfs seated themselves, he remained standing, once again assuming his stance with his mug held tightly in front of him.

'I have been king of Zhufbar through tough times,' he told the throng. 'We have fought wars and battled vile enemies, to protect our realm and to protect our honour. I am proud to be your king, and we have achieved much together.'

He stood silent for a moment. He was unsure about the next part of his speech, though he had practised it many times. Finally he took a deep breath and then spoke again.

'But there is one duty of a king that I have not fulfilled,' Barundin said, to the obvious puzzlement of his guests. 'I am healthy and in the prime of my life, and though I would like nothing better than to be your king for centuries to come, there is a time when one must face their own future.'

By now the dwarfs were thoroughly confused, and looked at each other with quizzical expressions, whispering to one another and raising their eyebrows. Some scowled in disapproval of the king's teasing speech.

'I am of a mind that Zhufbar needs an heir,' said Barundin, to a mixture of gasps, sighs and claps. 'I shall take a wife, and provide Zhufbar with a king to be, or a queen as nature sees fit.'

'I accept!' declared a voice from the back of the hall.

The dwarfs turned to see Thilda Stoutarm standing upon her bench. Her offer was greeted with laughter, including her own. Thilda was nearly eight hundred years old, had seven children of her own and owned not one of her original teeth, although her mouth was filled with gilded replacements. Now thane of the Dourskinsson clan after the death of her husband over seventy years ago, she was the terror of the bachelor thanes.

'Your offer, I must gratefully but politely decline,' said Barundin with a grin.

'Suit yourself,' said Thilda, downing the contents of her mug and sitting down again.

'I decline not on personal grounds, but on principal,' Barundin continued. 'I intend to wed a bride not of Zhufbar, to strengthen our ancestral bonds with another hold. For all of my reign, we have for the most part battled alone, for they have been our wars to fight. However, times are not comfortable, bad news increases by the month. I fear a time when the strength of Zhufbar alone will not hold back the enemies that will come against us, and for this reason I seek alliance with one of the other great clans, to bind their future with that of mine, and through that to secure Zhufbar for future generations.'

Though there were a few moans of disappointment from thanes that had perhaps hoped Barundin would choose a wife from amongst their clan, for the most part this announcement was greeted with claps of approval. It was a long tradition of the dwarfs to intermarry between clans and holds, to secure trade deals, renew oaths and sometimes, though rarely, even out of love.

'In the morning I shall send forth messengers to the other holds,' declared the king. 'Let it be known all across the dwarf realms that Barundin of Zhufbar seeks a bride!'

There was much cheering and clapping at this, even from those miserable dwarfs who had had their hopes raised, then dashed. If nothing else, a royal wedding would mean visitors, and visitors always brought gold with them.

IT WAS SEVERAL months before the first of the replies came back to Zhufbar. The cousin of the king of Karak Kadrin offered his daughter's hand in marriage, as did several other thanes from the hold. From Karaz-a-Karak, heads of important mining and trade clans offered hefty dowries for Barundin to court their daughters and nieces, while a lone offer from Karak Hirn promised Barundin a mine in the Grey Mountains. Others arrived, week after week, and Barundin put everything in charge of the Loremaster Thagri.

Declarations and histories were sent, extolling the honour and virtues of the prospective clans and brides, and for each one, Thagri searched the records of Zhufbar to find common history with the clans entreating the king. Some were dismissed out of hand, for being too poor, or not the right sort. Others made the second stage of selection, and servants of the king were sent forth to talk directly with the thanes making the propositions, not least to prove the existence of the proposed betrothed.

The accounts of these fact-finding missions began to dribble in, brought by runners and gyrocopter from across the World's Edge and Grey Mountains. Some included pictures of the prettiest candidates, drawn by Barundin's agents to help the king make his choice.

It was nearly a year after his announcement when Barundin had narrowed down the field to half a dozen likely looking lasses, and then the real horse-trading began. The question of dowries and wedding expenses were raised, of payment for Barundin's warriors to escort the bride-to-be to Zhufbar, and many other financial details, all of which Barundin and his advisors scrutinised, reread and checked through countless times.

Finally a decision was made, which Barundin announced on the first day of the New Year. He would marry Helda Gorlgrindal, a niece of the king of Karak Kadrin, three times removed. She was said to be of good health, strong of arm, and was only a little younger than Barundin. As a brother-in-law to King Ironfist, her father was considerably wealthy, and also commanded the king's ear on occasion. Barundin had agreed a date for the wedding, to be held on the summer solstice that year.

A LOUD KNOCKING on his chamber doors roused Barundin to a semblance of consciousness. His head pounded, his mouth felt like a rat had crawled into it and died, and his stomach was turning loops. He was sprawled on the covers of his bed, half dressed and covered in flour. The stench of ale permeated the room. He rolled over, ignoring the banging that was surely only inside his head, and came face to face with a plate of fried potatoes on top of which sat a half-eaten sausage. The banging continued, and he covered his head with a pillow. 'Bog off!' he grumbled.

He heard someone calling his name through the door, but diligently put them out of his mind, instead trying not to concentrate on anything because it simply made his head hurt more. He knew it had been a mistake to agree to Hengrid's invitation to organise his boar's night, his final day of celebration of bachelorhood.

Hengrid's plan had been simple: to disguise the king and go roistering through the pubs of Zhufbar. He had dyed the king's beard and, through a judicious use of rouge obtained from a lady of the Empire in some shady deal that Hengrid had not detailed, darkened the king's skin to appear like an old miner.

With several of the others, including Thagri and his cousin Ferginal, they had spent the night carousing in the many taverns of the hold, unfettered by the king's status. Now the ale, of which he had consumed more than he had ever done before, was returning to haunt Barundin.

He felt a hand on his shoulder and he spun over and slapped it away, eyes tightly shut against the light of a lantern held close by.

'I swear if you don't leave me alone, I'll have you banished,' the king growled.

His stomach lurched and the king sat up, eyes wide open. He did not even see who was beside his bed, but simply shoved them out of the way before stumbling to the cold fireplace and throwing up noisily. After several minutes, he was feeling a little better, and drank from the mug of water that had been thrust into his hands some time during the unpleasant proceedings.

Splashing the remainder on his face, he pushed himself to his feet and stood wobbling for a moment. He staggered backwards and sat down heavily on the bed, the mug dropping from his fingers, which felt like a bunch of fat sausages. Blearily, he focussed on the room, and saw a stone, roughly conical in shape, leaning against the wall in one corner. It was etched with several runes and painted red and white. There was a helmet of some kind atop its tip.

'What is that?' he muttered, peering at the strange object.

'It is a warning stone used by miners,' a familiar voice said. 'It is used to block the entrances to unsafe passageways or corridors still under construction. And on top of that, I believe, is the helmet of an Ironbreaker.'

Barundin looked around and saw Ottar Urbarbolg, one of the thanes. Next to him stood Thagri, looking slightly better for wear than the king, but not by much. It was the loremaster who had spoken.

"Where did I get them?' asked Barundin. 'Why are they in my room?'

'Well, last night, you thought the wardstone would be a great gift for your betrothed,' explained Thagri. 'The helmet, well that was Hengrid's idea. Something about a boar's night tradition. Luckily, all the ale had washed the dye from your beard and face, and the Ironbreaker from whose head you removed it thought better of lamping the king, though he was undecided for a moment.'

'And my ribs ache,' moaned the king.

'That would be the belly punching competition you had with Snorri Gundarsson,' said Thagri with a wince. 'You insisted since he beat you in a rorkaz.'

'Nothing wrong with a friendly skuf. Anyway, what in the seven peaks of Trollthingaz do you want at this hour?' demanded the king, cradling his head in his hands. 'Can't it wait until tomorrow?'

'It is tomorrow,' said Thagri. 'We tried to wake you yesterday, but you punched Hengrid in the eye without even waking up.'

'Oh,' said Barundin, flapping a hand ineffectually in Thagri's direction.

The loremaster understood the vague gesture, as only someone that had been in the exact same predicament the day before could. He poured another mug of water and passed it to Barundin, who took a sip, retched slightly and then tipped the contents down the back of his shirt. With a yell and a shudder, he was more awake, and turned his attention to Ottar.

'So, what are you doing here?' he demanded.

'Our family records have something that impacts on the wedding, my king,' said Ottar, glancing towards the loremaster for reassurance, who nodded encouragingly.

'What do you mean, "impacts"?' said Barundin, his eyes narrowing.

'I'm afraid you'll have to cancel it,' said Ottar, stepping back as Barundin turned a venomous glare towards him.

'Cancel the wedding?' snapped the king. 'Cancel the bloody wedding? It's only a month away, you idiot, why would I cancel it now?'

'There is an ancient dispute between the Urbarbolgi and the Troggkurioki, the clan of your intended,' said Thagri, stepping in front of Ottar, who was now decidedly pale with fear. 'You know that as king you cannot marry into a clan that is at odds with a clan of Zhufbar.'

'Oh, buggrit,' said Barundin, flopping on to the bed. 'Send for my servants, I need a wash and some clean clothes. And I've got the rutz very badly. I'll attend to this matter this afternoon.'

The two hovered for a moment, until Barundin sat up, the mug in his fist. It looked as if he was going to throw it at the pair, and they fled.

Barundin winced heavily as the door slammed behind them, then pushed himself to his feet. He gazed at the sausage on his bed, picked it up and sniffed it. His stomach growled, so he gave a shrug and took a bite.

'THE WHOLE MATTER revolves around Grungak Lokmakaz,' explained Thagri.

It was in fact evening before Barundin had felt like facing anything except the inside of his water closet. They were sitting in one of Thagri's studies, and the loremaster had a pile of books and documents spread out on the desk in front of him. Ottar sat with his hands clasped in his lap, his face impassive.

'That's a mine up north, isn't it?' said Barundin. 'Not far south of Peak Pass?'

'That's the one, my king,' said Ottar, leaning forward. 'It was dug by my forefathers, an offshoot on my great-uncle's side. Those thieving Troggkurioki stole it from us!'

'But isn't Peak Pass the ancestral lands of Karak Kadrin?' said Barundin, rubbing at his forehead. His head was still sore, although the excruciating pain he had felt for most of the day had been staved off with another couple of pints of beer before the meeting. 'Why is a Zhufbar clan digging around there?'

'That doesn't matter,' said Ottar. 'We found the gold, we registered our claim, and we dug the mine. It's all perfectly accounted for.'

'So what happened?' asked Barundin, turning to Thagri in the hope of a more unbiased account.

'Well, the mine was overrun by trolls and orcs,' said Thagri. 'The clan was all but wiped out, and those who survived fled back here to Zhufbar.'

'Then those damn Troggkurioki took it from us!' said Ottar hotly. 'Jump in our tombs just as quick, I would say.'

'They claimed the mine by right of re-conquest,' explained Thagri, holding up a letter. 'This was also properly registered by the loremaster of Karak Kadrin at the time, who sent a copy of his records to the Urbarbolgi.'

'At the time?' said Barundin, glancing between Ottar and Thagri.

'Yes,' said Thagri, consulting his notes. 'The original claim was made three thousand, four hundred and twenty-six years ago. The re-conquest took place some four hundred and thirty-eight years later.'

'Three thousand years ago?' spluttered Barundin, rounding on Ottar. 'You want me to cancel my wedding because of a dispute you had three thousand years ago?'

'Three thousand years or yesterday, the matter isn't settled,' said Ottar defiantly. 'As thane of the Urbarbolgi, I must dispute your right to marry into the Troggkuriok clan.'

'Can he do that?' asked Barundin, looking at Thagri, who nodded. 'Listen here, Ottar, I'm not happy with this, not happy at all.'

'It's in the book of grudges,' added Thagri. 'As king, it is your duty to see it removed.'

'So, what do you want me to do?' said Barundin.

'It's quite simple,' said Ottar, steepling his fingers to his chin. 'You must renegotiate the dowry to include turning over Grungak Lokmakaz to its rightful owners.'

'But the dowry and expenses have been settled for two months now,' said Barundin with a scowl. 'If I start changing the conditions of the wedding, they might pull out altogether.'

Ottar shrugged expansively, in a manner that suggested that although he understood the nature of the king's dilemma, it was, ultimately, not the thane's problem to deal with. Barundin waved him out of the room and sat growling for a few minutes, chewing the inside of his cheek. He looked at Thagri, who had neatly stacked his documents and sat waiting the king's orders.

'We'll send a messenger to start the negotiations,' said Barundin.

'Already done,' replied the loremaster. 'This matter came to light several weeks ago and, what with you being so busy, I took it upon myself to try to smooth things between the clans without having to bother with you.'

'You did, did you?' said Barundin heavily.

'I have your best interests at heart, Barundin,' said Thagri. The king looked at him sharply, for the loremaster seldom used anybody's first name, especially his. Thagri's expression was earnest, and Barundin realised that he had indeed followed his best intentions.

'Very well. So what has been the reply?' asked the king.

'You must travel to Grungak Lokmakaz yourself,' said Thagri. 'The thane of the mines, an uncle-in-law-to-be, wishes to speak to you personally about the matter and to sign the documents yourself. I think he just wants to have a look at the king that's going to be marrying his niece, because he's got nothing to lose by being connected to the royal family of Zhufbar.'

'Very well, I'll head north for a short trip,' said Barundin. 'Have arrangements made for me to travel three days from now.'

'Actually, the arrangements had already been made,' admitted Thagri with a sheepish look. 'You head off the day after tomorrow.'

'Do I indeed?' said Barundin, anger rising. 'And when did the loremaster inherit the right to order the king's affairs in such a way?'

'When the king decided to get married, but can't organise his way out of his own bedchamber,' replied Thagri with a smile.

IT WAS COLDER, Barundin was sure, than around Zhufbar. He knew that they were only some one hundred and fifty miles from his hold, and that the climate did not change that dramatically, but he knew in his heart that it was colder up north.

The mine itself wasn't much to look at; it was little more than a watch tower over the pit entrance, and a few goat herds straying across the mountainside. He could not see Peak Pass from where he stood, although he knew that it lay just over the next ridgeline. On the northern slopes of the pass lay Karak Kadrin, where his future rinn lived.

'Come on, you ufdi,' called a voice from the tunnel entrance, and he saw Ferginal gesturing for him to follow.

The king passed out of the mountain sun into the lantern-lit twilight of Grungak Lokmakaz. The entrance to the mineworkings was low and wide, but soon split into several narrower tunnels before opening up into a much larger space: the chamber of the thane.

The hall was thronged with dwarfs, and in their midst, upon a throne of granite, sat Thane Nogrud Kronhunk. Barundin felt rather than saw or heard Ottar beside him, bristling with anger, as he stood between the two thanes. He offered a hand to Nogrud, who shook it ferociously, patting Barundin on the shoulder as he did so.

'Ah, King Barundin,' said Nogrud, with a quick glance at the dwarfs around him. 'So glad that you have come to visit.'

'Always good to meet the family,' said Barundin quietly, keeping a smile fixed on his face, although he was seething inside.

'I trust your journey was uneventful,' continued Nogrud.

'We saw some bears, but that was all,' Barundin told him.

'Ah, good,' said Nogrud, waving the king to sit upon a chair beside his throne. 'I take it you came by way of Karag Klad and Karaz Mingol-khrum?'

'Yes,' said Barundin, suppressing a sigh. Why was it that relatives always wanted to talk about the route you took to get somewhere? 'There have been early snows around Karag Nunka, so we had to take the eastern route.'

'Splendid, splendid,' said Nogrud.

He clapped his hands and a handful of serving wenches brought in pitchers of ale and stools for the king's three companions: Ottar, Ferginal and Thagri. A wave of the hand dismissed the other dwarfs in the room, except for an elderly retainer who sat to one side, a book in his hands.

'This is Bardi Doklok,' the thane introduced the other dwarf. 'He's my bookmaster.'

'You are Thagri?' Bardi asked, looking at the loremaster, who smiled and nodded. 'If we get time before you return to Zhufbar, I would dearly like to talk to you about this word press contraption they have supposedly built down in Karaz-a-Karak.'

'The writing machine?' said Thagri with a scowl. 'Yes, we probably should discuss what we want to do about that. Engineers getting ideas beyond their station, if you ask me.'

'Perhaps,' said Barundin, interrupting the pair. 'However, we have other matters at hand. I want to be away within a few days, because I still haven't stood for my final measurements on my wedding shirt. These delays are costing me a fortune.'

'Well, let us endeavour to be as quick as possible,' said Nogrud.

'It's simple,' blurted Ottar. 'Relinquish your false claim to these mines, and the matter is settled.'

'False claim?' snarled Nogrud. 'My ancestors bled and died for these mines! That's more than you ungrimi ever did for them!'

'Why you wanazkrutak!' snapped Ottar, standing up and thrusting a finger towards the thane. 'You stole these mines, and you know it! That's my gold you're wearing on your fingers right now!'

'Wanakrutak?' said Nogrud, his voice rising in pitch. 'You big hold thanes think that you can throw your weight around anywhere, don't you? Well, this is my bloody mine, and no stinking elgtrommi clan is going to take it from me.'

'Shut up!' bellowed Barundin, standing up and knocking his chair over. 'The pair of you! We're not here to trade insults; we're here to sort out this bloody mess so that I can get married! Now, sit down, and listen.'

'I have found a precedent,' said Thagri, looking at Bardi more than the two thanes. 'Both clans have equal claim to the mine. That much can be deduced from the original founding and the right of re-conquest. However, since the re-conquest took place less than five hundred years after the abandonment, the Troggkurioki should have offered the Urbarbolgi the right to settle by means of a fighting fee; what you might call expenses of war. They did not do so, and thus they did not legally secure full rights to the mine.'

'And thus, the Troggkurioki owe expenses on one tenth of the mine's profits to the Urbarbolgi?' said Bardi.

'That is correct,' said Thagri with a sly smile.

Bardi scratched his chin and glanced at his thane, before producing a piece of parchment from the inside of his robe.

'Here I have a record that shows, without doubt, the expenses of the re-conquest campaign exceeded the profits of the mine for that first five hundred year period,' said Bardi with a triumphant gleam in his eye. 'That means that no right to settle need be granted, and thus the Urbarbolgi in fact owe the Troggkuri war expenses of not less than one third of their expenditure from the moment they entered the mine to the sealing of the claim by re-conquest.'

Thagri stared open-mouthed as the bookmaster, amazed by the guile of the dwarf. He turned to the others. 'This may take some time,' he said. 'I fear that you may also find it extremely tedious to witness us bandying claim and counter-claim. Might I suggest that you retire to more suitable chambers while your host entertains you in a more convivial fashion?'

'Sounds good,' said Barundin. 'Let's see what beer you've got, eh?'

'Ah,' said Nogrud. 'There we shall certainly find common ground. My brewmaster has a particularly fine red beer just matured two weeks ago. Smooth? I tell you, there's more grip on a snowflake.'

The two book-keepers waited until the group was outside the hall, then looked at each other.

It was Bardi that broke the silence. 'This could take weeks, and neither of us wants that,' he said.

'Look, let's just agree that the Urbarbolgi will pay right of settlement and war expenses in retrospect, and thus entitle them to a ten per cent claim,' suggested Thagri.

'Are you sure that'll be agreed by them?' said Bardi. 'That leaves them out of pocket for several centuries yet.'

'The king will pay,' explained Thagri. 'He's desperate for this wedding to go without a hitch. It's going to cost him more to delay it than to pay the settlement. Your lord gets a one-off payment from Zhufbar, Ottar's clan get an annual payment for the next five hundred years. Only Barundin loses, but he's losing already, so that doesn't really come into it.'

'Fair enough,' said Bardi. 'I've got a keg of Bugman's stowed away in my chambers.'

'XXXXXX?' asked Thagri, eyes alight.

'No, but it is Finest Dirigible, which I am told travels very well,' said Bardi. 'Let us seal the deal over a mug? We'll leave the ufdi to their own devices and tell them what we've agreed this evening.'

'Good idea,' grinned Thagri.

ALTHOUGH IT PAINED him to sign away so much gold in one stroke of the writing chisel, Barundin dragged the parchment towards him and dipped the pen in the inkwell that Bardi had provided.

'This is the only way?' Barundin asked Thagri, as he had already asked many times.

'In the longer term, yes,' sighed Thagri.

'Let's just settle the matter and your wedding will go without a hitch,' said Ottar, who stood to one side, running a finger along the spines of the books that were stacked high on the shelves of Bardi's library.

'That's all right for you to say – you're not paying up front,' said Barundin.

'I hardly call getting one tenth of my own bloody mine a good deal,' said Ottar, turning towards the king. 'There'll be some who think I've signed away our heritage. Look, I've signed, add your mark and we can leave tomorrow and forget the whole thing.'

'Where's Ferginal?' asked Barundin, laying down the pen and earning a scowl from Thagri. 'We need him as a witness from Zhufbar.'

'He went out drinking with some miners,' said Thagri. 'He can sign later.'

'It's not really a witness if they're not present when I sign,' said Barundin heavily. 'That's the point, isn't it?'

'Just a formality, really,' Thagri assured him. 'Nobody doubts the word of a king.'

As Barundin lifted the writing chisel once again, the door opened with a bang and Ferginal rushed in.

'Where've you been?' demanded Barundin. 'We've been waiting for you!'

'Don't sign it!' gasped Ferginal.

'What?' said Barundin.

'The agreement, it's a dirty trick,' said Ferginal. 'There's been no gold in these mines for six centuries!'

'No gold?' said Barundin and Ottar together.

'What do you mean, no gold?' said Thagri, gripping Ferginal by the arms.

'I was talking to some of the miners,' Ferginal breathlessly explained. 'There's plenty of iron ore and coal, but they've not seen a fresh nugget of gold here for over six hundred years.'

'The cheating swine!' roared Barundin, slamming down the pen as he stood. 'They tried to swindle me into buying an empty gold mine!'

'Does this mean the wedding is off?' asked Thagri, pulling a rag from his belt to mop up the ink spilling across the desk.

'By Grungni's beard, it does not!' said Barundin. 'For his elgi tricks, Nogrud is going to sign over this mine to me, lock, stock and every ounce of ore. He'll feel the taste of Grudgesettler if he tries to argue.'

'So it's war again, is it?' sighed Ferginal, leaning against the wall.

At that moment, Bardi entered. Thagri leapt upon him, snatching up the collar of his robe in both hands.

'Try to swindle us, would you?' snarled the loremaster. 'Thought you'd pull the mail over my eyes, did you? I'll see that the Council of Lore Writers has you chased into the hills for this!'

Bardi snatched himself away from the loremaster's angry grip and straightened the front of his robe. 'Nonsense,' he snapped. 'Not once did myself or my lord mention gold in the agreement, merely the profits from the mines.'

'The mine's almost worthless,' said Ottar. 'You've bled it dry.'

'Well, you'll not be wanting it back then,' said Bardi with a hint of smugness.

'Oh, we'll have it back alright,' said Barundin. 'By Grimnir's nose ring, we'll have it back! Just you think on that when our cannons are a-knocking at the doors to your room.'

'I came in to tell you that a messenger from Karak Kadrin has arrived,' said Bardi. 'Before you came we sent word of your coming and the, er, situation, and I expect this is King Ironfist's reply.'

'Like it or not, if he defends what you've done here, he'll face my wrath as well,' said Barundin.

'You would not go to war with another hold, surely?' said Bardi.

'Not if it can be avoided,' replied Barundin.

GRUDGE EIGHT
The First Grudge

WINTER LINGERED LATE in the mountains, and the slopes of Peak Pass were dusted with snow all the way to the bottom of the valley. The pine forests farther up the mountainsides were swathed in snow, barely visible as dark brown patches across the whiteness of the World's Edge Mountains.

Just visible to the east, before the pass turned somewhat northward, the silvery flanks of Karaz Byrguz could be seen, and atop it a great fire burned; it was a beacon tower of Karak Kadrin, the hold of King Ungrim Ironfist. Westward was the much smaller mount of Karag Tonk, its foot obscured by boulders and broken trees from recent avalanches.

The pass itself narrowed between the flanks of Karag Krukaz and Karag Rhunrilak; steep-sided and laborious to negotiate as the undulating valley crossed into the western mountains of the tall peaked range.

Just to the west was the summit of Karaz Undok, beneath which lay the gates to Karak Kadrin itself. Although many miles distant, Barundin could just see the great stone faces and battlements carved into the mountain tops surrounding the ancient hold, and the great span of the Skybridge that linked Karak Kadrin with the smaller settlements of Ankor Ekrund.

The wind was fierce, blowing down the valley from the east and north, with a biting edge to it that even the sturdy dwarf king could feel. His cheeks were red and his eyes watered in the early spring air, and he had to keep wiping a hand across his face to clear his vision. He held his helm under one arm, his shield propped up against his left leg as he turned his head to survey his force. The entire strength of Zhufbar had been massed for this battle, from beardlings that were raising their axes for the first time to veterans like himself that had fought in the foetid tunnels of Dukankor Grobkaz-a-Gazan.

Glinting ancestor icons were held aloft beside fluttering standards of deep reds and blues, amongst them the towering banner of Zhufbar held by Hengrid.

They stood on the southern flank of the pass, at the centre of the Zhufbar throng. To their right stood several thousand clansdwarfs, each carrying a sturdy axe or hammer and a steel shield embossed with symbols of dragons and anvils, lightning bolts and ancestor faces, each according to his own taste. Beyond them waited the Ironbreakers, formed into small, dense regiments. Little could be seen of the dwarfs themselves under their layers of gromril, rune-encrusted armour: even their beards were protected by articulated steel sheaths.

On the left of the line, Barundin had drawn up the greater strength of his missile troops. Rank upon rank of thunderers and quarrellers stood upon the mountainside, each row far enough back to overlook the lines in front. Behind them were the cannons, bolt shooters and stone lobbers of the engineers, who paced to and fro between their machines, making adjustments, throwing fluttering scraps of cloth in the air to judge wind strength and direction, and generally preparing for the coming battle.

Ramming his helmet onto his head and picking up his shield, Barundin picked his way down the mountainside, heading for his hammerers. As he did so, he looked across to the northern slopes of the pass, and the huge host of Karak Kadrin.

The first thing that caught the eye was its sheer size, nearly twice the number of warriors that Zhufbar could muster. Zhufbar, in its way, was isolated and well protected by the Empire to its west and the impenetrable mountains to the east. Karak Kadrin, on the other hand, held the pass, and here countless invasions of the mountains and the lands beyond had begun and been turned back by the might of the Slayer King and his army.

The slayers themselves were immediately noticeable, and though they stood far to the east, the splash of orange across the dirt and snow could not be missed. Forced to take the Slayer Oath for some real or perceived shame, slayers swore their lives to a glorious death, and for the most part wandered the world alone seeking out trolls, giants and other large monsters to defeat in battle, or die fighting a worthy foe. That was the only way a slayer could atone for his shame. They were dressed in the style that Grimnir himself was said to have done as he marched north at the dawn of time to slay the Chaos hordes that had been unleashed upon the world, and shut the gate that had been opened in the far north. They wore little more than trousers or loincloths, and their bare skin was heavily tattooed or covered in war paint, both with runes of vengeance and punishment, and geometric patterns.

The slayers' hair and beards were dyed bright orange, and heavily spiked using lime and other substances, so that their it stood up in great crests, and their beards jutted out in vicious points, often tipped with steel and gromril spikes. Some wore heavy chains piercing their skin, and nose rings and other jewellery. Altogether they were an outlandish lot, and Barundin was glad that their travels rarely took them to Zhufbar – although many passed through now and then – on their way to the flooded caverns of Karak Varn.

The army itself mustered under banners of gold and red and green, and under great scowling faces of Grimnir, most revered of the ancestor gods by the dwarfs of Zhufbar. It was in Karak Kadrin that the greatest shrine to Grimnir had been built, and for this reason the king was patron to many warriors, and his army was rightly feared and guessed to be second only to the great host of Karaz-a-Karak, serving the high king himself.

For all its size and ferocity, the army of Karak Kadrin could not compare with the army of Zhufbar in one respect: war engines. Zhufbar was renowned for the number and skill of its engineers, and above the mass of Barundin's warriors, gyrocopters buzzed to and fro, landing occasionally then taking off, like gigantic flies. The batteries of cannons behind the king were immaculately kept, and ammunition was in plentiful supply. Such was the demand to be in the Zhufbar Engineers Guild that applicants from across the dwarf empire came to study there, but only the very best were chosen to be admitted to the hold's greatest secrets. Every crew, from the swab-dwarf to the gun captain, was amongst the best gunners in the world, and utterly reliable.

A horn sounded from the east and was taken up by others along the pass, the warning note reverberating along the valley, until a deafening chorus of echoes resounded from both slopes. Barundin looked to his right and saw the slayers heading for the lower slopes, eager to get to grip with their foes.

Behind the horn blast, another sound could now be heard: distant drums. Steadily they pounded, a brisk beat that shook the mountain tops. For such noise, there must be hundreds of them, thought Barundin. The same thought must have occurred to many of the other dwarfs, for mutterings passed along both lines, some of excitement, others of consternation.

It was several minutes of the incessant beating, grinding on Barundin's nerves, until the first attack came. In a great horde they poured along the valley floor, coming from the east, jogging forwards to the beating of the drums.

The army of Vardek Crom, the Conqueror, Herald of Archaon.

The northmen were savages, dressed in crude furs and poorly woven wool. They wore scraps of armour, the occasional breastplate and a few links of mail, and carried vicious-looking axes and shields fitted with spikes and blades.

Horsemen rode at the front of the line, armed with long spears, axes and swords hanging at their belts. Their steeds were not the mighty warhorses of the Empire, but smaller, sturdier steppe ponies, sure-footed and swift. The horsemen peeled away as if part of some pre-arranged plan, allowing the first ranks of infantry to pass between them.

The marauders were arranged in tribal groups, gathered around their ghastly totems of bones and tattered flags, each bearing some mark to identify themselves.

One group had hands nailed to their shields, another had helms fashioned from the skulls of rams. Some wore intricate wolf tooth necklaces, while yet another group were covered in bleeding cuts, careful incisions made across their skin, their blood flowing over their naked bodies like a crimson layer of armour.

They were a fearsome sight, although Barundin knew they were just manlings, so their appearance was really the only thing about them that caused any dread. They would be wild and reckless, like all manlings, and easily cut down.

There were an awful lot of them, he thought as he watched the dark mass winding its way around the pass towards him. He could see why King Ironfist had sent for aid to hold back this host. The Slayer King had sworn that he would hold the pass against these incursions from the east, while the Empire mustered their armies to the west and took on the hordes of the dread Archaon that even now were hacking and burning their way through Kislev. If the army of Vardek Crom could not be held in check, they would pour through Peak Pass into the Empire, surrounding the forces of this new Emperor, Karl Franz. Such a thing would be disastrous for the dwarfs' allies, and thus Ungrim Ironfist had led his warriors forth to stand as a bulwark against the tide rising in the east.

The messenger had been well timed, for on the brink of such a war, Barundin had been ready to open hostilities on his own account. The matter of the mine had not been forgotten, but the threat of the northmen gave more common cause than the mine did differences.

The war drummers increased the tempo of their beating and the marauders hastened their pace, coming on now at a run, weapons drawn. Their shouts could be heard, yelling the names of the Dark Gods, swearing their souls away for victory, cursing their foes. As their pace increased, their cohesion began to disintegrate as the more eager or faster warriors broke into headlong charges and sprinted towards the dwarfs.

The slayers headed straight at the line of marauders streaming down the pass, waving their axes and yelling their battle cries. The horsemen rode forward cautiously, hurling javelins and throwing axes at the near-naked dwarfs, before retreating quickly lest the savage, doom-laden warriors catch them.

With a tangle of flesh, metal, bone and orange hair, the two lines of warriors met, as the slayers charged directly into the midst of their foes. The fighting was brutal, with both sides unprotected against the keen blades of their enemies. The marauders outnumbered the slayers by many hundreds of warriors, yet the fearless dwarfs refused to give ground and the barbarians' advance was halted by their attack.

In the valley to the east, the tribes were bunching into a great mass, stalled by the slayers. Already the bottom of the pass was stained with blood and littered with butchered bodies. The slayers, as their numbers dwindled, gradually became surrounded, until a knot of only a few dozen remained, a blot of orange amongst the pale skin and dark hair of the Kurgan tribesmen.

As the fighting continued, Barundin saw the great host further up the valley begin to split. As others saw the new arrivals, a great moan filled the air from the dwarfs. Between the lines of marauders, short, armoured figures marched in deep phalanxes: the Dawi-Zharr, the lost dwarfs of Zharr-Naggrund.

Clad in black and bronze armour, streaming banners of blood red stitched with fell symbols of their bullgod, the Chaos dwarfs advanced. In their midst, titanic engines of destruction were pulled forward by hundreds of slaves: humans, greenskins, trolls and all manner of creatures toiled at the chains, dragging the monstrous cannons and rockets into position.

Their crews bare-skinned, branded and pierced with hooks and spines, the hellcannons, earthshakers and death rockets were pulled up the valley. Once they were in position, ogres came forward bearing massive hammers, and drove pitons into the ground, nailing down the chains that hung from the immense war engines.

Priests robed in scale coats and wearing daemon-faced iron masks walked amongst the engines, chanting liturgies to the dark god, Hashut. They sprinkled blood onto the swelling barrels of the cannons and dropped burning entrails into their muzzles. With fingers coated in crimson, they scrawled wicked runes onto the rocket batteries and consecrated massive earthshaker shells to their master.

As the rituals were completed, the daemon engines began to wake. Where once there had been inert metal, now unnatural flesh began to writhe and turn, sprouting faces and fangs, claws and tendrils. Bound within the rune-scratched iron of their machines, the daemons possessing the engines began to buck and pull at their chains, and unholy screeches and roars filled the air. Crew dwarfs with smouldering brands prodded their charges into position, while burning skulls were laden into their furnace hearts, the heat shimmer boiling up the valley, melting the snow beneath the engines.

Blood poured forth from horrid maws, while oil dripped from cogs and windlasses. Flaming hammers scalded runes of wrath onto the bound creatures, infuriating them further, while rockets were loaded onto the launch racks and shells fed into the toothy muzzles of the squat earthshakers.

The slayers were now all dead, their bodies mutilated by the victorious marauders. But the Kurgan horde held back now, just out of range of crossbow and handgun. A runner from the cannon battery came to ask Barundin if they should open fire on the barbarians. But he told him no. Instead, he instructed the engineers to move their machines around to target the monstrous creations of the Chaos dwarfs.

Even as the engineers wheeled their cannons and bolt shooters towards this new threat, the first hellcannon opened fire. Its great bronze jaw opened, revealing a sulphurous gullet that squirmed with bound magic. From the depths of its gullet, dark fire churned as it digested the souls trapped within the skulls that had been shovelled into its burning furnace. With a belching roar, the cannon vomited forth a ball of fire that arced high over the marauders, descending towards the army of Karak Kadrin.

The Chaos fire exploded on impact with the ground, consuming dozens of dwarfs within its fiery blast, their ashes scattered to the spring wind within an instant. A gaping hole had been opened in the Karak Kadrin line, as those that had survived the attack retreated from the smouldering crater it had left.

More balls of magical fire stormed towards the dwarfs, and one looped high and began to descend towards Barundin and his hammerers.

'Run!' the king bellowed, and his bodyguard needed no encouragement. As one they turned and hurried up the slope as fast as their short legs could take them, abandoning their formation in their flight.

The blast hit the ground less than two dozen yards behind Barundin, and a moment later he felt a searing wind catch his back, hurling him to the ground. As he lay there dazed, he looked over his shoulder and saw the smoking crater where he had been standing only a few heartbeats earlier. Purple and blue fire still played around its edges, and the ground shifted and melted under the deadly burning.

Rockets screamed skywards, gouting tails of actinic energy, the daemons bound within them steering their explosive bodies towards the enemy. Rippled eruptions spread along the Karak Kadrin army as the death rockets slammed into the mountainside. These were soon followed by the detonations of earthshaker shells, which burrowed into the ground before exploding, hurling up rock and earth and causing the ground to tremble. One exploded not far from Barundin just as he had clambered to his feet, and the violent undulations of the mountainside knocked him down to his knees once more. For almost a minute the tumult continued as pulses of daemonic energy spilled from the impact of the shell.

Now the dwarfs' war machines were sighted on the enemy and cannonballs screamed back down the valley, crushing Chaos dwarfs and tearing great rents in their arcane machines. Rocks inscribed with ancient grudges and curse runes filled the sky as the stone lobber battery opened fire as one, their ammunition hurtling skywards then crashing down amongst the Chaos dwarf ranks.

Bolt shooters hurled their long harpoons at the marauders, pinioning half a dozen with each hit, ripping off limbs and heads as they sheared through the packed mass of barbaric fighters. The cannons were ready to fire again as the death rockets and hellcannons once more disgorged a hail of destruction from the eastern valley, ripping great swathes in both dwarf lines.

As he gathered his hammerers around him again, converging on the standard still proudly borne aloft by Hengrid who stood shouting defiantly at the twisted cousins of the dwarf, a cannonball bounced off the earth and sheared through the chains holding down one side of a hellcannon.

With its bonds weakened, the daemonic engine reared backward, its wheels grinding of their own accord, crushing the crew beneath the steel spikes of its treads. As it turned, the remaining chains snapped and tore from the ground and it vomited forth a stream of fire and filth that burned and corroded through the cannon next to it. Attacked by its neighbour, the earthshaker screamed in pain and anger and threw itself at its own chains, ignoring the shouts and prods of its crew.

The freed hellcannon rumbled forward, carving through the Chaos dwarfs and marauders, belching flame and trampling them under its armoured wheels. Malignant energy flared from pores and gashes in its structure and the marauders turned to battle against the creature that attacked them from the rear.

Those warriors that were not fighting the rampaging hellcannon streamed down the valley once more, shields and weapons held high, screaming war cries. Hails of crossbow bolts and handgun bullets that darkened the valley in a thunderous volley greeted them. Scores of barbarians fell to the first onslaught, caught in a crossfire from both sides of Peak Pass. Their tattered flags and icons of bones and metal were raised from amongst the bloody piles and they pressed onwards, more fearful of their dire masters than the weapons of the dwarfs.

It was then that Barundin realised he could not see the horsemen. While the attention of the dwarfs had been on the war machines and marauders, they had slipped out of sight, perhaps disappearing into the woods that grew on the higher reaches of the pass's slopes.

Barundin had no time to worry about them now, as a second volley of fire slashed through hundreds of marauders clambering up the pass through its narrowest reaches. It was because of this choking point that King Ironfist had decided to make his stand here, having sent advance forces to stall and waylay the marauders' approach. Barely two hundred yards wide, with the mountainsides almost too steep to climb on each side, the narrow area was a killing ground, and the bodies of the marauders lay in heaps. Some fled the fusillade, other groups were wiped out to a man, but still several thousand were pressing forward, accompanied by baying hounds and misshapen creatures that crawled and loped amongst them.

A staccato thundering from behind attracted Barundin's attention, and he turned to look up the slope towards the cannon battery. A pair of multi-barrelled organ guns were unleashing their fire into horsemen pouring from the woods towards the war machines. Barundin smiled grimly, for his trap had worked. Drumki Quickbeard and his runesmiths had worked hard, inscribing runes of invisibility on the short-ranged war engines. Such work was normally difficult; organ guns were a new invention, less than five centuries old, and such runes were not normally intended for the unstable machines. However, the trickery had worked and the horsemen had attacked, unaware that their doom lay just in front of them, hidden from their eyes by the magic of the runes.

Turning his attention back to the valley floor, Barundin saw that most of the marauders had now passed the narrow gap and were flooding into the main part of the pass. There was already hand-to-hand fighting amongst the eastern-most regiments.

A dark mass appeared from behind the dispersing marauders, compact and menacing. Marching in perfect unison, the elite warriors of Zharr-Naggrund advanced, the dreaded Immortals of the High Prophet of Hashut. Their armour was painted black, and they wore heavy steel from head to toe. Their curled, piled beards were protected by long sheaths of metal, and parts of their armour were reinforced with solid plates of marble and granite. In their hands they carried large-bladed axes, curved and deadly. Handgun fire and crossbow quarrels rattled off their armour, leaving only a few of them dead, the others quickly filling the holes in their formation.

Gyrocopters buzzed in on attack runs, firing hails of bullets from rapid-firing, steam powered gatlers, while pilots threw makeshift bombs from their seats. Steam cannons venting scalding vapours killed several of the Immortals, but they were undeterred, never once breaking stride, their bull-headed gold standard leading the advance, a great drum made from some monstrous skull calling the step.

Barundin sent word for the Ironbreakers to intercept the Immortals, and soon his own heavily armoured warriors were marching down to the valley floor, heading directly for their despicable foes. Like two great metal beasts butting each other, the two formations met, the enchanted gromril of the Ironbreakers matched against the cursed blades of the Immortals.

Barundin had no time to spare to see how his veterans fared, for something else was moving up the valley. It strode forward, a great mechanical giant, belching smoke and fire, the air around it shimmering not just with heat but also diabolical energy. Plated with riveted iron and fashioned in the shape of a great bull-headed man, the infernal machine was rocked back as a cannonball struck it in the midriff, leaving a tearing gate.

Oil spilled from the wound like blood, and smashed
gears and broken chains could be seen through the rent
in its armour.

'A kollossus,' whispered Hengrid, and for the first time
ever, Barundin could detect fear in the fierce warrior's
voice. Not when they had faced the disgusting rat ogres,
the whirling fanatics of the night goblins, the noisome
trolls, the crackling energy of the shamans had Hengrid
ever shown a moment's hesitation; now his voice qua-
vered, if only slightly.

From firing platforms on the behemoth's shoulders,
Chaos dwarfs spewed out gouts of fire, incinerating
dwarfs by the handful as the mechanical beast stomped
through their lines. Its heavy feet crushed them with
every tread, while they tried in vain to pierce its
armoured hide with their axes. Bullets whined from its
iron plates, while shells chattered forth from a rapid-firing cannon mounted in the mouth of its bull head.

By now the cannon crews were directing all of their
fire against the kollossus. One arm was ripped away,
spilling burning fuel onto the ground and setting fire to
its right leg. A ball trailing magical fire slammed into its
knee, buckling the armour and bending the gears.
Immaterial shapes began to writhe around the
wounded metal beast as they escaped the enchanted
machineries that held them to the Chaos dwarfs' bid-
ding.

A gyrocopter swept low, its cannon drilling the head
with bullets, and as it lifted its way out of the creature's
outstretched hand, Barundin recognised the flying
machine as the one that belonged to Rimbal Wanazaki.
The king gave a cheer as the mad pilot deftly dived his
gyrocopter beneath a swinging metal hand, turning in
the air to fire into the exposed innards of the creature's
midriff.

Like a creature beset by ants, the immobilised machine was soon swarming with dwarfs, hacking and tearing at the metal plates of its legs, climbing up and firing with pistols into the slits and rents in its armour. Throwing axes scarred its metal skin, and soon there were dwarfs clambering victoriously into the cockpit behind the armoured face of its head. They abandoned its still, metal form, and Barundin signalled to the cannon crews behind him to deal the final blow.

One cannonball struck the metal giant square in the face, tearing the head clean away and hurling it to the ground in an explosion of flames and sparks. Its already damaged leg buckled under another impact, and with a screech of tearing metal and the tormented screams of escaping souls, the kollossus collapsed to its right, shattering upon the ground. A cheer rolled along both lines of dwarfs as the marauders began to fall back.

The Immortals, now realising they could be surrounded, broke off from their fighting against the Ironbreakers, retreating eastward along the pass. Everywhere, the pass was emptying of enemies, as even the hellcannons were quieted, their magic doused by the priests, teams of slaves coming forward to drag them away from the battle, keeping the valuable machines out of the clutches of the victorious dwarfs.

From the other side of the valley, Barundin saw Ungrim Ironfist raising his fist in triumph and he returned the gesture. The odd cannon shot boomed out as the engineers vented their anger at the retreating horde, punctuating the cheers and jeers that echoed after the defeated host of Chaos.

THE LOSSES OF the dwarfs were comparatively light, most of them coming from the devastation wrought by the Chaos dwarf war machines. There would still be several hundred bodies to take back to the holds' tombs, but compared to the thousands of dead marauders and the hundreds of slain Dawi-Zharr, things could have been a lot worse.

Barundin was on the floor of the pass, sending and receiving messages, organising his army and generally dealing with the aftermath of the battle. He and King Ironfist had decided that a pursuit was risky, as they had no firm idea of the size of the horde that could be waiting further to the east.

Barundin looked up as Hengrid nudged him and nodded to his left. Ungrim Ironfist was striding across the bloodied snow towards him. The king was a strange sight, wearing plates of gromril armour and a dragon-scale cloak, with his hair and beard dyed and styled in the manner of a slayer. Barundin felt a strange thrill as he watched the other king approaching. He knew he was king of Zhufbar, and proud of the accomplishments of his reign, but he was in no doubt that he was in the presence of a genuine living legend.

The story of the Slayer King was a long and tragic one, and it began, as most dwarf tales do, hundreds of years ago, when Ungrim's forefather had suffered a terrible loss. Barundin did not know the details, like most dwarfs outside of Karak Kadrin, but knew that it had something to do with the death of King Beragor's son. In a fit of anger and shame, Beragor had taken the Slayer Oath. However, even as he prepared to set forth on his doom quest, his counsellors reminded him that he still had his oaths of kingship to fulfil; that he had sworn to protect and lead his people over all other things.

Unable to reconcile the two oaths, and just as unable to break either, the Slayer King Beragor built a great shrine to Grimnir, and became a patron of the slayer cult. From across the world, slayers travelled to Karak

Kadrin to give praise at the shrine, and to take the weapons forged there under the king's instruction. When Beragor died, not only did his oath of kingship pass to his son, but also his slayer oath, for neither could be met. Thus was the line of the Slayer Kings founded, for seven generations.

Ungrim was broad and burly, even for a dwarf, and his armour was resplendent with gold and gems. He raised a hand in greeting as he neared Barundin, and the king of Zhufbar self-consciously waved back limply.

'Hail cousin,' Ungrim boomed out.

'Hello,' said Barundin. He had forgotten that his new wife had been a cousin of the king, and that they were now related. That made him feel better and his confidence grew.

'You'll be heading back to Zhufbar, then,' said Ungrim, his gruff voice making it a statement rather than a question.

'Well, the battle is over,' said Barundin, looking over the corpse-strewn pass.

'It is, it is indeed,' said Ungrim. 'Although my rangers tell me that we have only faced the vanguard.'

'Just a vanguard?' said Barundin. 'There are more?'

'Tens of thousands of the buggers,' said Ungrim, waving a hand eastwards. 'Vardek Crom still holds the strength of his horde in the Dark Lands and the eastern valleys of Peak Pass.'

'Then I must stay,' said Barundin.

'No you bloody won't,' said Ungrim. 'You're to give my cousin a son or daughter before you go risking your neck fighting with me.'

'I swore to come to your aid,' protested Barundin. He flinched as he said the next words, but couldn't stop them coming out. 'I shan't be known as an oath-breaker.'

'Then fulfil your marriage oaths,' said Ungrim, not noticing or choosing to ignore the implicit accusation in Barundin's ill-chosen words. 'The high king has promised me an army, and they march north from Karaz-a-Karak at this very moment. Go home, Barundin, and enjoy your new life for a little while.'

Thagri came over, carrying with him the Zhufbar book of grudges. His face was grim as he handed the volume to Barundin.

'All the names of the dead have been entered,' said the loremaster, handing the king a writing chisel already inked. 'Just put your mark to this page, and they will be entered against the grudges of the northmen and the... the others.'

'That it is a long list,' said Ungrim, peering over Barundin's shoulder as he signed the page. 'I think not in your lifetime will they be all crossed out.'

'No,' said Barundin, blowing the ink dry and flicking through the pages of the heavy book. So many grudges, so few of them drawn through. 'The list is longer than when my father died.'

'Still, plenty of years left in you yet,' said Ungrim with a lopsided smile.

'And plenty of pages still to fill, if need be,' agreed Barundin with a nod, snapping the book shut.

'For me, and for my heir.'

ABOUT THE AUTHOR

Gav Thorpe works for Games Workshop in his
capacity as Lead Background Designer, overseeing
and contributing to the Warhammer and
Warhammer 40,000 worlds. He has a dozen or so
short stories to his name (maybe less, he can't
remember), and over half a dozen novels. Dennis
the mechanical hamster is now enjoying a small
amount of infamy on the internet, and is
embarking on a career as an international pet
of mystery.

READ TILL YOU BLEED
DO YOU HAVE THEM ALL?

WWW.BLACKLIBRARY.COM